THE MILCH BRIDE

J.R. Biery

ABOUT THIS BOOK

A dear friend I taught with planned every day for the birth of her son. She died a few days after he was born, never realizing her dreams. I couldn't stop mourning her until I wrote this book. I believe she is like the mother in this story, an angel who is hovering over her son.

(I was surprised it ended up being set in Texas in 1872, but there you go, writing is always a trip.)

DISCLAIMER

DEDICATION

Dedicated to Jerry, my patient and loving husband, who has always supported and encouraged me to follow my dreams, and to the members of Cookeville Creative Writers' Association who prodded and nudged me forward to actually publish some of my books. Special thanks to Sarah Holloway for reading and providing me with a great critique.

CHAPTER ONE
March, 1872, Mill County, Texas

Jackson Harper stood at the edge of the grave and strove to hold back the tears. Donna was gone. Gone with her, all the joy and excitement about J.D.. Gone her hours of planning, sewing, and talking about how wonderful life would be when their son was born. None of her dreams included death, leaving him alone with their helpless son who was now growing weaker every day.

He knew women died after childbirth, but not women like Donna. A rancher's daughter, tall, strong, self-assured, she had been confident that Jackson Dawson Harper would be a boy, healthy and handsome like all the Harpers.

Why had he believed her? Because she had lived the charmed life of the beautiful only daughter of the town's biggest rancher, a powerful man who was also president of the bank. She knew that whatever she wanted she would have, even Jackson.

He had resisted at first, not interested in her father's money or in Donna for that matter. Finally, he found himself enjoying her charms, her happy laugh and her bold, daredevil ways. When the baby became a possibility, he had done the honorable thing. Their marriage had been a happy union with the promise of the child and a stable future.

Charles Dawson moved over, scowling at him. "Son, you don't have to worry about the baby. Irene and I will be happy to look after him. She's already planning to send to Austin for a wet nurse."

"Thanks, but I promised Donna I would raise our son."

"According to Doctor Jenkins, your baby isn't able to digest cow's milk. He predicts that J.D. won't make the week if you don't find a woman to nurse him."

"I'll handle it." Jackson stormed away before Charles could argue. He didn't believe the quack. Hadn't he assured him Donna would stop bleeding and be fine? Doc was wrong, but what if he were right about the baby. They had tried canned milk, cow's milk, even goat. None worked.

The doctor was waiting for him on the board walk, his bulk well clothed in a brown wool suit. "You could steal a Choctaw squaw, if you find one with a papoose board on her back. But the only lactating female in Star is Tom Stoddard's daughter."

Jackson stood beside the buckboard and accepted the tightly bound bundle from the doctor. He checked that the quilt was still inside the emptied wagon toolbox and tucked the baby inside. Then he pushed the wooden box back into place beneath the seat.

He stepped up, exchanging nods with the last somberly clad friends and neighbors who were leaving the graveyard. Most of the church people had stopped work and come to town for Donna's funeral. But Jackson could not respond to their sympathy the way they wanted.

The woman they had helped him bury was not his Donna. He felt the sudden cold tightness in his chest and clucked at the horses to clear the feeling and get things into motion.

"If she's the only woman available, then I'm going to fetch her home. I'm not losing J.D."

Even as he wheeled the buckboard to head out of town, he wondered if Indian milk wouldn't be easier for J.D. and him to swallow. Tom Stoddard had been a good man, but he had avoided town after the disgrace of his unwed daughter's pregnancy became common knowledge. According to some of the owl-hoots that hung around the saloon, the girl didn't even know who to name as daddy.

The morning rain which had stopped as if by the banker's order, so they could bury his daughter 'properly', once again poured down. For once, Jackson appreciated the cold rain. He didn't need the town folk's pity, any more than he needed Charlie Dawson's suggestions about the proper thing for him to do. They had come storming out to the ranch on the baby's arrival. His mother-in-law shooed him out of the bedroom, grabbing his new son from his arms. She acted outraged that he had been in the room at all.

Never an easy relationship, at first he had been grateful for their help. His father-in-law's effusive confidence that everything would be great. J.D. would be the first of the half-dozen he and Donna could expect to have. Charles had strutted about the study, crowing about how J.D. had the best bloodlines in Mills County. The boy would be enrolled at Harvard, the best Eastern college money could buy. Jackson wouldn't have to worry because Charles would pay for everything.

Jackson protested he would provide for his son if he wanted that much education. Charles laughed, reminding him it was what his Donna would expect. Who else would he spend his money on, if not his daughter and his first grandson?

Jackson had swallowed his pride, along with a couple of glasses of the bonded whiskey Charles had brought out for their celebration. When he checked on Donna she had been pale and exhausted from the long labor. But she had insisted he take her dad out to see the new bull and the other spotted cows he had purchased during the last drive to Abilene.

Relaxed, his fears gone now the baby was here, he had listened to them all. He should never have gone.

Charles had admired the stock but resumed their long-standing debate about the new Hereford cattle that some of the cattlemen were bringing into Houston from England. He was thinking of changing his herd to the thicker, red stock and had already ordered a breeding pair for himself. That had decided Jackson; he would never have anything to do with them. If Charles thought they were so perfect, then they were too good for him. Besides, with cattle still free-ranging, hornless cattle wouldn't stand a prayer grazing on the rough pasture around Star.

Maybe if he hadn't gone…He had wanted only to sit beside Donna and watch her and the baby.

By the time they had ridden back, it was dusk. Doc Jenkins was gone, and Irene was frantic. He knew everything was wrong from the loud wails of his son.

He hadn't followed his father-in-law to the barn to unsaddle, merely swung down at the house.

"I sent one of your men after the doctor," Irene wailed. "It's Donna, I can't wake her, the baby is hungry and I can't keep him quiet."

Jackson had rushed into the bedroom, ignoring his mother-in-law's shocked protests. When he turned up the lamp, he recognized the waxy pallor at once from men he had seen on the battle-field. Throwing back the covers, he groaned and sank to his knees beside the bed. The heavy towels he had helped the doctor position under her hips as birthing pads were red from her blood.

The doctor burst into the room behind him. "Jesus, why didn't you send for me sooner?"

Jackson sat rocking, devastated. Why had he listened to any of them? If he had stayed, stayed beside her, he would have seen what was happening in time. He would have known to call the doctor back sooner.

Instead, he lifted her to let the doctor and housekeeper rush to move the soaked towels into a wash basket, hurriedly piling clean ones on top of the stained oilskins.

He laid her down, muttering his agonized apologies against her cheek, listening to her shallow breaths. He had stayed this time despite Irene's protests, letting the housekeeper deal with his outraged mother-in-law and the baby.

When he yelled at Doc Jenkins, the quack had paled. "You know where I learned my trade Harper? As an orderly for an eastern doctor on the battlefield. Do you know how many women were on the battlefield?"

"You have to try. You have to do something to save her."

He had held his wife while the ignorant fool of a doctor heated a polished metal rod to white heat. He had held her, feeling her horrified scream in every inch of his body, as the doctor inserted it inside her to cauterize the bleeding.

The first tears were for Donna. The next were for the other children they would never have. After the first scream she had passed out, a mercy if ever there was one.

When he was forced from her side, he left her mother and father holding her hands as she lay, unknowing, hopefully unfeeling. The rest of the night, he sat outside her room until his in-laws went to bed, then kept vigil beside her. It was nearly dawn the next day when she finally slipped away. It happened quietly.

Numb, he had walked to the barn, grabbed a shovel and headed to the hill behind the house where he had buried his dog Henry. He marked off the grave, six by three feet, and dug in the hard rocky soil until he was below six feet.

They had carried the baby to nurse twice during those last twenty-four hours. They fed him with sugar water in between, and when he stayed ravenous, canned milk in a bottle.

The canned milk gave him colic. They tried boiling cow's milk for him. It streamed out nearly as fast as he sucked it in. Desperately, he demanded Doc Jenkins help him find a wet nurse.

In the meantime, his in-laws ordered a casket and arranged for Donna's funeral in town.

As the baby's cries grew weaker he fled into the night long enough to dig another grave on the hill, this one shorter and shallower. He prayed until he had himself in hand, and then returned to the house to sit beside his dead wife and listen to the weak cries of the baby.

Listening to the baby, he had almost run back to fill in the small grave. He wasn't going to die. Jackson was determined to do whatever it took. Even if it meant having a trollop like Harriett Stoddard hold Donna's child to her breast.

CHAPTER TWO

Hattie felt as cold as the dead babe in her arms. God had taken him back because she had never wanted him. Sickly from the start, he had come into the world on a whimper, blue and lifeless. Without help, he would have been stillborn. How many times had she prayed it would be so?

She had been terrified she would not find him in time or that the same men who had destroyed her life would find her first. Thanks to her racing into town, gun in hand. But the doctor had been there.

Her father had been grimacing in pain, holding his arm, his whole body contorted. Pregnant as she was, she had headed into town, afraid to leave him, terrified of what would happen if she didn't go.

The Doc had driven them back in his buggy. Her labor began before they reached the ranch, but she insisted the doctor continue the race to reach her father in time.

When they arrived, her father's attack was over. His breathing was shallow and the right side of his body sagged as though an avalanche had happened inside, everything on that half of his body had slid downward.

The doctor admitted he wasn't sure if the attack had been Dad's heart or merely apoplexy. He gave him one of the new "trinitin" pills containing nitroglycerin, a compound that had been proving magical in treating heart attack patients. Her Dad's color had returned immediately, and the doctor had turned his attention to Harriet and the sickly slip of a child that she delivered.

He had cleared the baby's throat, breathed into his mouth a couple of times, and Hattie had watched the baby go from blue to gray.

At least coming a month early, the delivery had been easier than she had feared. For the last few weeks, she worried that its delivery would kill her and she would leave her father all alone. When Hattie accepted the child from the doctor, she waited, wanting to feel the sweep of emotion, the love of a mother for her child. Instead, she was swept with a heavy wave of sadness. Her child, created in pain and violence, weak and helpless, was blameless in the crime against her. She knew it, but it did not change how she felt.

Passively she waited while the doctor laid the child on top of her; placed her nipple in the baby's mouth. At his weak tugs, the doctor showed her how to stroke his cheek to help him nurse. When he let go, she collapsed. The doctor spent the night, guarding all three of his patients and Hattie slept.

When the doctor left the next morning, Hattie's two weeks of unrelenting toil began, working to tend her father and the struggling infant. She cooked, cleaned, washed bodies, did laundry, and then fed each in turn. Doc Jenkins thought her father was having a heart attack when she described his symptoms. But the drawing on his right side was clearly the result of apoplexy.

He left her a small can with twenty of the precious miracle pills with instructions to use only one if her father showed the symptoms of another attack. She watched him for chest pains, shortness of breath, flushed face and severe pain. Blessedly, all twenty of the little explosives still rested in the small metal can.

Doc came by a week later and patted her shoulder. He was shocked to see her sitting with the babe at her breast, her free hand spooning gruel into her father's crooked mouth, mopping it up, and refeeding it to him. Doc agreed to spend the night to relieve her.

As Doc left the next morning, he told her to prepare to lose one or both. The baby still showed little interest in feeding. His skin was so pale it was translucent, and his breathing so shallow his little chest barely moved. The doctor explained that the reason her father could not get out of bed, even with help, was because he'd had one or more additional seizures. When he told her the strong man who had always taken care of her would never be able to take care of his own needs again, she knew he would not want to live.

Her father died a week later. At the end, Hattie had held his head up, trying to help him breathe. He had smiled his new lopsided grin, his eyes speaking to her. She heard in her mind the words, "Buck up Hattie, you're my brave girl, you can do it."

She had smiled back at him. Even as he took his last, gasping breath, she had whispered her reassurances. "I'll be brave, Daddy. I'll be all right."

But she had not been. When the realization came that she would need to prepare her dad for burial and dig a grave, she felt a despair so heavy it made her want to give up. Only the weak mewling cries of her newborn put her back on her feet. First, she would clean and feed the baby. Then while he slept, she would eat a bite and rest. In the morning, she would prepare and bury her father.

She had finished bathing her father, putting him in his best pants, shirt and black frock coat. It was a suit he had worn at his own father's funeral, his wedding, and on the rare Sundays when her mother had been able to coerce him into accompanying her to church, and finally at her mother's funeral. He had scoffed when she suggested he buy a new one. "It's my pall-bearer suit, probably be my burying clothes."

With everything done, the bag of spices in his mouth, his blue eyes closed forever, she turned to check on the baby.

Shocked at his stillness, the coldness of the soft skin, she realized with pain why he had not stirred nor cried yet. He had died in the hour just before dawn. The poor child was gone, lost, never loved, never to be loved. He would never grow into a man like her father, or as she had feared, like the animals who sired him.

She had been tearless for so long, tearless despite the ordeal of the terror and shame of the pregnancy, and then her father's suffering. There was too much to cry about, if she ever started, she would never stop. There was no time for self-pity, and that was what crying felt like. Besides, crying for her father seemed wrong, knowing he was free and happy again to cast off his helpless body. She had remembered his smiling eyes at the last and knew he was now in heaven with her mother.

When she lifted the babe to her chest, no tears would come. She wanted to shed hot and scalding tears for him, tears for herself, and tears for the misery of her condition.

It was nearly noon before she could release the tiny body. She had rocked and screamed in rage, but the emptiness would not leave her. Finally, she forced herself up to do the rituals, to bathe another Stoddard for burial. Even as she tucked the tiny closed fist into the sleeve of the drawstring gown, she bent to kiss the downy head. When she laid the dressed body down, she tucked the baby into the crook of her father's arm.

She wanted to move but couldn't, held by the beauty of the two together in endless sleep. For the first time she noticed the dimple in the boy's chin, just like the one in her father's. Why hadn't she noticed, why hadn't she allowed herself to love him before it was too late?

Trembling, determined not to break again, she went to the barn for the shovel. Dragging it behind her, she plodded toward the tall walnut tree in front of the small cabin.

◇◇◇

The wagon wheeled into the yard so quickly, Hattie raised the shovel in defense.

"Whoa."

The loud yell could have been aimed at the foam-flecked mustangs or the soaked girl waving a shovel. As soon as he pulled the team to a halt, he wrapped both reins around the brake handle and swung down to snatch at the shovel in her hands.

Hattie fell backward but retained the shovel, as insubstantial a weapon against the towering man above her as her clawing hands had been against those men.

"Whoa," he surprised her by backing away, holding both arms in the air. "I'm not here for trouble. I'm looking for a young woman to help me care for a baby."

At the last words, Hattie surprised herself by letting the shovel drop across her lap where she sat in the muddy yard. Her dry eyes burned as tears pooled behind them. She sniffed to keep them at bay lest he think her crazy.

Slowly he reached down; lifted the tool from her lap. Then he placed both hands on her arms and hauled her to her feet. She took a step backward, pulling free. It was then that they both swiveled at the loud bawl of a baby. Hattie turned to look up at the man.

"My son will die if you don't help us. My wife passed two nights ago. J.D. can't keep anything down and is starving to death. Canned or cow's milk, both come back out one end or the other about as quick as he's fed. Ma'am, you're the only chance we have, according to Doc Jenkins."

"Well, if you're looking for desperate, you've come to the right place. Bring him inside, Mr...."

"Harper, Jackson Harper, ma'am, and J.D.'s my son."

The first thing Jackson noticed was the smell. He stood with the wagon toolbox in his hands, and then waited as she picked up a towel to wipe her face and dirt streaked arms. She stared at him, shrugging. "They're in the back room. It's why I was digging."

Jackson put the box down gently on the table, noting the broken backed chair that wedged underneath one end to support it.

Dried off, Hattie leaned down to pull the squalling infant from the box. "Fill that dishpan with water, there's a rain barrel at the corner of the porch. I'll get him cleaned up so I can feed him."

He glared at her, surprised at the sharp order. But she was already removing the baby's soiled diaper and wiping him clean with the front of it. When he returned a minute later, the baby was undressed, angrily kicking his feet and waving fists at her.

Jackson paused to stare as she wiped tears from her eyes, her hand gently reaching to wipe the tears from the baby's cheeks. The boy was long and soft and very red, but even Jackson could tell she saw how perfect and beautiful the baby was. Carefully she scooped him up from the table, cradling him against her chest, tucking his face toward her neck as she cooed soothingly to him and kissed his wet face. Instantly he stopped raging, making small gasping sounds against her skin.

When Jackson moved forward to set the basin down, she shook her head and sniffed. Using the clean front edge of his cast-off gown, she dipped and scrubbed the baby tenderly, slowly removing all the waste, then again pressing the naked, squirming body close.

"There are baby things," she pointed, "on top of the dresser."

He carried them forward, shocked when she unbuttoned her damp shirt and used it to dry and wrap the boy. Her chemise was gray and thin, but he was relieved when she used the baby and old blouse to hide herself from his view. He grinned, half apologetically, as he heard the greedy suckling sounds of his child. A few minutes later, she raised the babe, rubbing his back as she rearranged her clothes, then positioned him to nurse from her other breast.

Jackson stood embarrassed. There was nowhere to sit. He noticed there was a pot on the stove and he lifted the lid to see bean soup. Restless, he busied himself opening the oven, searching for wood, and then leaving to return with three small logs, the only dry wood he could find. As the beans heated, he leaned against the wall and watched them. Clearly, the child was asleep, but he would suddenly start and make suckling sounds whenever she moved even the slightest.

"Could you look in the bedroom for a clean shirt for me?"

A minute later he returned and shrugged his shoulders, "I only found men's shirts."

"The red plaid will be fine, I'm cold."

He brought both back, held the red one open while she put an arm through the sleeve, and then leaned forward so he could wrap it around her. She struggled to get her hand started in the other sleeve but when she could not manage, he held it until she succeeded. Trying not to, but unable to keep his eyes from the white fullness of her breast where the child was attached. He pretended not to be looking when the baby's head rolled back releasing the dark nipple, a bubble of milk on his pursed pink mouth.

Blushing, she quickly grabbed and held the front of the shirt closed as he reached for the baby. Timidly Jackson held him with his bottom resting on one big palm, his head cradled in the crook of his arm. He gently rocked his arm back and forth, terrified that the child might reawaken with more crying.

As soon as he stepped back with the child, Hattie rose, turning her back while she rearranged herself, buttoned, and tucked in the shirt. Turning around, she busied herself, replacing the soiled quilt with a clean blanket. Jackson gingerly nestled J.D. back inside the toolbox.

In whispers she said, "I need to get back to digging."

He held up a hand, shaking his head and pointing at the chair. "Just sit and eat while the food's hot, I couldn't find enough wood to keep things going. I have a little ground Arbuckle's out in the buckboard, it looks like you're out of coffee and lots more."

Hattie sagged into the chair he pointed out and waited. Warily she watched him carry the only bowl and spoon left on the shelf, as well as a tin mug that he had brought inside with the coffee grounds.

"There's a bit of corn pone in the pan inside the oven - molasses on the shelf," she said, even as she started to eat the warm beans.

He brought the warm bread and sorghum, and then looked around again. He went outside and brought in the rocker from the front porch. Then he used the empty coffee can to hold a cup of coffee. Breaking the bread in two, he handed her half, then brought the bean pot from the stove.

He watched her eat like someone who had not stopped to eat in a long time. Satisfied when he saw the bottom of her bowl, he refilled it, then using a bent fork, crumbled his crust of bread in the liquid and ate just as hungrily. When her coffee cup was empty, he refilled it and poured the remainder in his empty can. "Tasted mighty fine," he grinned at her, pleased when she grinned back.

Even as the grin faded, he pointed with his fork toward the back room. "Dead long?"

She shook her head. "Dad died yesterday, his heart, or maybe another stroke. He quit eating and then he seemed to just let go."

"The baby?"

"Sometime before daybreak, I was preparing Dad's body. He was just gone when I went to check on him."

She could not look at the man, instead she stared at the stove. "I should have gotten them in the ground. I just kind of …" her voice broke, and she shook her head, even as she felt the tears gathering.

His voice was thick as he whispered, even though his blue eyes remained clear and intense as he stared at her. "Well, it looks like you've done a good job in getting them ready for burial. While my wife, Donna, was fading, her parents came out. They insisted we had to get a proper box built for her, had to have a proper funeral for her at the church and a burial in the town cemetery. While we were waiting on the carpenter, J.D. started to really struggle. I dug another grave, one more his size. Guess I should have filled them in, but I didn't. What I'm saying is, if you aren't too proud to use it, we could bury your folks in those graves that are already dug."

"On your place?"

"They'd be close to you that way, while you're at the ranch tending to my boy. Then if you want them moved back here, we can do that when the time comes."

"You think I'm going to leave my ranch and move in with you?"

"Ma'am, I intend for my son to live. He needs you and your milk to do that. Yes ma'am, I reckon you're moving into my place until he's weaned."

Hattie glared at him, knowing she again had no choice, but hating him and fate for forcing her life in a direction she hadn't chosen.

"You have other plans, do you?"

"Yes. I need to find and herd up the cattle on this place. Three weeks ago, there were about fifty head left. I intend to trail them to town to sell in order to have sufficient money to pay the taxes on this ranch. Otherwise, I'll lose it." With each word, she grew a little louder, and by the time she finished she was standing and shouting at him. "Our ranch may not look like much to you, but my Dad spent his life trying to make a go of it. I owe it to him to not let the bank take it from us."

He stared pointedly at the sleeping baby and kept his voice low, his eyes staring directly into hers. "Fair enough, I'll pay you for wet nursing my son, whatever you owe in taxes. I will send my men out to round up all your cattle and move them, pack up any of your furniture or what not that you want, and move it all to my place. When you're done, when J.D. is weaned, I'll have them move it all back." He too rose and grew louder as he answered her. "I reckon we can keep up with another fifty cows and whatever else there is for a year or so."

She stuck out her hand, shocked when it was engulfed by his. Here she was nothing but a milk cow, but she felt more like herself then she had in months.

Quickly she tugged her hand free. "I'll make a list of the animals. It won't take long to pack up what little is left." She quickly cleared the table, pulled the family Bible out of the drawer of the only dresser, and then sat at the table with a piece of butcher paper and a flat pencil.

"I accept your offer of the graves. My father wouldn't care about proper caskets or burials in town, even if I had the money to pay for them. Besides, I believe he is home in heaven with my mother."

"I need something to put down in the wagon-bed, before we load them."

Hattie turned back and bent to the bottom drawer and pulled out a thick-woven Indian blanket.

"It doesn't look like the rain is going to stop. Do you have any oilskins?"

Hattie handed him the thick blanket, blushing furiously. "They're still on the bed."

Jackson stopped, accepting the heavy blanket and staring down at the slender girl before him. Had it been such a short time since she underwent the same ordeal that had claimed Donna's life? According to Doc, she had ridden to town on a galloping horse to get help for her father on the day she delivered. Now she looked painfully shy over even the mention of it.

"I'll be just a minute."

When he returned, Hattie had a bag full of clothes, a rifle and her father's pistol on the table. He called her to take her father's feet, then they lifted the bodies together, careful to secure the baby in her father's arms as they lifted and carried them out. As soon as he had the bodies in the wagon bed, she turned and ran back into the cabin, returning with two quilts and the oilcloths, balled up with the yellow-coated canvas side out. Standing in the wagon bed, he took the edge and covered the top half of the bodies, making sure not to disturb either body in their peaceful pose.

He covered the bottom half just as carefully, then used the bag of tools that he had removed from the toolbox to hold the top right corner. Hattie handed him the guns and he rolled them under the edge of the tarp to weigh down the left upper corner. She carried out a wooden box, loaded with the broken remains of a blue and white square canister set, and a small set of oil and vinegar jars. He put it as a weight at the tailgate on a bottom corner and he set her bag of clothes on the last corner and jumped down.

While he gathered up the baby, she pulled on a heavy barn coat and grabbed the family Bible, and a tattered cookbook. He was loading the box and baby when J.D. began to fuss. Hattie reached in the box and felt his bottom, then wrapped the blanket closer around him, before tucking the baby inside the folds of her heavy coat. She accepted a hand up onto the buckboard seat. Since the baby continued to fuss, she reached in to free her breast for his searching mouth.

Hattie was not sure if it was the baby who was comforted, or herself. As soon as she tucked him in against her, she felt a swell of warmth rush through her.

Jackson studied her profile, and then clucked the team into motion, putting an arm out to steady her as he circled out of the yard. She stiffened away and he dropped his arm, as struck by her reaction as his guilt for forgetting. The babe J.D. was his, but the woman would never be his Donna.

CHAPTER THREE

It was mid-afternoon when he pulled the buckboard up to Thompson's store. Jackson sprang down, but Hattie remained on the buckboard seat.

When he stepped up on the boardwalk beside her, she asked, "Why are we stopping here?" Hastily she rearranged herself and the baby.

"I promised the cook I'd bring back some stores." Not giving her a chance to hesitate, he lifted her down with the baby still in her arms. He sprang over and opened the door to the store.

Jackson stood there, holding the door open even as he talked to the storeowner. Hattie inched inside, backing up to blend with the barrels and tack by the door while Jackson stepped forward and handed the shop owner his list. Both men stared at her as Jackson leaned closer to whisper to the store owner. "Mr. Thompson, as you can see, she needs clothes, everything, head to toe, including all the female fripperies." Loudly he added, "I'll be back within the hour. There are bodies in the buckboard, be extra careful when you load up."

"Bodies?"

However, the question was directed toward his back and the closing door. The store owner turned his head and hollered at his wife. "Lady out front needs help." He nodded at her and went to work filling the order.

Several minutes later, his wife finally arrived. "Lady, humph, that's nothing but Stoddard's dirty slut of a daughter."

"Hush. Jackson Harper wants her to have clothes - head to toe - from the skin out," he whispered angrily. "Keep a civil tongue in your head and make the sale."

She snorted again, and then waved at Hattie, unconcerned that she had heard every word. "This way."

The woman eyed her critically and Hattie realized she could not remember the last time she had bathed or combed her hair. Why hadn't she thought of it before letting Jackson drag her in here?

"Could you take off the coat so I can better judge your size?"

Hattie hesitated; dreading the woman's reaction, then opened the coat and shrugged out of one sleeve. When the clerk's wife saw the baby's feet, she screamed.

"My God, you've brought your bastard into town."

Hattie flushed with anger. "My son is dead. This is the Harper boy."

"Emma, mind what you were told," the owner yelled at her.

Hattie managed to bunch up the coat as she removed it and laid it on top of two full crates of potatoes, then swaddled the boy and stared up at the woman. She was thoroughly embarrassed, aware of her matted dirty hair, the baggy flannel shirt of her dad's and the mud- stained skirt. She prayed she would not have to feed the baby again and expose her gray, stained, underwear.

"Good Lord, you do need clothes."

Hattie kept a hand on the swaddled baby, but this time her blush was shame, not anger.

"We really don't carry ready-to-wear for women, other than shirt-waists and skirts."

"Fine, I don't care, as long as it's black. I'm in mourning. My father is dead, too."

The woman stared at her, and then pursed her lips. "I'm sorry for your loss. Tom Stoddard was a fine man."

Hattie bit her tongue then nodded. "Thank you, anything in black, if not I'll need a box of dye."

"Widow's rags it is. There are two skirts, one you will need to hem. Both black. The shirts are black, one with red stripes, the other with blue. I just have the two."

"Fine, they sound fine. I can make do with them."

"Over here are the undergarments," she whispered.

The baby interrupted with a cry and Hattie moved quickly to lift him up, finding him wet. "Whatever you think, basic is fine. I'm sorry, but the baby needs changing."

"I can sell you a yard of swaddling. We can cut it to make four nappies, you can hem them later.

"Good, those first please."

The clerk shook her head but grabbed the bolt of cloth, quickly cutting off a yard and quartering it.

Hattie moved back to the coat and made quick work of changing the crying newborn. His bottom was already chapped, and she did not want it to get raw. "Do you have salve, something I can use for the baby's bottom?"

"I'll get you a tin of balm. Make sure you keep him clean and dry."

Hattie glared at the woman, but nodded.

◇◇◇

Jackson crossed the street to the bank, bustling into the small brick building and knocked on the office door at the back of the room. He barely acknowledged the greetings from young Smith, the only teller.

"Hello, Charlie."

"Hello, son, where's the baby?" Charles Dawson said as he rose, an anxious expression on his face.

"Over at the store, with the wet nurse."

Dawson shook his head, scowling. "That Stoddard tramp, I can't believe you left Donna's son with that woman."

"Enough. We don't know that all the gossip about her is true. There are a lot of things that make me wonder if somebody lied. If you saw how busted up their house was, and Tom Stoddard looked broken down too. It could all be stories told by the men who should have been hung for what they did."

"Bah, you're more gullible then I thought. A Jezebel like that could fool any man"

"Let's agree to disagree. Why I'm here is I've hired her to care for J.D. I told her I would pay their back taxes."

"Ridiculous. Do you even know how much they owe?"

"A ranch a fifth the size of mine, one year's taxes. I figure I can handle it."

Charles Dawson moved over to the ledger for taxes. In a small town like Star, he was rancher, bank president, and tax assessor.

"You're going to regret your offer, Jackson. Might make you question your judgment all around."

He spun the ledger around and pointed to the number. Jackson sank into the chair in front of the desk and tented his fingers as he thought what he should say. Finally anger got the best of him.

"What the hell is going on Charlie? You set this damn number. I'll pay the same rate as last year's taxes on the property, or I'll meet with the city council and you can explain this number."

For the first time, Charles Dawson seemed to lose his composure.

"The damn council are the ones who wanted the tax rate raised…"

"Hell, I could buy the land for that much money."

"Wait a month, and when it goes on the block for back taxes, if yours is the highest bid, then you can buy it."

"They only owe one year's taxes. If you weren't trying to steal the ranch, the number would be affordable."

"Watch yourself, Jackson. You don't have Donna any more. You don't want to become my enemy."

"I'm the father of your damn grandson. Hell, you know this isn't right. I expect you to do the right thing. Someday that little boy will want to be proud of his grandfather."

Jackson rested his hands flat on the desk, leaning forward to stare into the eyes of Charles Dawson. It was a moment before the other man blinked and looked down.

When he raised his head, he said. "Pay the bill. I'll deed the property to you. There's no reason for a farmer like Stoddard to have ranch land with a natural spring."

"Tom Stoddard is dead. The land belongs to his daughter."

"Not when she owes taxes she can't pay."

They were again staring. This time Jackson blinked first.

"Hell, Jackson, make up your mind. The land will sell for the back taxes. I have the power to sell it. If you want to have it, pay the bill."

Jackson groaned. It would put a dent in his cash reserve. With an operation the size of his, anything could happen and he would be back in this office, asking Charlie Dawson for a loan. He could just tell Hattie the taxes were too high and pay her the amount they should have been.

No, he had given her his word. He could pay, shake his father-in-law's hand, and take a deed to the ranch. At the end of the year, he could deed it back to the girl. He could help her fight the assessment, get it changed. But now he had to act.

"Write it up. But remember, I need enough left to keep up my ranch and raise the boy. There are also the funeral expenses."

"Nonsense, Irene wanted it, we insisted, we'll pay for it. We've already paid." He handed Jackson the receipt from the funeral home. While Jackson read it, he pulled a sheet of foolscap from his desk and checked the nib on his ink pen. Then he flipped the ledger to the forms listed at the front of the book and wrote two paragraphs, then turned the book back to the listing. When he had filled in the form, he turned back to the front for the closure paragraphs needed on the form.

Jackson stood behind him, reading over his shoulder as he created the document. While Charles copied the boundary and specifics of the property, Jackson noted that Stoddard wasn't the only small rancher who had an inflated tax bill.

As he signed the debit form drawing out the money from his account, then the deed, he has a new realization. As steep as the bill was, it was only a tenth of what the four-hundred acre spread was worth, especially since the natural spring on the place made it priceless. The fact that the land fell between his and Charlie Dawson's ranch probably accounted for the high assessment more than anything else did.

As a last thought he stood, "I'll need a receipt and my account balance. Smith can bring them as he comes in to notarize the deed."

His father-in-law gave him a hard stare, and then stepped out to confer with the teller. As soon as he returned, Jackson had to force out the words. "Thanks for the funeral, it was beautiful. I'm sure Donna would have approved."

Charlie's eyes filled with tears. "It still doesn't seem real."

Jackson felt his own eyes fill as well and for the first time since entering the confined, stuffy office, he saw Charlie Dawson as a human being. He had lost a beloved child just as much as Jackson had lost a wife. It was comforting to know the grave at the top of the hill in the cemetery would soon have a marble slab with a carved angel and the words "beloved daughter, wife, and mother."

When Charles sniffled, he surprised himself even more by wrapping a big hand around the banker's upper arm and giving him a firm shake, just as Smith came in.

He handed Jackson the debit slip, showed him his current account balance, and showed the subtraction at the bottom of the debit, along with the date and his initials. Then he removed a clamp from a small case, squeezed the parchment, then signed and dated as witness and notary.

Jackson folded the documents, slipped them inside his jacket pocket, and then shoved his hat back on. He shook Smith's limp hand, listened to the usual obsequious statement of sympathy, and then gave Dawson's hand another firm shake before leaving. "Thanks Charlie, thanks for everything."

◇◇◇

Hattie had the baby diapered and cradled against her when the door from the store to the saloon swung open. Her heart raced and her tongue turned to cotton as she was faced with her daily nightmare. Unshaved, smirking, dirty, she had thought she would never clean their smell from her skin and hair. Rafe Hogue and his shorter, smellier partners, Silas and Able Sweat appeared.

"Lookie, lookie, I told you she'd be coming to work at Thelma's."

He walked toward her and Hattie shrank back, the baby giving an alarmed cry as it sensed her fear.

"Hey, look what sweetie has," Rafe cackled. "Come on girl, let's see who the little bastard looks like."

Horrified, Hattie pulled the baby even closer, raising the blanket to protect him. The store owner's wife gasped in shock and turned to find her husband.

"I told you about that girl," she whispered furiously, "now what are you going to do?"

"Hey, fellas, she's acting shy again. Help me get her cornered so we can examine our work. Five dollars says he looks like me," Rafe boasted.

Hattie looked around, wishing she had her gun. The first time they came, she had been too shattered to think of pursuing them. She would have gone to town for the sheriff anyway but her father was so badly beaten. She had forced herself to pull her torn clothes around her, choke back her tears and help him to bed.

She had been terrified when her dad was unable to talk to her, but mortified by the tears that leaked down his cheek every time he looked at her.

The next time they came, she was sitting at the window, her guns ready beside her. She began firing as the first man stepped on the porch. She heard one man holler when he was hit, another scream when splinters from the porch rail hit his face.

Now in this store, the only thing at hand was the crate of potatoes. She gripped one tightly.

"Watch out boys, she wants to keep the papa a secret."

The bell over the door rang behind them, but they were all focused on the terrified girl. Hattie was studying them, looking for the mark of splinters or gunshot. Able Sweat had three red spots on his cheek; his older brother seemed to favor his leg. On Rafe's face were five streak marks from where she had clawed, trying to get his eyes.

"Cowards," she hissed. Each had noticed her eyes catching their marks.

"Maybe we need to mark her up a little this time," Able growled.

The sound of a gun being cocked behind them brought them up short. Hattie realized she had dug her nails into the potato.

"Far enough boys, move away from my son."

Rafe recovered first. "Wow, our little wild girl's been busy on the side, boys."

Hattie felt her face flame with the insult. Wasn't it enough to be raped and beaten by these savages? Why did they need to destroy her reputation, too? She shoved past Rafe and when Silas grabbed at her, she fired the potato at his head as hard as she could.

There was a pop as it splattered and she was rewarded by his angry yell, then angrier curses.

Able clapped his hands and laughed. "Got you again, brother."

Silas swore and swung at his brother and they grappled as Jackson reached for Hattie, pulling her and the baby behind him.

"Hey," the storeowner raised his shotgun and the loud racheting sound as he cocked it stopped everyone.

Rafe raised his hands and backed toward the saloon door. "Come on boys, we'll visit the little lady later. See if she has time to put us on her dance card."

"No need men. She is going to have all her time taken up caring for Donna's and my son. If you want to lay claim to her son, you're too late, he's dead." Jackson's cold voice filled the store.

Hattie had been frightened and angry before. Now she felt humiliated. Her father was gone. There was no one left who knew and loved her, who knew she was not a fallen woman, who knew she was a person, not just a wet nurse. However, to everyone in Star, she would never be anything else.

When they were gone, Jackson holstered his gun, and then turned to examine the woman. She shushed the crying baby and would not look at him or anyone else. She turned her back and let him settle with the clerk. When he looked at the invoice, he was surprised at how brief her purchases were. Well, there were Donna's clothes that could be made over, a room full of them, if she needed more.

"Thanks Thompson, for grabbing the shotgun," he added as he paid the bill.

"Those rowdies, I figured you deserved someone to back you. I'm sorry about not getting the supplies loaded, but it's been raining."

Jackson knew it was not rain, but the man's fear of the dead bodies. He let the man carry out the box, while he lifted and toted the sack holding flour, dried beans, and corn meal. As Jackson carefully loaded everything, the store owner complained. "It seems wrong that Tom's daughter isn't burying Tom in town," he added, then realized the girl was already seated on the buckboard.

"Maybe, she doesn't care anymore for this town than they seem to care for her" Jackson said, as he climbed up to sit beside Hattie and the baby. He had noted her curved back and bowed head as he stepped up, but he was surprised to hear J.D. slurp loudly as he released the nipple. Jackson scooted the box out between their feet, and then took the boy.

Hattie started when he did, then quickly fastened her coat and struggled to sit upright, her eyes half-closed in weariness.

Jackson tucked the small boy into the blanket lined box, surprised when he lay there, staring up at him, opening and closing his mouth. "It's all right boy, you can have more when we get home." Smiling, he secured the box and started the team.

CHAPTER FOUR

When he pulled up at the ranch house, it was almost dark. He moved his shoulder to jostle the sleeping woman leaning against him, startled by the vivid blue eyes staring up at him. "I'm going to unload the wagon, and then try to drive the team up the hill to the graves."

Hattie nodded, and then started to get down when a small voice began a high-pitched squall. A couple of people came out of the house, one a woman who started to talk, then froze as he reached under the seat for the baby. As he pulled him out and up to her, he whispered, "He's wet again."

The cry was growing in intensity. She laid the babe onto the high seat as Jackson swung down, passing the box and bag of groceries to the waiting hands. "There's clean cloth in the top of the bundle of clothes," she said.

The woman on the porch harrumphed as Jackson hurried to hand her the diaper. "Miss Harriett Stoddard, my housekeeper, Rubye White."

Hattie looked past the waving tiny feet at the scowling face of a tall, angular woman who stood with arms folded across her chest. Before Hattie could speak, Rubye raised her apron to cover her mouth and nose.

"Rubye, we've got some folks to bury first, before Harriet can come in. But I know she'd like to clean up and get settled."

Another man came out on the porch, and both men uncovered their heads in respect. Even as Jackson finished giving Rubye orders, the loud frantic cry changed, and then abruptly stopped as Hattie lifted the child to suckle, her back to all the people on the porch.

Rubye disappeared into the house with a disapproving cluck, ready to heat water and set up the tub in the pantry off the kitchen.

Hattie stared down at the small baby in her arms, grateful for the fading light that helped to mask them from all the staring eyes. Jackson handed out the last bundle, removing the Bible and putting it on the floor of the buckboard beside her.

"Hank, can you give me a hand to get the team on up the hill."

Hank walked up to the head of the lead animal as Jackson sprang up to the seat beside her.

"Hold on to your hat, Miss Stoddard," and he snapped the reins.

Hattie braced forward, hanging onto the baby who frantically held onto her nipple. She managed to clasp one hand on the back of the seat as they began the steep incline. Through it all, the babe continued to nurse.

At the top of the hill, she continued to tend the baby, grateful to be able to watch as Jackson shook out an oilcloth into the bottom of each grave. At least here on the hill, the water had already run through the soil and she was glad not to hear a splat.

For the first time, he lifted the tiny scrap that had been her son, pausing with the baby beside her. Hattie fought back tears at the sight of the tiny bundle, dressed in his flour-sack gown. Unloved, unwanted, he was about to be buried. He was about to be buried in an unhallowed grave without even a name. Hattie choked back a sob as she nodded and Jackson lowered the tiny babe as gently as though he were sleeping into the small hole in the ground.

She returned the sleeping boy in her arms into his box and straightened her clothing yet again. She wiped at her eyes even as Jackson and his cowhand paused again beside her, waiting silently with her father's body. This time she had to bite her lip to swallow the sobs, wondering even as tears streaked down her face if they were for her father, or for herself.

Finally, both bodies had been moved, each one once again covered with the quilts from the cabin. Although not wooden coffins, Hattie felt that both were now wrapped protectively in love. The quilts made by her mother had always been important to her father and herself. She was comforted knowing they would cover them in their final sleep.

Jackson reached up to help her down and Hattie accepted his hand, feeling awkward in the twilight in this strange place. "Is the Bible still in the wagon?"

The tall cowboy reached around her and lifted the worn and torn bible from the floor beneath the seat. "I grabbed it before they carried your belongings inside. But I don't think there's enough light to read. Do you know the words you want us to say?"

She shook her head, clutching the old book close against her chest. "Begin with Dad," she whispered.

Both men uncovered their heads and moved to the foot of the grave, framing Hattie. Jackson placed a hand on her shoulder and she lowered the Bible toward him. Taking it, he began to speak.

"Tom Stoddard, beloved husband, father, and grandfather…"

Hattie gasped. She clenched her jaw to keep from fresh sobs.

Jackson continued as though she had not interrupted, holding the Bible forward in both hands, the brim of his hat clutched beneath the book.

"Never heard any man say a bad word against you, so I'm sure God has welcomed you home, that your wife and parents have greeted you in their loving embrace. Your daughter here is grieving, but she knows you are in a better place. As the good book says, 'dust to dust, ashes to ashes.'" He knelt down to drop a hand of wet dirt onto the soft quilt.

Hattie followed his motion, scooping the pebbly soil into both hands and sprinkling it over the quilt.

Jackson extended a hand to her elbow to help her rise. "Tom, as hard as it is to let you go, we rejoice knowing you are in a happier place, Amen."

Hattie and the other man echoed, "Amen."

When he turned to the grave holding the baby, Hattie sank to her knees between the two graves, dropping a handful of dirt onto the babe.

Jackson waited expectantly, but was surprised when she rose and took the Bible from him, choking back tears until she could speak.

"Go with your grandfather, little one. I'll join you soon. Amen."

There was a dissatisfied silence, then finally the men added, "Amen." She scooped up another handful of dirt and sprinkled it over the quilted form.

Jackson lifted out the sleeping baby and Hattie clasped the Bible to her body once again, before letting the strong man beside her lead her down the hill toward the house. In the shadowy light, she was grateful for his support.

◇◇◇

On the porch, the hands gathered for dinner. Jackson acknowledged their greetings, ignoring the jibes about his carrying the baby. Rubye tsked and took the infant, then scowled at Hattie.

"Vittles are ready, and I set up for her bath in the pantry."

Jackson patted Rubye's shoulder as he gave up his son. He turned and steered Hattie toward the pantry and held the door for her.

◇◇◇

The water was cold and Hattie shook her head, rousing enough to rinse the second soaping from her hair. It had been ages since she had the time to relax and enjoy a hot bath. She heard the baby cry and realized J.D. was gaining momentum. Sighing, she rose to towel off, dressing in the stiff new clothes. She felt strange, embarrassed by her uncertain status. The housekeeper had propped a mirror on a pantry shelf, setting a brush and comb in front, a lighted oil lamp beside it.

Hattie lifted the gilded handle of the brush, noticing dark hair caught in the bristles. She dipped it in the cold bath water, and then used the comb to clean it. Gratefully she toweled her hair and furiously attacked it.

J.D.'s angry cries and Rubye's frantic pacing warned Hattie to hurry, but the knock at the door still made her jump. Hattie laid the brush down and hastily twisted her hair into a clumsy braid before opening the door.

◇◇◇

She was surprised to find the big dining table empty of all but Jackson and the cowboy Hank. Hank rose, tipped his hat, and then bowed out of the room.

Hattie opened her arms for the baby and the housekeeper gladly turned him over. "He's hungry," Rubye snapped.

She wanted to answer back, he's always hungry, but she bit her tongue. She sniffed the good smells that lingered on the empty plates. The table was set for eight and seven of the plates sat with only crumbs and smears of grease to indicate they had ever held food.

Rubye bustled into the kitchen with a tray of stacked dirty plates and glasses. Hattie draped the blanket higher on her shoulder, aware of the sharp tension in the room. The housekeeper bustled back for a second load of plates, wiping down the table this time, then carried the last load to the kitchen.

Hattie could feel the baby already slowing down in his feeding and automatically stroked his cheek to cause him to remember to eat, just as she had her own weak baby. But he had never suckled like this boy, never bawled from hunger, never drank so deeply. A wave of sadness swept over her again, a desolate sense of loss. Was it her fault he was sickly, that he died?

The sound of Rubye washing dishes in the kitchen was very loud. Hattie raised the baby to examine him when he whimpered. Even though his eyes were closed, his little face was scrunched into complaint and he made a small, whining sound.

Rubye bustled back from the kitchen, setting a small skillet of food along with a tall glass of milk down before Hattie. "Did you burble him?" she asked accusingly.

Hattie raised her eyes to the woman, "Burble?"

The older woman sat down on the chair beside her, took the clean cloth she had used to grip the skillet, shook it out, and then draped it over her shoulder.

"Got to burble a baby so he don't get colicky." She stretched him against her shoulder, and then very softly patted his back.

Hattie laughed, surprised at the loud burp from the tiny baby. Jackson smiled proudly as though the boy had just recited a poem.

The housekeeper gave him another couple of pats and a smaller noise and a splash of milk decorated her shoulder. Satisfied, she leaned the child down in her arms. "Now he's ready for bed."

Rubye dabbed at his pursed mouth with the clean end of the towel. "You'd best eat up, it won't take another warming, probably dried out too much already."

Hattie tried to find a smile for the brusque words but the woman was gone. Timidly she broke off a pone of bread, hard and dry, just like the cook said. But it tasted so good she leaned forward and grabbed a fork to get at the fried pork and potatoes, the thickened beans. Washing it down with the cold buttermilk, she enjoyed it all.

◇◇◇

Then she heard the loud voices, whispering, but all the angrier because of the hissing low tones.

"Where do you plan for her to sleep, out with the hired men?"

"What's wrong with in here, near the baby?"

"In your wife's bed? You plan to put that tramp in your Donna's bed and her not cold in the ground yet? If you do, I'm leaving."

Hattie waited for Jackson's voice, calming, pleading, but when he answered the whisper cut like a knife. "Then leave, but I'll be damned if I'll lose my son because of what people might say. I'll get a cot set up in the study for me."

Rubye's shocked silence was all the angrier.

"The men will like that, seeing her when they come in to eat."

"Hush. We'll work all that out, it's the boy that matters."

Rubye clearly wanted to argue more for she stomped past, glaring at Hattie. Minutes later she returned with the package of clothes and the sack holding Hattie's few possessions from home. This time her chin jutted forward and she didn't even bother to glance at the quiet girl.

Hattie felt the chill of resentment and swallowed the pride that made her want to leave this place where she was unwanted.

Jackson remained at the door a minute then walked to the dresser. Slowly he pulled out one of his wife's nightgowns, hesitating a moment to ball it up and bury his face in, breathing in Donna's scent. He shook out the gown and draped it across the bed, then glanced around the room. He could still feel her presence and hear Donna's voice. To the unasked question, he thought he heard her answer. "Take care of J.D., whatever it takes."

◇◇◇

Hattie carried her empty pan and glass to the kitchen, looking about at the big black stove, the full wood box. She had already marveled at the pantry, stocked with food yet still with room enough for her to bathe. When she stepped back into the main room, she again counted the eight chairs at the long table, and then stared at the other half of the long room to the big stone fireplace. Along the back of the house there were three rooms, the bedroom where she could hear more arguing and two other rooms. Curious, she stepped closer to the open door in the middle. The desk and book shelves made it clear it was Jackson's office. The third door was closed, but she knew it had to hold Rubye's bedroom.

◇◇◇

Jackson's voice made her jump, aware that she was guilty of snooping. He nodded toward the bedroom and she followed him to step inside. Weary though she was, she was aware of another presence in the room. According to Rubye, it was his wife's room. Across the end of the bed hung a yellow nightgown, clearly the object of the argument she had overheard. She reached to finger the soft thin cotton, aware of being watched.

"I could sleep in the front room on the settee," she said.

He shook his head. "You need to be here with the baby; the gown is for you." Then he closed the door.

A gas lamp sat on the bedside table, softly glowing. Hattie stood and stared in the mirror. Her hair had worked loose from the braid and looked neither combed nor as wild as when she had been in town. She unbuttoned the dark shirt waist and looked for a peg to hang it up.

The room contained a high bed with curved headboard and footboard, the dresser with its mirror, and a tall wardrobe. All were made out of the same dark, red stained wood. Hattie removed and folded her new clothes, pulling the soft gown over her head before removing the new undergarments. She folded them and stacked them on top of the other clothes. On one end of the dresser sat the paper bundle of store things and beside on the floor the canvas sack from the house. Maybe she should put away her clothes.

Looking over her shoulder, she slid a dresser drawer open. The top drawer was full of baby clothes. Each garment was soft, clean and new, little caps, sweaters, gowns, booties and blankets. The other end held diapers like the one she had first removed from the baby. She lifted the soft white cloth, noticing the neatly hemmed edges and the blue initials J.D.H. in the corner. Had his mother picked two names, a boy's and a girl's?

Suddenly her eyes were pooling with tears and she sank back onto the bed. She lay, pressing her hand against her mouth, willing herself not to sob. She felt icy cold suddenly, unwilling to crawl under the covers, helpless to move.

The sounds were soft, little hiccupping noises. Hattie rolled off the bed pausing to pull back the covers before approaching the crib. Tiptoeing she gazed down at the stirring baby. He was covered by a blanket so soft and white it seemed to glow, making his skin look very red and new in contrast. So tiny and helpless, he was totally dependent on her now.

Gently she gathered him into her arms, then laid him on the bed to make quick work of changing him. She moved a pillow to form a barrier on the side of the bed, then rolled the crib up against the pillow and bed, even as the baby continued to fuss. Satisfied that he wouldn't roll out when she fell asleep, she walked around the bed and climbed into the other side.

Cuddling him close, she unbuttoned the loose gown and began nursing him. Even as he fed, she let the sorrow slip from her. What if his mother had been rich, had time and means to make so many lovely things for him. The thing she had wanted to give him was her love. Now Hattie would have to be the one to hold him, feed him, and give him the love he needed to grow. Cocooned in the soft bed, she felt content, promising the shadows in the room that she would do just that.

CHAPTER FIVE

Voices woke them, although Hattie had been up and down with J.D. twice during the long night. Even though her own baby had not been as loud or demanding, he had taught her how to grab sleep between interruptions. She felt rested but groggy-headed.

As soon as she had tended J.D. she dressed. This time she took the time to brush her hair and coil it atop her head in a loose bun secured by pins, pins that like the brush, still held dark hair that must have been Donna's. Fed and dry, the baby fussed about being left behind. Hattie picked him back up realizing she would have to find a way to put him down or grow an extra set of arms.

Primly buttoned to the chin, she opened her door, surprised to be stared at by seven sets of eyes. One of the cowhands held out a chair, and Hattie took a seat, casting a questioning glance toward Jackson. He ignored her and the men turned back to eating and talking, but she could feel most of them peeking glances at her.

Rubye walked behind her, set a cup of coffee by her plate, then took her plate and filled it with grits, eggs, and salt pork. She set it down and when Hattie reached out for the last biscuit, one of the hands held the plate out to her. Another moved the sorghum pitcher closer, and a third passed the butter dish.

The housekeeper grunted behind her, and Jackson made an echoing sound. In minutes he had assigned all the men tasks, including three he handed her list to. He ordered them to return to the Stoddard ranch to bring her cattle, as well as the chickens, two mules and saddle horse that were still in her barn. He told one to drive the buckboard with orders to load the rocker and crates for the chickens, as well as any feed left in the barn or any food left behind in the house.

Hattie interrupted. "We have a wagon and harness in the barn, you won't need to take the buckboard."

He arched a brow and glared at her. Obviously Jackson was a man who didn't want to be corrected.

Hattie blushed, embarrassed at how little they would find to pack. She had already taken everything of value, her momma's cook book, the family bible, and dad's guns. While Jackson was loading her books and guns, she had removed the brick under the stove and pocketed the twenty-two dollars and change that was still hidden there. She had been tempted to pay for her clothes yesterday, a show of pride that seemed meaningless to a woman in her circumstances. Instead, she had kept quiet, taken the clothes as part of her compensation, and held the money for future emergencies.

Rubye set down the coffee pot and moved over into the chair beside Hattie as soon as one of the cowboys stood up. She held out her arms and Hattie was surprised at how reluctant she was to surrender the baby.

She worked on breakfast, aware that Jackson had come around the table, standing over the housekeeper to look at the baby, as though making sure he was still the same.

Hattie was glad she had taken the extra time to change his gown and add a pair of the soft blue booties. When Rubye unwrapped the tight blanket, they were not the only ones to smile at the waving fists and little booteed feet. A couple of the cowboys cooed and Jackson reached out a hand, delighted when a wet little fist grabbed a finger and tried to guide it toward his mouth.

"Hungry, boy?"

Hattie set down her coffee cup. "He ate all night, and has already had breakfast."

Jackson nodded, still enjoying the wet gnawing of his son on his finger. "Well, you better eat up so you can keep up with him."

One of the hands made a joke to one of the others and Jackson glowered at him, "You men wait outside for me."

As soon as they left he turned on her. "My apologies for my men, but maybe it would be best for you to eat in your room or wait until they aren't here to come out. Especially if you intend to draw attention to your bosom when they are present."

Hattie rose in a flourish. "I did nothing to warrant that comment from your men or from you. But if you want me to eat in my room and stay hidden, I'll be glad to do it."

"I think it would be for the best. Your reputation precedes you. There's nothing you can do to change it. Men will be men. J. D. needs you to survive, but I don't need to run interference between you and a bunch of randy cowhands."

Hattie knew her face was on fire, since it always flamed when she lost her temper. She should just bite her tongue and storm into the bedroom, but she had never been one to run from a fight.

"I've done nothing to warrant my reputation. Watching my father be beaten nearly to death, robbed, then tied and forced to watch my rape by three drunken cowhands is not my fault. If you are like the rest of the gossips in town, then so be it. But if you cannot guarantee my safety here, you and your son had better find another wet nurse."

The words were brave but she was trembling. Hattie felt the tears gathering and clenched her fists at her side, her nails digging into her palms.

Once again, Jackson doubted the gossips. He had seen the evidence of broken furniture and the damaged body of her father, the pathetic scrap of a baby. But what kind of town was Star if it would let a young woman be brutalized and do nothing to her attackers? It just couldn't be true.

He stared at her small angry face, gritted teeth, and tear brightened eyes. She was a feisty little thing. Again he wondered. He recalled the streaks on the face of Rafe Hogue, the limp of Silas

Sweat and the ugly red spots on the cheek of Able Sweat. He had a feeling he knew who had given the marks to them. What was the truth? What had Able called to Silas, "Got you again, brother."

Rubye held the baby who was emitting a half-hearted squall and moved to the other side of the table, staring from one to the other. "Hey, is this row necessary?"

Jackson lifted his hat, set it on his head. "I'll set my men straight. It would still probably be easier for you if you ate before them or after they leave."

He stopped at the door, tipped his hat at her. "One thing I can promise you Miss Harriett Stoddard, as long as you're in my house, you will be safe. We made an agreement, and J.D. still needs you. I'll make sure the men know that."

The door slammed shut and Hattie sank into her chair. The baby gave a little whimper at the loud noise. Rubye walked over to the fireplace, then turned to pace back.

Hattie stared at the half-eaten plate of food and tried to make the knot in her stomach relax by breathing deeply. Slowly she raised the coffee cup to her mouth and drained the cold, bitter liquid. Determinedly she ate, swallowing anger, shame and frustration with each bite.

◇◇◇

Hattie carried her dishes to the kitchen, standing to stare out the window for a minute. Three men rode out of the yard south, hopefully they were heading to her ranch. Then Jackson and the remaining three rode off in the opposite direction. She washed and rinsed her dishes, then dried them, looking around, she attacked the others waiting to be washed. The activity helped restore her calm.

Glad that Rubye was still happy to hold J. D., she finished clearing the table and washing up, then found the broom and swept out the kitchen and dining room. The hardest part of the agreement would be staying inside, out of sight of the men. She was used to tending the animals, riding fence, and spending most of her day out-of-doors. But she had also been her dad's 'little housekeeper' from the time her mother died when she was nine. As long as she stayed busy, she could do this.

She scooted the chairs back, making sure she caught all the dirt that had fallen off boots under the long table. She was stooping to brush the last pile of dirt into the pan when the whimper changed in tone and Rubye stood, bouncing the babe on her ample shoulder.

Hattie said, "Just a minute. She returned the broom and pan and rinsed her hands, then came back to take the baby, but they were no longer in the main room.

Hattie walked to her bedroom, glad she had made the bed. Rubye was finishing with changing the baby who was in full squall. Hattie extended her hand, feeling a strange clutching in her chest with the tremulous sound of desperation in each cry. Without hesitation she leaned forward and put her face against his, kissing his cheek and crooning to him. Immediately, the pitch of his cry softened.

Rubye stepped back and Hattie gladly raised the baby to her full breast. Perhaps it was his constant nursing; perhaps the fact that she'd actually taken the time to eat three meals in a row, but she could tell the difference in the amount of milk that was flowing at his ravenous suckling. She would be able to do this, this baby would live. She used her left hand to cup his little bottom and fit him into the curve of her right arm against her body.

"Go on, lay down with him. I'll bring you something when the vittles are ready at noon. If you wait and eat after the men, there won't be enough left to keep you fed."

"Thank you, Rubye," Hattie muttered, "Is there water in the pitcher?"

The other woman raised her hands to her hips as though ready to comment on people who wanted you to tote and fetch for them.

Hattie stood up and the baby pulled loose from the nipple and started to protest.

Rubye shook her head, "never mind. We've a pump in the kitchen, I'll bring you some."

Hattie settled back, bracing her back against the headboard and swung her legs up. "I'll get it next time. I'm just thirsty. Also I need to wash out his clothes and hang them out to dry."

Rubye stopped at the door, one hand again on her hip. She was going to make another protest, but mumbled under her breath, "I'd like to see that, missy."

"When he's finished," Hattie added.

◇◇◇

When J.D. finally quit, Hattie made sure to place a cloth over her shoulder before coaxing a burp from him, remembering the sour smell of milk on her gown this morning. No doubt about it, babies were smelly little creatures. She downed a glass of water, then filled it again. J.D. tried to raise his head up, his head wobbling on his weak neck. She cupped his head and before he could change from a fuss to a cry, went ahead and offered him the other breast.

This time he suckled only a few minutes before dropping into exhausted sleep. "You just wanted to know it was there, didn't you little piggy," she whispered stroking his cheek to make sure he was finished.

She ran her fingers over his scalp, playing with the soft dark hair there. She could probably put him in his bed and get back to helping Rubye. She knew the woman resented her, for reasons too numerous to list. Perhaps, if she helped her with her work, she wouldn't resent her as much.

Instead, she removed her shoes and scooted down to stretch out beside the sleeping baby, again using the other pillow to hold him wedged against her. Maybe she could just lie here a minute, then she could get up and help.

◇◇◇

Rubye stepped in with a plate of beans and a thick piece of cornbread, already buttered, and then set a tall glass of cold milk beside it.

Hattie sat up slowly, then wrinkled her nose. The baby lay looking sweetly up at her. Rubye stared down at him. "I believe J.D. has a present for you too."

Hattie smiled and for the first time, Rubye smiled back.

◇◇◇

The first group of men, including Jackson, came and went quickly. Jackson knocked at the bedroom door, and Hattie hurried to open it, but he was already hurrying away. "Brought a present for you," he called.

She held the baby in her arms and he stopped and walked back, leaning to stare down at the sleeping boy a minute before reaching out to rub his downy head. The baby was sleeping, a pink sausage in the snug blanket. He stared at them a minute, looking confused, then hurried out.

Hattie looked around, not spotting anything. She looked over at Rubye, who nodded toward the living room. A crude wooden cradle sat rocking before the empty fireplace. Hattie smiled, noticing the still damp wood.

"Men found it out in our barn and cleaned it up. Missus didn't want it, preferred her fancy new contraption. But we thought you might find it handy to have a place to set the baby down when you're out here, if you want to use it," Rubye said.

Hattie smiled her thanks, "I'll need something to dry it out and then something to pad it. I don't have a quilt left, or that would work."

Rubye lifted a hand. A minute later she was back with a towel and a folded quilt. Hattie walked over a few minutes later, keeping an eye out for the other men. Relieved, she put the sleeping baby down on the soft quilt. She held her breath, sighing when he stayed asleep as she set the cradle to rocking.

Quietly she headed back to the bedroom to gather the basin full of damp and smelly baby clothes. Rubye had already put water to heat on the back of the stove and there were two washtubs set up in the pantry, one with soap beside it and the wash board standing up. The second tub held cold, clear water.

Hattie had grown used to washing smelly clothes during the last two weeks, but she had washed them out in the sunlight, not in a closed room.

Her eyes burned from the ammonia fumes and she felt frustrated when she splashed both her shirt and dark skirt while rinsing the garments. Finally she had a basket of clothes ready to hang, including the yellow gown and her dirty clothes from home. All had been washed, rinsed and wrung out by hand. Her knees and back ached.

Rubye picked up the clothespins and started to take the basket. But J.D. slept on and Hattie held onto the clothes. "I need to dry out a little. The sunshine will help me."

Rubye harrumphed, but walked her to the end of the porch and pointed out the clotheslines.

Hattie raced across the yard, quickly shaking out and pinning diapers, gowns, booties and her own clothes. She shook her loosened hair, letting the wind whip it around to cool her, already feeling her shirt drying. She stood, just letting the breeze dry and cool her sweaty body, hoping the dampness under her arms and down her back would not leave stains.

She was hanging the yellow gown at the high part of the line when she heard the horses and wagon pull into the ranch yard. She heard the squawk of chickens and the bray of her mules, Henry and Pepper. Horses in the yard nickered in greeting.

Hattie yelled at the mules by name and they gave a second bray and her old pet Nugget tugged at his rope tied to the back of the wagon. Hattie swung the empty basket onto her hip with the leftover pins and moved to touch each animal in welcome. Then she leaned close to hug Nugget. She turned toward the house when Rubye appeared with a fussing J.D. and a huge scowl on her face.

Hattie gave the horse a last rub down his dusty head. Quickly she bounded up to the porch, trading her basket for the baby and disappearing inside.

CHAPTER SIX

Only when she had changed J.D. did she glance in the mirror. She gasped in horror. Her hair was a tangled, stringy mess. She put the crying baby into the crib for a few minutes and took time to wash her face, hands and arms. Then she brushed and repinned her hair. Finally she used the damp washcloth to wipe around her neck and clean both breasts before offering the fussy baby either one.

She could hear Rubye warming food for the men, sympathizing with their tales of chasing chickens.

"I hope Miss Stoddard isn't too disappointed. We brought a chest, rocker, one cane seat chair, the tools and harness from the shed, along with three saddles and bridles from the barn. We couldn't find but the one old horse and two mules."

"The boss will be ticked for sure. We have 32 head outside, twelve are calves. If she had 50 head three weeks ago, we couldn't find them."

Hattie wasn't sure if they thought she couldn't count or that she had lied. She sat up, her shoulders tightening as she grew angry. If they doubted her, what would Jackson think?

J.D. leaned back and gave one sharp cry.

Hattie stared down at him. He seemed to be studying her, quietly staring up at her with his misty blue eyes as though to say, "Hey pay attention to me." He made a soft bleat of sound and she leaned down to kiss him.

His tiny hand touched her face and she felt her worry and anger go, sinking into the pleasure of the moment. She moved her head enough to catch the tiny fingers in her mouth and he turned back to nuzzling, hunting his nipple. She relaxed and stretched out on the bed to feed him and rest.

<><><>

She did not wake until much later. The bedroom was dark and quiet and she realized that J.D. was winding up to cry again. Quickly she tended him, then remained still in the dark while he fed, listening to the conversation through the door.

Rubye must have been too busy tonight since there was no food, no glass of water or milk. The more the baby nursed, the hungrier and thirstier she felt. She was annoyed that there were lots of voices, but she could not discern what anyone was saying.

As soon as the voices died down, she picked up the baby, patted him on her shoulder, made sure he was still dry and clean and she was neatly buttoned and pinned. Then she opened the door to peek outside.

Two people remained at the table with Jackson, but he looked up and motioned for her to come forward. She stopped at the chair where she had eaten before but Jackson indicated the chair beside him. As she started to sit, both men stood up and the cowboys bowed toward her and left.

Jackson reached out toward Hattie and though surprised, she handed the child to him.

Jackson unwrapped the baby, touching the soft legs, cupping the small feet, then putting a hand on the full rounded tummy. J.D. raised both hands to put on top of the big hand, catching two fingers, one in each fist. Slowly, lazily, he leaned his head back to reveal his soft throat, yawning contentedly before managing to open one eye half-way.

Hattie hadn't realized she was holding her breath until Jackson smiled, setting the boy down on one long thigh, placing his free hand beneath the wobbly head as J.D. turned his head, trying to pull a finger to his mouth.

Jackson glanced up then and the look in his eyes made her let out her breath in a single gasp. 'Gratitude,' if she had to label the look. She waited to hear the words and realized they would not be coming. The man seemed content to just bounce his knee and stare at the baby.

Rubye set the food down but Hattie barely noticed, draining her milk instead and gladly accepting a refill. She whispered, "Thank you," when Rubye set the half-full pitcher beside her dish.

Next Rubye brought the basket of clothes she had pulled off the line. Hattie started to say, "I'll fold those," but the housekeeper plopped the basket in the chair beside her and it was obvious Hattie would be the one doing it.

Hattie ate quickly, anxious to move to the next job. The tension in the room was unsettling. While Rubye cleaned up Hattie rose and stood to fold clothes, item by item. Soft booties, embroidered diapers and baby gowns, each was tiny and precious like the boy mindlessly relaxed on his father's gently bouncing leg. Hattie was embarrassed at the flour-sack gown and diapers she had dressed the baby in at the ranch, even more so by her own dingy, worn clothes. She folded them quickly, tucking them into the bottom of the basket as soon as she could. She was folding the yellow night gown, the last item, when Rubye came out of the kitchen and moved the basket to the bedroom. Then she bustled back to take the limp baby and cradle him as she carried him to bed as well.

Jackson waited as Rubye returned to collect the empty milk pitcher and last dishes. They both listened to the sounds in the kitchen until five minutes later Rubye blew out the light and breezed past them toward her own bedroom.

Twice Hattie had started to rise but Jackson had signaled her back to her seat. Each time she had felt another set of muscles tighten. What now! By the time the housekeeper stopped puttering and disappeared, Hattie's legs were bouncing under the table from nerves.

She stared at him, wary and suddenly aware of him as a man and the fact that they were alone. She tried to tamp down the fear that roiled through her. She imagined he had heard about the men seeing her in the yard hanging clothes. Perhaps he wasn't pleased with how well J.D. was keeping down her milk; after all he was always hungry. Maybe he had heard how she petted the mules and Nugget, certainly unladylike, yelling hello to mules.

She gripped the edge of the table and waited for what he had to say. The grandmother clock resting on the mantle gave a light musical chime and they sat while it went through all eight counts. On the last chime she spoke.

"What does J.D. stand for?"

"Jackson Dawson Harper, its Donna's maiden name and my name."

At the reminder, he glimpsed Donna as she used to sit and chatter about this time of night. She would give reasons she knew it was a boy. The way he kicked, the way she was carrying him in front, the fact that both families always had boys first, although her brother Charles had died as a baby. She would show him the clothes she had made that day, protesting when he would ask if she hadn't made enough. She claimed you could never have too many things for a baby.

Slowly the image with its head of glossy chestnut curls faded and instead of the stout familiar figure he was staring at this thin, nervous woman with her wispy blonde hair, huge blue eyes, and timid manner. God, you would think she was afraid he was going to beat her as tensely as she sat and as high-pitched as her voice had been. Carefully he began his questions.

"Fifty head of cattle is far fewer than your 400 acre spread should carry."

"We had nearly two hundred last year about this time, too many, and then Dad got the tax bill. After spring calving, he and our two hands branded and treated the cattle, then we separated about a hundred head and drove them to Abilene to sale. He let the hands go and they stayed in Abilene to find work. The night we made it home, that's when the robbers came. They knocked Dad out in the barn, then tied him up. Then...." her voice trailed off.

He stared at her, not commenting. Hattie swallowed, then continued.

"When they left, the cattle money and our two saddle horses were gone."

"Why didn't you report it to Sheriff Tate?"

"It was a week before I felt Dad would be all right alone. I wore his six guns and a pair of pants to ride old Nugget to town. The sheriff laughed at me. Told me he'd heard a different story. Three men had been bragging about how I'd invited one or the other out every night, how I would slip out to the barn to be with them."

"I told him they were liars, and if he didn't do something, I'd shoot them myself."

The sheriff came out to the ranch. But when he asked Dad, Dad said nothing. He just teared up and looked ashamed when he looked at me.

"Outside, the sheriff told me that even my Dad wouldn't defend me. To him that meant that what the men said was true and if he saw me dressed like a man again in town, he would arrest me for indecency."

Jackson swore. "What did he say about the money and horses?"

"He told me he knew nothing about missing money or horses, he hadn't heard of us being in town to sell our cows."

"Of course, Dad hadn't wanted to sell them there. Everyone knows the only buyer is Charles Dawson, and he only pays a fraction of what they are worth."

Jackson stared at her. He knew his father-in-law ran things, but he had always paid more than a fair price for the cattle from the Harper spread. Apparently, he hadn't realized a lot of things about Dawson's dealings with others.

"Then what did you do?"

"With no hands and Dad laid up, I had my hands full tending the stock, moving them to new pasture. That fall, we were only able to get part of the feed crop put up. Dad was able to help by then, but I had figured out I was expecting and wasn't as much help as we needed. After what the sheriff said, I avoided town, only going in early when I had to go for supplies."

"You had over a hundred animals last winter, but this spring you only located 50 or so."

"The round-up wore Dad down. It was too much for him. When he had his attack, I was able to get him home and inside, then I rode into town for the doctor. I've already told you what happened after that, the baby and all."

Jackson nodded, unwilling to give her the pity she was asking for. "Fifty is a big loss for a mild winter. Any idea what happened to them?"

"No, we never saw any carcasses or bones left by predators. Dad and I felt they were being rustled."

"It's a possibility. We have the herd penned. There are a lot of calves that need branded and cut, plus I want to make sure the herd's healthy before I let them loose with the other animals."

She nodded. "Did your men bring Dad's branding iron?"

"Yes, that's what I wanted to go over with you, the list of what they brought, compare it to the list you sent them with."

He handed her both pieces of paper. Hattie noticed they had brought her plow, her seeds. Seeds that had been passed down from gardens her grandmother had grown, through her mother, carefully saved and labeled for the next garden.

She stared at him, looking up hopefully. "They brought Momma's seeds. I wonder if you would let me add them to your garden."

"I thought your mother died when you were a little girl?"

"She did. Dad and I always saved seed and labeled them, Momma's beans, Momma's cucumbers, etc."

"Rubye has a small garden out back. James helped her plant it a couple of weeks ago. I'm sure she wouldn't mind adding a few more rows of whatever you want to plant. I can have one of the men plow it."

"Thanks. If it's all right with Rubye, I can use Pepper or Henry to plow it. I always did the garden at home."

He looked doubtful. "Its hard pack, I'm not sure if you ever had to break soil before or just till up old garden space. But I'll have one of the men stand by to help if you need it."

Hattie started to rise, but hesitated.

"I thought you would be angry, because I went out to hang the clothes."

"I can't expect Rubye to handle all the extra work. It was just chance, that you were outside when they came back."

Hattie seized the chance. "About the laundry..."

"What?"

"It would be a lot easier to wash the clothes outside. It made a lot of extra work for Rubye, my doing them in the pantry."

"Maybe, if you wait until after the hands are out on the range. The side yard would probably work since it's fenced."

He hesitated, then added. "I told the men they need to treat you the way they'd want their sisters or mothers to be treated. I warned them if they didn't, they'd be looking for another job."

She started to thank him, but he shook his head. "You still need to be careful, stay near the house, and be sure Rubye is nearby." He shook his head, "It would be a lot easier if you weren't so young and attractive, but they're only men."

Hattie rose, suddenly wobbly again with nerves now that he had reminded her of all there was to fear.

"Goodnight" she whispered stiffly, "Thank you, Mr. Harper."

He rose to stare after her, answering just as formally. "Goodnight and thank you Miss Stoddard."

CHAPTER SEVEN

Hattie rose early, fed and dressed the baby before dawn, then straightened the room and left him sleeping in the crib. She felt excited about the day. Gardening and washing clothes outside would allow her to enjoy the sunshine again. Crossing the empty house to the kitchen, she stirred the fire, adding wood and emptying ashes. She was setting the table and had coffee and a pot of water on to boil when Rubye entered the kitchen.

The housekeeper was clearly surprised but only gave her usual harrumph and Hattie was glad she had not started to cook. Rubye walked into the pantry and came out with a jar of jam, a slab of bacon and the tin of grits.

"Do you need me to milk the cow?"

"No, James does that after he feeds the stock."

"James?"

"James Boyd, the older man. He's chuck cook during round-up, stock wrangler every day."

Hattie nodded and looked around. Rubye stirred the grits, then pointed to the pantry. "Get three potatoes and an onion. If you're so antsy to work, hash 'em up."

Quickly Hattie peeled and diced the vegetables. Rubye lifted the last thick slabs of bacon out of the grease, poured half of the oil off into a crock, then took the bowl of potatoes from Hattie and added them to the hot skillet.

A cowboy entered the warm kitchen, looking from one woman to the other. He set the can on the floor by the sink and Hattie looked to Rubye. This time she nodded and pointed to the left drawer of the tall cabinet on the left wall. Hattie opened it and pulled out a clean square of cheesecloth and then opened doors until she found the wooden churn. She removed the lid and paddle, making sure it was clean and smelled sweet inside before stretching and knotting the cheesecloth over the top. Slowly she lifted and filtered the fresh milk into the churn.

The old cowhand nodded to her. "Morning, Miss Stoddard."

"Morning, Mr. Boyd. "Do you know where the cold milk is?"

He grinned at her. "I'll get it Miss, but if you need milk or butter next time," he lifted the trap door and pointed.

Hattie smiled as she watched his graying head disappear down the stairs to the cellar. While he was gone, she walked over to watch Rubye stirring up a slurry of flour and cold water for the gravy.

The older woman glanced up at her from the corner of her eye.

"They brought our plow and my mother's seeds. I wondered if there might be room for them in your garden."

Rubye snorted. "If the boss said you could, it's not my place to say yea or nay."

"It's your garden. I want it to be all right with you."

"You're a funny girl. Nothing here is mine. I work for Mr. Harper, same as you. The garden was Mrs. Harper's, but I guess it would be hard to ask her."

Hattie looked chastised, then a voice said, "Here Miss."

Hattie jumped at the head appearing through the floor and accepted the heavy pitcher of milk and cold crock full of butter. He was looking past her to Rubye, "You need me to fetch up grub for supper?"

"Yeah, a sack of red beans and a slab of ribs, cut one, no cut three more onions from that braid."

"You any good at making bread?" Rubye asked.

Hattie smiled, "Biscuits or corn bread?"

Rubye snorted. "No sense spoiling 'em. Just stir up some meal for corn cakes. Skillet will be ready again, time you're through."

Hattie whirled across the kitchen, heading for the side cupboard in the pantry where she had seen tins of meal and flour. The second door she opened held a mixing bowl. Quickly she added three big handfuls of meal, then added two small handfuls of flour before using a spoon to add baking powder. She used the pitcher of milk and some water and stirred them even as she walked across the floor.

She heard boots and voices in the other room, but over it all, the thin sweet warble of the baby's waking cry.

She handed Rubye the batter, then turned back to the bedroom. As the one or two voices said good morning, she nodded, the whole time looking toward the floor. As she hurried past them to the baby, she was aware of the tall man emerging from his room, scowling at her.

When she had bathed, changed, and redressed the baby, she settled on top of the bed to feed him again. She listened to the quiet conversation of Jackson and Rubye.

"I told her you wouldn't mind if she added a few rows to the garden. James, I'd like you to stay close to hand, once she's laid out the plot, move the end fence and add a length of posts to it."

"Rubye, I also told her she can wash clothes outside, as long as she keeps to the back of the house near the well and clothesline. I'll expect you to keep an eye on her and the baby anytime she's outside."

Hattie knew if she had been in the other room, she would have seen resentment in the other woman's eyes. She was requiring extra work for everyone, of course they would get angry and argue.

She strained to listen but heard only a grunt of agreement from Rubye. She realized James must have nodded. Bundling J.D. to her shoulder, she decided to face the music.

All three sets of eyes followed her to the table. Before sitting down, she walked to the kitchen and returned with her warm plate of food. Then she poured a glass of milk and sat down.

She was surprised when the old cowhand asked, "Can I hold the little fellow."

She looked up to Jackson but it was Rubye who clucked. "Nonsense, what do you know about babies?"

He made a face at her like soured milk. "Reckon I've held every kind of baby critter without hurting nary one, even the human kind."

Jackson nodded and smiled and Hattie rose and gently placed the baby in his arms. He cooed and made faces at the baby, waggling his mustache as he smiled.

J.D. yawned, turning his head in a long stretch, and then made a small fussing sound.

Rubye scolded, "See there, that ugly face of yours has made him cry." Gingerly the old cowhand let her take the baby from his arms to pat against her shoulder. J.D. made a few more fussing sounds, burped, then curved into her shoulder. When Jackson rose to look over her shoulder, she leaned the baby back, rocking and crooning while both men stared down at him.

Hattie smiled. The boy was a wonder and worth all the fuss, but he was sure to be spoiled rotten. While they focused on him, she ate greedily of the slab bacon and crispy potatoes smothered in gravy. She used the corn cake to mop up the thick white gravy, washing it all down with milk.

It was Jackson who poured coffee for her and passed the plate with the last hoecake. She made a puddle of sorghum and mashed butter in it, then slathered it on the cake. No matter how well she ate, she was always ravenous. Sipping the warm coffee, she tried to eat the bread slowly. They all probably thought she was a pig, the way she bolted her food.

"When you finish, I'd like you to look over the herd from your ranch."

Hattie stuffed the last half of the bread in her mouth, nodded, and rose immediately. She downed the coffee as she walked, pausing at the door to set down the empty cup.

"Ready." She opened the door and sailed off the porch and across the yard toward the corral, satisfied when he had to take long strides to catch up.

"I worried all night about which animals were missing. The herd often split up for grazing, the young cows with the bull, the yearlings and older cows with Birdie. She's a brindle coated cow, with a black circle around one eye and extra-long straight horns. She climbed onto the bottom rail, leaning forward to study the milling animals.

"See, that's Birdie," she pointed toward the reddish cow. "That's Suke and Blaze, Beverly, and Sunday."

"You name all your cows?"

"Dad didn't like me naming them, because it's a beef herd, but I always named a few of the calves. Especially, if we had to keep them up and feed them." One of the cows moved toward the girl perched on the fence. Jackson made an involuntary move to pull her back but she reached down toward the animal. He watched as the girl pulled an ear on the cow she'd called Sunday.

He remembered the battle it had taken him and three hands to catch, tie, and finally milk a beef cow the first night when J.D. kept bawling. He bet she could have cornered anyone of these and sweet talked her into being milked, beef cow or not.

If his father-in-law hadn't bought a milk cow and sent it out from town he'd decided to feed the baby on canned milk. That was better than having someone stomped to death or gored by the wild animal.

"This is Birdie's herd, right, and 33 counting new calves. Oh, there he is, I thought you said 32 last night, but that little ghost makes 33." He followed her pointing finger and saw the still damp white and dusty calf.

"At least they all seem healthy. Do you have any idea where the bull and the other eighteen or so might be?"

"Blackie is a bull you can't miss, black of course with horns like Birdie, but one tips up and the other down, like he has it put on backward. Dad got him for a great price, because the owner figured he might throw some three headed calves or mistakes. He never did." She looked at him for confirmation of her Dad's wisdom.

"No, they're good looking animals."

"Three cows I know should be with him are Frenchie, Birdie and Blondie. Frenchie is Birdie's calf with a coat just like hers from two years back. Blondie is colored like little Ghost, white and tan. And Pinto is a black and white spotted cow with a coat like an Indian pony. They could be down where the spring burbles up and the ground stays wet. That old bull loves the mud and the fresh water cress that grows in the seep."

"They probably looked there, but I'll have them go back in a couple of days, when they finish branding and get the bull calves cut. We'll need to move these animals into the herd and watch to make sure they work out together"

"We treated for worms and threw out two salt and mineral blocks after the last snow. I reckon Blackie's calves are as good as any bull throws."

He heard the defensive pride in her voice. "I'm sure they are, Miss Stoddard."

She acknowledged his apology with a nod.

"Hattie. I wanted you to see the chickens too; apparently five of them are missing."

James Boyd had come out to the fence leaving Rubye standing on the porch, rocking the baby.

"They're in the barn, the mules and that old gelding are in the back paddock."

But Hattie was already gone, opening the barn door to disappear inside. By the time the men caught up, she was outside the door with a pan of grain. As she walked outside she clucked softly, shaking the grain in the pan, "Here chick, chick, here chick." In minutes eight red hens boiled around her feet, pecking at the grain as she scattered it. One of the hounds stood on its haunches and barked, but Jackson called him back down.

"Reckon you'll need to put up a coop for these, if they're to last more than a day or two," Boyd said.

"Probably easier if we just add some wire to the garden fence. The chickens can work it and keep the bugs down. They're used to roosting in our barn, so that shouldn't be a problem." Hattie patted the flat pan against her hip and added. "Dottie and her sisters are gone, along with Gaylord, the rooster. The hens were setting so they may have stayed with their nests. Gaylord should have been out cutting up to protect the hens."

"No way could we miss a flogging rooster. Looked through that barn pretty close too," Boyd protested.

"Dad had a board just under the eaves where they roosted. We used to have a yellow cat, Purdy, who liked to move through them at night teasing them awake. So there are poles outside the barn where they can swoop up in stages then fly into their nests. There are probably one or two eggs in the nests of those that are not brooding."

"I hope you don't expect me to go back and wrangle chickens, because that was the meanest job you ever gave me boss."

"If they're nesting, we'll move nest and all for those four. I'll bet the roosters gone. Didn't you leave any dog or cat behind?" Jackson barked.

"Purdy died last year. Bert, our cow dog, was shot when the yahoos rode in."

Jackson shook his head. Had he really thought she was timid and quiet?

◇◇◇

"I'll ride out after we finish here and take Cliff. We need to chase down that black bull and any heifers he's guarding. James, you stick close. See if you can help get the garden in."

He turned back toward the corral as Hattie moved back to the house when she heard her name called. She stepped up onto the porch to take J.D., not surprised to feel a damp bottom.

James was walking toward the house, and Hattie waited until he was in easy hearing. "Can you tell the boss I need to talk to him before they leave?"

He tipped his hat in acknowledgement and Hattie took the crying infant inside.

◇◇◇

It was an hour later when she carried the padded cradle and sleeping boy to rock gently in the warm shaded breeze of the back porch. Hattie smiled, happy for the first time in weeks. She heard the hens clucking and scratching through the garden. She had lined up the seeds, each labeled and saved in its packet made from old catalog pages.

In the distance she could hear the men working in the far corral, smell the scent of singed hair and hear the painful bawls from the calves. Even the yearlings needed branding and snipped, being changed to steers before the men finished.

Ignoring the sounds, she went to the paddock for Henry. Although Pepper could outlast the younger mule, Henry was quicker to obey her commands and responded well to her lighter hand.

Harnessed to the plow, she entered through the gap in the fence that James had made earlier. She backed the mule to the edge of the current garden, set the plow blade then snapped the reins and yelled, "Giddy-up"

Exuberantly the mule leaned his head forward, putting his chest muscles into the task, ripping down the yard and opening out a shallow furrow. At the end of the thirty foot row, she yelled "whoa" and pulled on the reins. Henry stopped like a dream.

She lifted the plow blade, turned Henry and plowed up to the edge of the garden again. Quickly, she and Henry set a pattern.

Boyd came around the house to watch, marveling at the ease with which the duo worked. "Setting you're rows too close, ain't you Miss?"

She finished the fifth sequence, then turned Henry again, carefully setting the plow within six inches of the last furrow. "We're not plowing yet, just breaking ground. When I finish this, we'll need to cover the ground with some of that aged manure, spread it out, maybe wait a day or two, then run the plow through it deeper and set actual rows. But I'll harness Pepper to a dray to haul it over here. Both these long-eared guys love to work."

"I can get to loading that, have it ready to spread when you finish. I didn't figure a little girl like you would know anything about this work."

"My mother was German. She loved to garden and to work. She insisted Dad change the garden plot every two years. One year he didn't get to it in time, and I watched her dig one just like this. I've always wanted to try it myself."

He laughed and she laughed too, pushing herself and Henry, trying to finish before J.D. grew fussy. She was on the last furrow when he started crying.

Hattie wiped her face with her long sleeve. She was surely a sight, sweaty and red faced, with the fine dust sticking to her skin with each step she made over the roughly tilled ground.

She unhitched Henry and led him to the trough in front of the paddock rail, loosely hitching him and patting the dark, dusty neck.

James was already driving the other mule and the load of manure toward the garden.

By the time Hattie reached the porch, Rubye had arrived with a pail of fresh water and a towel. Hattie gratefully accepted both, stepping on to the porch where she could reassure J.D. that she would pick him up in a minute.

Rubye stepped between her and the baby. "Well, I never."

Hattie looked down at her dusty skirt and red hands, her pride of minutes ago vanishing. She reached for the fussing baby, but Rubye picked him up. "I'll change him, you get some of that dust and sweat off you so you're fit to feed him. The men will be in to eat soon, let's not waste time."

Hattie tapped her feet, knocking the dust off her boots, then hurried after them to the bedroom.

It was later, the men fed and gone, before Hattie rose from her nap. She pulled on her old skirt and the flannel shirt of her father's over her old chemise and petticoat, realizing that this was the outfit she should have worn this morning. Once again she laid the sleeping baby in the cradle on the back porch. Taking time to shade him with a protective cloth spread over the top of the cradle, she hurried to drag washtubs, washboard and soap into the side yard, drawing water to fill both. Then she brought out the pan of dirty clothes and the basket and clothespins.

Satisfied, she made short work of washing out baby things, hung them, then washed the soiled dress and under things, plus the baby's crib bedding to hang. Finally, she washed out towels and washcloths. With three lines full, she took her time in carrying the dirty water to water Rubye's rows. When she had the tubs emptied and rinsed, she stacked them on the end of the porch and stood to admire the darkened end of the new garden, already covered with the manure spread by James and Pepper.

Rubye came out, then took the washtubs and proceeded to fill them. She had two hampers of clothes, hers and Jackson's, as well as household linen.

"Do you need help?" Hattie asked.

"Nope, it's Tuesday. I always do laundry on Tuesday. Besides, James plowed that garden. You probably want to get busy and get it planted."

She heard a snuffling sound from the cradle and peeked in, patting the little raised bottom. "Such a mite for making work, little Jackie."

He squirmed a little under the weight of her hand, rooting around in his sleep until he found a fist and settled back down.

Quickly, she picked up the first bag of seeds and used the hoe that James had left beside the plowed garden. She was surprised at how deep the soil seemed. James must have plowed a lot deeper then she had, but she was pleased to note he had avoided damaging the original garden. By the time she was on the third type of seeds, Rubye was finished.

Hattie could hear the baby and dusted her hands, stopping to pull up a bucket of sweet water to drink her fill, then wash her hands and face. She walked up onto the porch and took the squalling baby that Rubye was trying to calm.

The housekeeper scowled at her muddy feet and wrinkled her nose. "Humph," she said patting the wide awake and complaining J.D. "Might as well run you through the tub as well. Hurry, if you want a chance to eat before supper."

"I didn't finish all the plantings."

"It's called tomorrow," the housekeeper said. "You can finish it in the morning while I iron, then you can iron."

Hattie raised her brows. "Right, ironing." She didn't want to admit that she usually didn't bother with her old clothes or her father's. There had been no one to see how they looked unless they were going into town.

CHAPTER EIGHT

Hattie relaxed in the tub, the baby naked and floating on top of her, his little unbound belly button and stub of cord exposed. Rubye had carried the cradle in to put him in, but Hattie had barely finished soaping and rinsing before he had begun to fuss. She had been unable to resist the opportunity to soap and rinse him, even the soft dark hair on top of his head. In the high setting tub, she had easily been able to keep his belly dry. At first he was frightened, but like her, the warm lap of the water soon relaxed him. Now he lay, completely clean and relaxed, gazing at her cooing voice.

Rubye knocked on the door, then opened it to shake her head at them. "The men are out cleaning up, you better hurry."

Hattie stood up, surrendered the baby to the housekeeper and toweled off. Then she slipped into the clean gown and robe that the housekeeper handed her. She shook out a baby blanket and took the naked baby back from Rubye, then followed her out of the door.

"Wait." The voice was loud and commanding and Hattie froze in horror. She was barefoot, her wet hair in a towel, and she clutched the top of the robe closed and the baby even tighter against her.

The terror must have shown in her eyes and Jackson felt confused. He nodded toward the bedroom and Rubye put her hands on her hips and looked scandalized. He gave her a hard look, and she turned back to the kitchen to get the food on the table, still keeping an eye on both of them.

Jackson made sure the door was open and remained in sight as Hattie entered the bedroom and laid the baby in the middle of the bed. She reached behind her for baby clothes. Even though he knew he should stay at the door, Jackson felt drawn into the room by the baby. It was the first time he had seen him completely naked since the delivery. Hattie backed up, staring at both of them.

Jackson uncovered the boy, just standing and staring down at him. Nervously, Hattie pulled the collar up on the robe, moved one foot behind the other, even though both the gown and robe drug the floor. "Is there something wrong?"

He shook his head, stepped aside and moved back to the open door. "He's just so beautiful."

She stared back at the baby and nodded. "Perfect, Donna, gave you a perfect son."

The reminder of Donna made him straighten up and refocus. "I needed to tell you that we didn't finish in time to go to the ranch today. But James said you needed to talk to me."

For the first time he stared at her, taking in the towel wrapped head, her red, embarrassed face, and the way she kept fidgeting with the robe. Even in Donna's clothes, she looked strange. Not only looked, but was strange. Earlier in the day he had needed James, but the cowhand had protested that Hattie had broken the ground for the garden. If he didn't hustle, she would be back plowing it. Donna would never have plowed a garden, never have done anything to get all sweaty and dirty. He shook his head and smiled in spite of himself.

J. D. made a sound and Hattie grabbed the blanket to block the stream of pee that arced upward. Suddenly her nervousness was gone. Quickly, she dried him, wrapped a clean band around his tummy, and then diapered him. Despite his protest, she threaded his rubbery arms into the clean gown. She had moved the damp blanket aside and checked the cover on the bed before sitting down with the fussing boy.

Jackson coughed and she looked up, suddenly embarrassed again to realize he was still there.

"I wondered if you could dig the herbs that are at my place and bring them for the new garden. They'll be the only really green plants, well, the marjoram, looks blue, but they're probably the only things growing there."

He nodded, smiling in spite of himself as the fussing baby nuzzled the front of her robe, obviously upset that she wasn't feeding him. He wondered if he hadn't coughed if she would have forgotten him and opened the robe. Blushing, he knew it was time to leave. "We'll try. Nesting hens, herbs, and look for the cows. Anything else, let me know in the morning."

He closed the door and Hattie sighed with relief. Like all men he made her nervous. But as she fed J.D. she realized in surprise, she wasn't afraid of this man.

◇◇◇

The next day, Hattie finished the last row, planting the seeds for tomatoes on the outside rows in little hills. Then she dug four big holes at the end of the new garden for the herbs, confident that Jackson would bring them home.

James Boyd had Pepper harnessed and ready to haul new pickets and rails for the garden. She enjoyed his expression when he pulled the mule to a stop, "Girl, I don't reckon I've ever worked with a better pair of mules."

"This garden is the best plowed land I've ever planted. You must have gotten Henry to outdo himself."

"I learned by watching you. That animal just about did it all by himself. I swear he remembered each turn from when you worked him in the morning."

She laughed, and from the porch they heard Rubye's strident voice. "If you two are through bragging on each other, there's a little stinker up here calling your name."

Hattie abandoned the shovel and stepped up on the porch. Leaving her smelly boots outside, she used the bucket of water she had waiting to wash her hands, arms, feet and face.

It took several minutes after she had him changed to calm the baby enough to nurse. He seemed outraged at her for taking so long and Hattie felt guilty. After all, helping in the kitchen, planting the garden, even doing laundry was secondary. Her most important job was J.D. She kissed him and held him close, crooning to get him calmed. Finally, he began nursing hungrily.

Still crooning, she rocked him back and forth, kissing the pulsing spot on the top of his head. "I'm sorry sweetheart, I'm sorry. Donna, I'm sorry. I'll stay closer, I promise little man. I promise."

Leaning back and relaxing with the baby, she wondered at herself. She had come to the ranch in rage and desperation, determined to save her home and to regain her confidence and pride. Instead, she was lost in the simple joy of holding this baby. Every day, her heart opened a little more. If she weren't careful, she would be more lost than ever.

◇◇◇

After napping, eating, and feeding J.D., Hattie made quick work of the laundry. At least today, there were only a few nappies, baby clothes, and blankets. As soon as she finished hanging clothes and watering the newly planted seeds, she carried the cradle and sleeping boy inside.

She finally managed to iron the clothes from yesterday. Rubye scolded her when she was eating lunch that if she didn't do them soon, she would have to rewash and starch them. Hattie had never boiled starch so she was grateful that Rubye had starched and rolled them when she did her clothes and Jackson's.

Fortunately, Rubye had a shoulder roast in the oven. Soon the housekeeper would add potatoes, onions and turnips to roast as the meat finished browning. It was quick work to heat the iron on the hot stovetop, but a labor in frustration to get both shirtwaists and skirts ironed. Unfortunately, Rubye had also starched her petticoats. Hattie knew they would be scratchy and stiff the next time she wore them. At least when she ironed them, she didn't worry about pressing in wrinkles like she had on the skirts and blouses. No one would ever see the undergarments.

By the time she finished, she was burning up, the front and back of the flannel shirt soaked with sweat. When J. D. started fussing, she dragged the cradle and boy outside. As soon as he felt the cool breeze under the big porch, he settled back down. Hattie set the cradle to rocking and hurried to collect the dry, clean clothes and set them inside. By the time she reached the porch again, he was awake and winding up for a cry.

Quickly she removed the soaked diaper, wet gown and even added the folded quilt from the bottom of the cradle to the diaper pail. Relaxing, she smiled as she held the squirming baby, naked except for his belly band and booties. Quickly she draped the lacy baby blanket over her shoulder and the baby curled against her, snuggling into the crook of her arm to suckle. Rocking and cooling them both in the bright sunshine, she let her hand cup the small bottom, her other hand play across his soft naked skin beneath the blanket. She felt great satisfaction in how rounded and full he was becoming, especially the snug, rounded tummy. In minutes they were both dozing.

<><><>

The wagon pulling into the yard startled them both. Her first instinct was to grab the baby and run to hide. The next was just to bow her head and become invisible.

"Oh my Charles, she's feeding the baby on the porch!"

"I thought Jackson said he didn't want to have an Indian feed his son," Dawson said.

Hattie's face flamed even redder. When Rubye came out on the porch to greet her visitors, she tried to signal her but didn't catch her eyes. Why hadn't she gone in to change the baby where there were clothes? Then the horror really hit. They would come over to see the baby and be scandalized.

Ignoring everyone, Hattie dashed past them into the house.

"What is that smell? Why are there clothes and washtubs on the porch? Rubye, has my son-in-law gone mad? What was that girl wearing? They looked like rags but I heard in town that he bought her clothes to wear?

The questions pelted after her as Hattie made it to the bedroom. Quickly she cleaned and dressed the sleepy baby. Then she frantically washed her own face and changed clothes for the third time in the same day. Dressed in the starched black dress with its navy stripe, she felt armored. She parted, then twisted her hair into a tight controlled bun and pinned it at the back of her head. Staring in the mirror the only thing she could think was why had she been so foolish to work in the sun all day without her bonnet?

Clicking her tongue at her reflection, she gathered the beautifully dressed baby and carried him out to the waiting couple. The banker and his wife were seated on the settee in the living room and Rubye had left them to fetch some cold glasses of tea. Hattie sank primly into the chair across from them, lowered her bundle and turned the blanket back.

"Oh, how precious," the woman cooed and held out her arms. Hattie surrendered the baby, aware of how critically the banker was staring at her.

"Rubye, where's Jackson?" Dawson asked.

"He rode out to look for stock. We don't expect him until suppertime. Would you like to join us for dinner here?"

"And eat with his cow hands, no thanks," Irene said.

Hattie pictured the hands sharing dinner with her father and her. It had never occurred to them that one wouldn't share food with the people you worked with every day. Clearly Jackson worked with these men, led them, and ate with them.

Of course, the banker and his wife would not sit down to eat with their hired help. Had Donna, the perfect wife, complained about sharing meals with the hands?

The woman was talking, asking her something. Hattie realized it by the sharpness with which she repeated the question.

"He is nursing well?"

Hattie nodded, feeling a strange wave of protectiveness as the woman prodded and peeked under the baby's gown, at his feet, checking his belly, then examined his fingers. When she started to pull at the belly band, Hattie wanted to snatch the boy back.

"He eats every two hours, day and night."

"Is he always so sleepy? He's not waking up at all. Look at him Charles. He's dead to the world."

The baby protested the inspection by giving a soft cry, as though to prove her a liar, scrunching his face and almost opening an eye.

Hattie moved her hands to the edge of the chair and sat on them to fight the strong urge to grab the baby back.

"You buried your father and son on your ranch?" Dawson asked.

Hattie sat up straighter, moving her hands to her lap and folding them together. "No, there wasn't time. They are buried here. When I go back next year, we'll move the bodies."

"Go back?" There was something in the way he said it, like the mere suggestion was ridiculous. It made her swallow hard. But those cold blue eyes had moved off. He sat forward, studying the baby.

"Let's go, Irene. You can see him at church Sunday."

Hattie expected her to protest or resist giving up the baby, but she let Rubye take the child so she could rise.

"Doesn't he seem lighter to you?" She looked at Rubye. "Maybe he is eating all day and night because there is no nutrition in what he eats. Our wet nurse for Donna was a large woman with plenty of fat in her hips and breasts. Our Donna was such a lovely, plump baby. You remember what a chubby darling she was, Charles?"

Hattie rose to reach for the baby, but Irene Dawson turned. "You seem awfully scrawny to me." She stared accusingly at Hattie. "Are you eating enough? What does Dr. Padgett have to say about what you should eat and how often you should nurse the baby?"

There was no chance to answer any of the rapid-fire questions. But when she finally paused to breathe, Hattie asked. "Who is Dr. Padgett?"

"Dr. Padgett is the author of *Advice for Young Mothers*. His childhood manual is the standard. You have been reading and following the child care manual? You must follow all his instructions, my dear. After all, you are so young and have no experience with raising a baby."

"I had a child."

"He died," Charles and Irene chimed in together.

Hattie felt the words like a physical blow. "He was born too early. I've fed and kept calves and baby goats alive before. All of them ate frequently, night and day, and slept between feedings."

"Cows and goats!" she shrieked. "I insist you find and read Dr. Padgett and follow it to the letter. You can read?"

"I can read and write in English and in German. I promise you I'm doing everything I can to care for this baby."

Irene Dawson moved past her, whispering to her husband as they left. "We can wire Austin for suitable help, Charles."

Hattie stood rooted, waves of emotion sweeping through her. The baby sensed her turmoil and began to cry in earnest. Hattie raised the child to her shoulder then moved backward toward the bedroom as Rubye escorted the angry grandparents out the front door.

She could hear Charles Dawson firing questions at the housekeeper standing in the door to glare back at her.

"She's sleeping in our daughter's bed!" Again Hattie heard gasps and whispers as Mrs. Dawson's voice rose louder. "That's outrageous! Really Charles you need to talk to Jackson, that boy has no sense of propriety."

"Is he sharing her quarters?" This time Charles voice was the one rising in shock.

"No, no. His bed is in the study. I'm in the house at all times. There have been no real improprieties, I can assure you."

"See that there aren't," he said.

"What do you mean real improprieties? Why did he give her Donna's bed?"

Hattie sat on the edge of the high bed, the baby greedily tugging at her breast.

"He wanted her to be next to the baby, to take care of his every need. She has been diligent in taking care of him. I can assure you they are both getting enough to eat."

With Rubye's defense she relaxed and so did the baby. In minutes he was asleep, still fastened to her breast, but as his head started to fall back, he jerked awake and suckled fiercely. Hattie smiled and rubbed his silky head. She would find and read the baby manual, but she could not leave yet.

Through the open door, she could hear the distant voices, but no longer make out what they were saying. She pushed her fears away, it had to turn out all right.

◇◇◇

It was late and Hattie sat in the rocker on the porch, folding the last of the clean baby clothes. Finished, she stood and looked out at the ranch yard, picking out the barn, paddock and garden in the fading light. Strangely, it felt as though she had lived here forever.

She was surprised when Jackson came outside and moved to sit on the porch rail, sipping a last cup of coffee. As he too stared at the vista, she wondered if he was aware that she was there. Then he spoke. "We brought back your hens, even found some eggs for breakfast."

"Really, you found Dottie and her sisters. Were you able to save the eggs they were setting on?"

"Yeah, Cliff figured it out. He slipped the nests into sacks, put food on the rail where they had been, then when the hens resettled on the nests, he pulled the sacks up and tied them. I would never have had the patience."

"How long did it take?"

"Not that long. I was digging plants in the garden, bagging them. We finished about the same time."

"Did you find Blackie and the cows?"

He stared off into the distance. "You hear that young bull bawling in the paddock."

Hattie nodded, not sure if he could see her.

"He's black and has the curved horns you described on your bull, only they both point in the right direction. I figured if we found the missing animals, we could castrate him and let him join the rest of the herd, if not, you'd still have a bull."

She smiled tightly, stunned by the unexpected kindness.

"You didn't find them," she said.

"No," he stared down at her, surprised at how hard it was to tell this strange girl bad news.

She squared her shoulders, took a deep breath. "No sign of where they went, no bones, no carcasses."

"No trace. Cliff and I figure rustlers."

It was a bitter blow, but that was what she received these days, blow after blow.

"Thank you for looking, for everything."

"It's not over. I figure if they would rustle your cows, they could be taking others. I plan to do a count of our brand, compare it to last year's tally, now that the boy is safe and you're settled."

"Did Rubye tell you we had company?"

"My in-laws. I heard they gave you a hard time."

"Your mother-in-law suggested they send to Austin for another wet nurse."

When he waited she forced the words out, "Because he seems smaller and is eating and sleeping all the time."

"That's what babies do, never seen a critter that didn't start out that way, most lose a little at first, then start to gain."

"They told me I should read Dr. Padgett's *Advice for Young Mothers* and follow it to the letter."

"Not surprised. Irene had Donna reading it and fretting about his advice for months. It's in the study. I'll get it for you."

Harriet couldn't tell if he agreed or disagreed with what they thought. He hadn't told her not to worry about the nurse from Austin.

She carried the basket of clothes to the bedroom, grateful that J.D. was still asleep. She was standing, staring down at the baby when Jackson tapped lightly at the door, then crossed the threshold to hand her the book. He took her place, leaning over to listen to the baby's chest, placing a large hand on his soft head while he listened.

"Try to ignore them," he whispered as he straightened. "That's what I always told Donna. Trouble is, she could never do it. Her mother and father ran her life, even picked me out for her husband. It surprised me, since Charles never really seemed to think much of my opinions."

Hattie stared up at him. "I don't believe that. You were her choice and they agreed to her wishes."

He felt the tightness in his chest. For the first time he considered their summer romance in a different light. What if it hadn't been the banker that threw them together, but Donna who had arranged all the meetings, the dances, and events? Just the thought of it made him sigh. He realized how much he wanted it to be all Donna's doing.

Hattie stared up at the tall, handsome cowboy, noticing the dark hair and light eyes that were the baby's. She set the thick, small handbook down on the dresser next to her family Bible. Running her fingers along the edge of the pages, she sensed the trace of Donna's fingers on the smooth paper.

Jackson remained beside the crib but stared across at the nervous girl, fingering the handbook as nervously as Donna had. So far she had taken care of the boy by instinct, rushing to take care of his needs with calm confidence. He hoped the book wouldn't make her as nervous and indecisive as it had Donna.

"Remember we have an agreement. I've paid your back taxes, so I'm not paying someone else for the same work. You believe you can handle him, don't you?"

Hattie nodded, "I promised you I'd do my best. I do try my best every day."

Rubye stood in the doorway, staring at the couple beside the crib.

"What's all the jabber about? Something wrong with J.D.?"

Jackson looked at her with a scowl at being interrupted. But suddenly he felt as guilty as Hattie looked at being found together in her bedroom.

"Just giving Miss Stoddard the copy of Dr. Padgett mother Dawson told her to read."

He walked past Rubye and murmured as he left, "Goodnight, ladies."

CHAPTER NINE

The rest of the week passed without another word between them. Hattie watched for him, followed his movements, and listened to him give orders to everyone in the house, everyone but her. She had become invisible to him. Crazily, that made her both relieved and disappointed.

Every day, Hattie rose early. She changed and fed the baby, then hurried to the kitchen to start the fire and put on coffee and oatmeal or grits, whichever Rubye had set out the night before. She also helped to put together the basket that James Boyd took along each day for the men and their lunch.

All six men rode out together, and then spread out over the area Jackson assigned. They joined James at the spot set up for lunch. They would compare their tally, then move to the next sector and work through it. The plan was to take the next two weeks to finish the survey of the over two thousand acre ranch.

At night, the women worked up a bigger meal and added a dessert. With the hens laying they had eggs. Hattie had only made one cake in her life and it was a disaster. But Rubye stirred up one most nights after the men had to be away from the house.

Although each cake tasted different, they began with the same recipe: two cups flour, one cup sugar, one half cup butter, two eggs, one cup buttermilk, one teaspoon vanilla, two teaspoons baking soda, and a pinch of salt.

Rubye kept a pair of vanilla beans in a small bottle of whiskey, and used the strong liquid to flavor the cake, replacing the whiskey as needed but keeping the beans in the jar. Sometimes she used the vanilla, sometimes cinnamon and brown sugar. To the next cake she might add chocolate powder and pecans. All were baked in the largest iron skillet. If it was a plain yellow cake, she glazed it with a caramel made of sugar browned in the big skillet and thinned with rich cream then left to bubble and thicken before being poured over the big round cake. After a couple of days, Hattie could help bake the cake, but always waited for Rubye's instructions.

After the hard days, working cattle and checking boundaries, the men enjoyed the big meals, always with beef-- steak, stew, roast, braised ribs, or chili. They seemed to enjoy getting even with the animals who had worked them so hard during the day. Meals were quiet affairs, with everyone hungry and too tired for anything but eating, eager to rest for the next day.

◇◇◇

By the second Sunday they had finished the count so everyone dressed, the men in black suit coats, the women in starched dresses and petticoats. Hattie wore the black blouse striped with red and the solid black skirt. She wore a stiff, black, poke-bonnet that had been her mothers. Now it was starched and ironed with a big black bow tied beneath her chin. On her hands she wore her mother's gloves, bleached white, with a briar stitch along every seam. She clenched her fingers inside the tight cloth of the gloves, nervous as they approached the church.

The Dawsons would be waiting. That woman would be waiting to take J.D., to bounce him and show him off. To cluck over the sweet sleepy face, to silently weigh him, and tell Jackson how wrong she was as a wet nurse.

Hattie stiffened on the hard bench beside Jackson, recalling the first time she had ridden here nearly a month before. Two benches had been added to the back of the buckboard. Rubye and James rode behind them, Cliff, Hank and one of the young hands rode on the last bench. The remaining three hands rode on horseback alongside.

Hattie looked over her shoulder, smiling at Rubye sitting stiffly beside James Boyd. For the first time, she noticed him turn and smile at Rubye. The woman looked forty, maybe forty-five, tall, homely, and strongly opinionated. But that shy smile could have been given to a young girl. For the first time that morning, Hattie smiled.

Jackson glanced at her and smiled too "Finally, you've had a pleasant thought?"

She looked up at him, wondering if she dared to say it. "I wondered, Rubye and James?" She whispered.

He laughed, "Anything is possible."

She nodded, staring down at the baby, once again tucked into the wagon toolbox for safety and riding at their feet. "I can't help worrying, whether mother Dawson will think he is growing fast enough."

He glanced down at the baby. "Don't worry about them. I know what you've done for him." He gripped the reins in his left hand, reaching down to squeeze her hand. Even through the glove she felt the warmth of his fingers. Nervously, she pulled her hand free and folded both hands primly in her lap.

He pulled the team in beside a shade tree, and then raised the sleeping child onto her lap. Jackson dismounted and then reached up to firmly grip her waist, lifting her and the baby to the ground.

Hattie stood, waiting until the taller woman could stand beside her. Rubye wore a hat, a small blue bonnet studded with a white silk rose, a trail of veil draped across her upper face. She too was gloved, her dress a stiff blue bombazine. Hattie noticed Boyd had stepped down first, then walked around to lift a hand to help Rubye down.

Using a spoke of the wheel as a step, she still weighed enough, for the man to make a woof of sound as she settled.

As they walked around the wagons near the church, Hattie heard quick catches of breath and murmurs of disapproval. "I'll take the baby," his strong voice startled her. "Rubye can show you where to sit."

Hattie bit back the retort. I can sit where my father and I always sat, midway back, on the left side. But she didn't say it out loud because with everyone pointing her out and whispering, she knew she would never have the nerve to walk in and sit in that pew.

◇◇◇

Suddenly, Hattie felt absolutely alone. The brief moment of understanding was gone. As she watched, the tall cowboy climbed the steps of the white frame church. She heard the kind murmurs: "Oh, Mr. Harper, he's beautiful; well done, Jackson; too pretty to be yours, old son."

For a minute, she thought she saw a tall, young woman beside Jackson, her hair pinned in an upsweep of brown curls, smiling at everyone. Hattie imagined her tugging his arm to reveal the baby's blue booties, perfect little blue cap and blue sweater over the immaculate white gown. The lacy baby blanket spilled over the black-sleeved arm holding the little miracle. It seemed everyone had something to say until Mrs. Dawson swept back down the aisle to fuss.

"Cover him back up, Jackson; it's a cool morning for a baby. Here let me have him." When she moved in closer, the ghostly shadow of his wife disappeared. For a minute, Hattie felt her loss as acutely as the tall man who looked totally bereft. Then his mother-in-law paraded down the aisle, showing the baby, accepting the accolades and murmurs of sympathy for the daughter who would miss the boy and man the child would become.

Hattie followed the ranch hands and Rubye to the last pew on the right side and filed in first as Rubye indicated. This put her on the inside wall and she knew if the baby fussed everyone would have to rise to let her out. Then she realized they wouldn't. She would use Rubye's tall frame and a blanket to hide what she was doing and she would nurse J.D. in pretended privacy.

Hattie settled into her corner, aware of the couple in front of her pew, arguing, until the woman stood and the man followed. The woman gave her a scandalized look as she rose and Hattie felt her face flame with shame. Then she reminded herself, she had nothing to apologize for, it was that trash that hung around Thelma's in town, bragging and making up lies about her that should be ashamed. Let God take care of those liars and these self-righteous people who were so eager to believe gossip.

So she made herself sit straighter, raised her head higher, and managed to lock eyes with the departing woman. "Fool," she said without speaking a word.

Hattie tried to relax, but the sermon seemed dry and overlong, the emphasis was on prayer to stay away from temptation. Then suddenly the preacher was in a thunder, warning that the rewards for sin were damnation, with fire and brimstone awaiting all those who fell from the straight and narrow. As one, the congregation turned to stare in her direction, as though to add, "He means you, harlot."

Hattie felt a quiver of despair. Was there no way to remove this stigma? True the town had seen her pregnant and unwed; she had borne a child and lost it. But she had not surrendered to temptation but to force. Hattie's legs began to shake with nervousness. It was all she could do to sit quietly and not scream in protest of her innocence. When the tension became unbearable, she heard a high-pitched squall, and then a gasping, warbling cry.

In a minute, she knew J.D. would be in full cry. Fortunately the preacher called everyone to their feet to sing a hymn. Moments later she saw Jackson at the end of the row, passing the baby from hand to hand down to her. When he arrived, she sank back into her seat, unbuttoned her dress and draped the lacy blanket over the fussing baby and herself. By the time the hymn ended and everyone was seated again, J. D. was happily nursing and Hattie relaxed, shutting out all the scorn and judgment. She felt at peace just holding the baby. He was the one person who did not label or judge her, only needed and trusted her in the most basic of ways. She would have to be like this baby and just accept and trust that life would be all right for her too.

Finally, the service ended and Hattie was relieved to have her row exit first. She carried the satisfied baby out to the wagon, and then changed him before tucking him back into the tool box under the seat. She accepted a hand up from Boyd and settled on the buckboard seat to wait. Through the trees, she watched Jackson standing on the top step of the church, talking with his in-laws and exchanging words with others from the congregation. Please don't let them invite us all to dinner.

What was she thinking? They would never invite her to the house for dinner.

Minutes later Jackson strode back to join them.

◇◇◇

"If those eggs ever hatch, I could stand a pan of fried chicken," Cliff muttered.

"It takes three weeks to become a chicken. Everybody and everything seems to be thinking of eating my poor chickens, even the ones still in the eggs."

Jackson laughed. "If my hounds don't get them, I would be happy to get a chance at them."

Hattie scowled, sat forward in a huff, as they all laughed softly.

◇◇◇

Finally, the first clutch of chicks hatched. Cliff had put the nests up in the loft, so when Hattie went to feed them, she always checked for chicks. When the whole nest finished hatching, she scooped the first set of chicks up and carried them down from the loft, placing them in an empty stall.

It was three days later before the last clutch hatched. Jackson and the men were once more riding the range. Hattie had managed to scoop up the last fluffy chick and was resting on the top rung, her skirt swept up to ensure her firm footing before carrying them down.

"Well, boys, look what we've found here. Our own sweet wild girl, already in the hay loft waiting for her first caller," said Rafe Hogue.

Hattie sat, her throat frozen with fear. Her rifle was still on the porch, where she set it close to hand each morning before leaving the house. When the men were gone, Jackson had made her promise to keep it ready when she was outside.

If only she had taken her daddy's pistol. She looked about for some sort of weapon and spotted the hand scythe hanging on a nail to the right of the ladder.

Able rode into the barn and leered up at her. "First, I owe her a bullet, let her feel how it is to be shot." He raised his pistol and Hattie flipped the hand scythe through the air. His scream came with the thud of the bullet into the ladder below her feet. When the gun dropped, his finger fell with it.

Silas swore and turned his mount to ride over to his brother. "Damn you, you've cut off his finger. I'm going to cut you up bad for that."

They heard the ratcheting of a shotgun behind them and Rubye's hard voice, "Move and I'll blow you in half."

Rafe swore. "I thought you said she was here alone."

Rubye let out her usual harrumph. "Get your sorry carcasses off this ranch. Jackson Harper will string you men up for this if you ever set foot here again."

"Let me get my finger, won't you?" whined Able.

Hattie stepped down as soon as she heard Rubye's voice, racing to pick up the fallen gun, while managing the apron full of chicks.

Crouching she raised the pistol, cocked, and aimed it at Rafe Hogue's head. "The hens have already eaten it, move before I shoot off some more food for them."

She saw the fury in Able's eyes, heard all three mutter threats, but as quickly as they rode in, they were gone.

Hattie squatted and shook the little chicks from her apron. Then she picked up the finger where it had dropped. She stuck the grisly trophy in her apron pocket, hooked the scythe over the stall wall, and followed Rubye across to the porch.

◇◇◇

By the time she reached the steps her legs felt rubbery and she sank on the bottom riser. Rubye moved past her before collapsing on the top step.

"Lord, girl, if the dog hadn't started barking, I wouldn't have looked out to see them."

Hattie looked up at her and then reached out to clutch her hand. "You were so brave, Rubye, thank you."

"Humph. I just didn't like their mangy manners. Are they the ones you were telling Jackson about?"

Hattie nodded as she gulped air, her heart still pounding in her chest.

Rubye looked grim, still staring down at her. "Next time, make sure you have a gun with you."

Hattie nodded. "I've got Dad's old pistol, and now I've got this one."

She turned the barrel, looking at the five bullets in the chamber, holding it at arm's length as she released the hammer to uncock it.

"Let me see it."

Hattie raised the gun but Rubye shook her head and Hattie looked down to where Rubye was staring. There was a blood stain on the pocket. "Do you have a box?"

Rubye stood up, went inside, and then came back a few minutes later. She handed Hattie the large box that until minutes ago had held kitchen sulfurs. Hattie solemnly removed the finger, studying its broken, dirty nail, and passed it to Rubye.

"Just two knuckles. He'll still have a stub."

She passed the index finger back and Hattie dropped it into the match box. Slowly she closed it. "Don't say anything to Jackson," Hattie pleaded.

"Don't be silly. I have to tell him. He'll want to keep more men here to protect you."

Hattie laughed. "I'm already boxed up. That would be one or more men who couldn't do their job, just hanging around to 'guard' me." She stared up at Rubye. "Please don't tell him."

The older woman shook her head. "I can't lie to him. What if he or one of the men heard the shots and asks me? I'll have to tell him then."

"I'm not saying lie if he asks you, but don't tell him anything if he doesn't ask."

Rubye stood up, shaking her head as they both heard the baby's first cry. "What about J.D.?"

"It was me they were after. The baby is safe."

Rubye gave her usual snort as both entered the house.

◇◇◇

The men came in that evening and nothing was said about the incident in the barn. They all wanted to talk about the little chicks milling around the yard. The biggest worry was the dogs. All but the oldest hound were always gone to work with the men, with the cowboys barking orders at them when home. But the hens had settled them down quickly. They would circle to protect the chicks, taking turns at pecking any part of the hounds that came forward.

"I'd feel better if they were in a coop. Boyd, I thought you were going to put wire around the garden," Jackson said.

"I think they'd be better off if I put it around the empty corral for now. Maybe set some boxes in for nesting. They might eat the seeds and the ladies plants if we keep them fenced in the garden."

"You could, but you'd have the chore of moving boxes and chickens when we need it for horses," Cliff added.

"We'll think about it, and then Saturday when we're in town, we can get the supplies," Jackson concluded.

CHAPTER TEN

Two months later, there was still no coop. Hattie was resting on the porch, rocking the sleepy baby after doing laundry and hanging it. She looked up at the squawk of a hen and stared as a red blur squeezed out from under the rail, a sagging bundle of feathers dangling from his jaws.

She gently dropped the baby into the cradle, then picked up the rifle and rested the barrel on the rail. The first shot sent up dust behind him, the animal was moving so fast. The second she aimed ahead and to the left of the last shot and was thrilled when he zagged into her bullet.

Rubye came running out. "Are they back again?"

"It's a different kind of varmint. I'm walking out for the coyote."

"Wait," Rubye ran back out, with a small knife. "For the tail, there's a bounty."

Hattie slipped the knife beneath her apron belt, grabbed the rifle. As she walked out toward the fallen animal she hoped her hen might still be alive in the coyote's grip.

As she approached, she saw a red form darting toward the fallen animal, another prey clenched in his jaws. She knelt and fired, overjoyed when the second animal dropped, a few feet from the first.

She made quick work, detaching tails and stabbing the animals in the neck to make sure they were dead. Disappointed, she lifted the still warm hen by the feet, her neck broken, probably in the fall. The second animal had caught a jack rabbit, clearly planning to trade up to the fat chicken.

She tucked the dusty red tails and knife back in her belt, made sure the safety was on the rifle, then clutched an animal in each hand.

A pair of riders appeared over the horizon. Hattie was relieved to recognize Cliff and one of the younger hands. She lifted her rifle and the game and grinned in salute, then marched back toward the house.

The third rider came up in a blur. For a moment Hattie raised the gun, then lowered it when he hollered. Jackson stopped quickly, his horse rearing beside her before dropping down. She saw the worry in his face and knew she should say something.

"Hand me the gun," he barked.

She swallowed at the look of anger in his eyes. She checked the knife and coyote tails at her waist, switched so she held the rabbit and chicken in the same hand and handed up the rifle.

He leaned over, grabbed her by the waist and lifted her up before him, his arm around her waist like an iron band.

"The coyote grabbed one of the hens, so I shot it. This one came in to trade his rabbit for her and I shot him too."

He pulled her back hard against him, his voice a fierce whisper in her ear as he slowly walked the horse back to the house. "I thought it was one of those two legged coyotes again. Or did you think Rubye wouldn't show me that finger and tell me what happened?"

She felt a shiver of fear at the accusation in his voice. "She promised not to tell. It was all right. We chased them off."

"But it could have gone the other way, if Rubye hadn't been there."

Hattie swiveled in the seat, trying to look up at him. "I'm not helpless." She spat out, trying to hold back the rage she felt.

"You are when you're out here away from the house."

She started to protest, but felt his arm shift, his hand grasping her shoulder to trap her other arm by her side. He planted his hand in her hair and forced her face up to his. Angrily he kissed her, his lips punishing. For a minute she struggled, pushing at him in panic. As she shrank in fear, he loosened his grip, softened the kiss, held her gently.

Panic and fear vanished as he gentled his hold and Hattie lost her breath in the fierce soft sweetness of it. She stared up at him, confused. When she saw the same confusion in his eyes, she turned away. Face flaming she faced forward as he rode into the yard, setting her off on the porch. Hattie stood there, her legs shaky, as he stared down at her. "Remember to stay close to this house to be safe." Then he handed her the gun and turned his horse. In minutes he was gone.

◇◇◇

She plucked and cut up the chicken, adding the meat to the skinned and cut up rabbit. She cut the little puff tail to use to powder the baby. He was already big enough to need things to distract him. Not her, her mind kept returning to Jackson. She hung two tail feathers from the handle of the cradle where they could flutter above him. According to Dr. Padgett, babies needed distractions for mental exercise when awake, especially after three months of age.

She wasn't sure if everything the man wrote was true, but she found it comforting to read what to expect the baby to be able to do at each age. So far he had been right. Just in the last two weeks, Jackie had begun to make sounds and faces back at her when she talked.

She focused on the baby, noticing how he was staring up, at the fluttering feathers. Even as she watched, he waved a fist as though he would grab the feathers fluttering overhead.

He had definitely smiled at her, she knew they were real smiles, not gas, as Rubye stated. Any day now she expected a real laugh. Three months last week.

Rubye stood on the porch, staring at the baby reaching up for the floating feathers. "You want me to fry that up?"

Hattie shook her head. "It's too tough. I was thinking dumplings."

Rubye put her hands on her hips. "Never heard of dumplings and rabbit."

"Dad liked dumplings with any kind of stew, we often added them to rabbit stew. I'll cook it, if you'll watch the baby?"

"Humph. What else you going to cook with it?"

"Wilted salad, from the lettuce and garden thinnings."

"Maybe you want to do a peach cobbler, with those canned peaches."

"Sounds perfect."

<><><>

Despite her wandering mind, she was able to make the meal. As Hattie browned the meat in the heavy stock pot, she relived his angry words. Then added three quarts of liquid to cover the meat while it boiled. She prepared vegetables to add, potatoes, onions, carrots, thinking of what she should have said with eat cut. While the meat continued to boil, she slipped out to the garden to pick herbs and fresh lettuce, along with young carrots, pea plants and turnips as she thinned each row.

By the time the meat was starting to fall off the bone, she scooped it out to cool, dropped in the vegetables to boil, and then stopped to feed J.D.. Holding him, she relived it all again. As soon as he was asleep, she hurried back to finish her cooking. She pulled all the meat loose, added it, herbs, salt and pepper to the boiling vegetables. By now all she could remember of the incident was the kiss.

She cracked three eggs, added a splash of oil, and two tablespoons of buttermilk into a pile of flour on the dough board. Scolding herself to stop thinking about it, she quickly stirred the liquids, then folded flour in until she had soft dough ready to roll out. She rolled out a huge rectangle and cut it into thirds, then rolled each smaller rectangle and cut long strips. Using a big spoon, she dropped dumplings into the broth, letting them spiral out into the boiling stew, feeling her mind spiral with them.

Making the cobbler she kept remembering how suddenly the punishing kiss had changed. She quickly thickened the peaches, poured them into a pan and stirred up a different batter, one sweetened with sugar, and dropped it by spoonfuls into the peaches and liquid, sprinkling it with sugar and cinnamon before adding it to the oven.

While the cobbler and biscuits baked, she moved the dumplings to a back-eye to stay warm, and then cut bacon into the skillet. Why had he grabbed her? He had no right to do that. When it was fried, she added three tablespoons of sugar to the hot grease, then added a half cup of vinegar to the pan, finally adding all the washed lettuce and snipped greens to the pan, tossing them in the hot spicy liquid. She diced a hard- boiled egg, crumbled the bacon, and added both on top of the wilted greens as soon as she lifted them to the big flat bowl.

◇◇◇

Hattie was back in the bedroom, the window open and a cool breeze fluttering the curtains, when she heard the men ride in. She could hear them at the well washing up, talking excitedly about the good smells from the kitchen.

As the men came to the table and started to eat, all were complimentary about the food. Rubye took all the accolades in stride, saying nothing until one of the men asked how she had talked Miss Stoddard into killing one of her prized hens.

"Coyote did it for her. Thank her for the dumplings. But, half of its rabbit and you boys didn't even know it."

"Not mine, I et chicken. Best I ever had," Boyd said.

"How'd she get a rabbit, if the coyote caught her chicken?"

She listened to Rubye tell the story of the two coyotes, making Hattie sound like a real sharp-shooter. The men were laughing, trying to imagine the young girl chasing after her hen.

The men were nearly as complimentary of her biscuits and the peach cobbler. For a moment she remembered her Dad and the hands going on about her cooking, felt the pride she had felt then.

But when she closed her eyes, she felt that iron band and breathless feeling from Jackson's kiss, and was instantly awake. What had he meant by kissing her?

◇◇◇

When Hattie came out after the voices finally left, Rubye was busy clearing dishes. Hattie walked over and handed Jackson the baby, then sat down at the empty table. Rubye bustled in with her plate, a few dumplings with a mouthful of wilted greens on the side and a cold biscuit on the edge of a small dish of cobbler.

"You're lucky they left any for you. Sweet or buttermilk?"

"Sweet, thank you Rubye, I can get it."

"Sit, you did all the cooking."

Jackson raised an eyebrow, stared at Hattie then smiled at Rubye. He was holding the baby under the arms, letting him push against his lap to stretch out with his little bowed legs. When J.D. pushed too hard in the wrong place, Jackson made a face and let out an 'ow.' The baby laughed and Hattie smiled.

Rubye walked in from the kitchen, smiling and laughing too. J.D. looked over at her and made a happy gurgle. "Do it again, make him laugh."

Jackson sat the baby on the edge of the cleaned table and laughed at him as he pretended to bite his neck. The baby laughed and rolled his head against him, trying to bite back.

"Now, that's a right sweet sound. Here let me take him."

Hattie sat mesmerized by the look on Jackson's face as he stared at the baby. When he looked over at her, she felt him studying her face, wondered what he was looking for.

Rubye sank down, drying her hands in her apron to take him. "Here you silly goose," she teased, laughing when the baby cooed up at her. At her laugh, he laughed too. "There, did you hear it? Donna's laugh?"

He nodded and Hattie felt a sharp pang in her heart. No wonder he looked so enchanted. The baby laughed like the woman he loved.

Rubye looked from one to the other. "Humph, you'd best eat up. This little man needs changing." She handed him back to Jackson and left the room.

Hattie ate, barely tasting the food. When she rose to take the baby she said. "He's right on schedule, according to Dr. Padgett. I wish I knew how much he weighs. He is getting bigger isn't he?"

"Bigger every day. Irene Dawson will be pleased when she sees him tomorrow. He's looking pudgy, and that's the way she likes them."

At Hattie's scowl he laughed. "Of course, you don't know what he weighed at birth, but Doc Jenkins put down seven pounds. Next time we're in town, you can weigh him at Thompson's store. Bet he's more than fifteen pounds."

She remembered how enormous the newborn J.D. had felt when she first lifted him. Of course, the tiny scrap that had been her son still was the baby she compared him too.

◇◇◇

That night as she gave him a sponge bath in the washtub on top of the dresser, she was careful as Dr. Padgett advised not to remove the protective oils found in every baby's skin. She studied the chunky legs and arms, the round pink tummy with its perfect little innie-belly-button. There were dimples on each knee and elbow. She kissed each then lifted him out over the chamber pot as Dr. Padgett directed she do every day. For only the second time, there was the little tinkle of success.

She wasn't sure if there were anyway the baby could know or control the event, but according to the good doctor, this repeated process would lead to a well-trained child by age one. She had promised Irene Dawson that she would follow the good doctor's advice. No matter how silly much of it seemed to her, she did it because she knew it was what Donna would want, would have done if she were still here. Smiling, she recorded the laugh and the successful potty experience in the baby book.

Clean and diapered, she deposited J.D. into his crib, where he could watch her getting ready for bed. He did so with the usual kicking of feet, waving of fists, and range of coos and gurgles. When ready, she stared down at him, trying to see his mother. Rubye claimed the boy looked just like Donna. Hattie loved his soft blue eyes, button nose and decidedly pointed chin. Even though he didn't look like Donna or Jackson in the tintype, Hattie loved his sweet face. "Your momma made a wonderful son, Jackie."

She picked up the baby to lie playing beside her, despite what Dr. Padgett said about never allowing a child into your bed. She could remember climbing into bed with her parents. Even the year that her mother died, she would let Hattie curl up beside her to read and talk about recipes and things she had seen that day working with her Daddy. She loved the shared time then, and she loved it now.

Each night, with pillows and crib fencing him in on one side, she played peek-a-boo and talked lovingly to the baby until they were both sleepy, then she blew out the light.

◇◇◇

"What's going on?"

Jackson stared at his housekeeper, surprised at her tone of voice. He studied the tall, rangy woman, a friend of the Harper family and his neighbor all his life. When he bought the ranch and needed a housekeeper, she was the first person he asked. Single, the typical old-maid, she had remained behind to care for her parents when the rest of the family married one-by-one and moved out. Mid-thirties, cantankerous as an old goat, her chances in life seemed limited. He tried to remember why she was bitter and tolerate her caustic tongue.

"What's going on between you and that girl?"

"You're asking me if there's something improper between me and Miss Stoddard." He felt the muscle in his jaw flex, he was gritting his teeth so hard. "Nothing."

"Nothing," she said the word with disgust, her hands on her flat hips. "Don't tell me nothing. I saw you two making eyes at each other."

"Making eyes? We shared a smile when the baby laughed. You smiled and laughed too."

"You weren't smiling at the baby. You were looking at each other, smiling and looking away. What's going on?"

"Nothing," he growled. "You're here every day with us, you know nothing is going on, for God's sake."

"Don't swear at me, Jackson Harper. Then why were you on one horse?"

He wondered if it was possible that Rubye had seen him kissing Hattie. He shook his head in disbelief. No, he had been in a swale below sight of the ranch. No one saw it.

Rubye was one cagey old bird. Somehow she knew about it.

"I heard the shots. Worried those no counts were back and rode in to help you ladies…"

"She was shooting coyotes. What kind of woman shoots coyotes?"

"Quiet down. Give me a chance to answer. She was out walking, and I only had one horse. I was bringing her back to the house to be safe."

"Donna would never shoot at coyotes. She was a lady. This girl is strange. You've heard all the whispers and talk at church. Mrs. Dawson says she can send for someone suitable, we don't have to have that trollop."

"Irene Dawson needs to back-off. She seems plenty pleased at how big and handsome J.D. looks when she's showing him off at church services as her wonderful grandson."

"When have you ever seen any lady act like she does?"

"No, she's not Donna. Her Dad taught her to shoot and ride and chase cattle," he continued.

"She's strange. Donna would never have scrubbed dirty clothes, or harnessed a mule to plow a garden, or skinned a rabbit. She was a lady."

"Her manners may be lacking, but you can help her with that. She's young and has grown-up with just her dad these last ten years."

Angrily he whispered as he stood over her, determined to shut her up. "Donna never chased or fed chickens, cooked a meal for a table full of cowhands or did any real work. She would plan meals, read Dr. Padgett, sew baby clothes, and read the catalog for things to order for the house or for herself. Hattie's a prairie girl. She's had to learn it all, do it all. But she can read and write and does every single day. She works hard, and judging from that meal tonight, she can cook as good as any woman in Texas."

"Humph," Rubye snorted and turned toward her room. "I'm watching you," she hissed before slamming her door.

Jackson paced angrily back and forth in the living room. Even after three months of working closely with her, Rubye still resented Hattie. He knew part of it was that the younger girl had beaten her in the kitchen today. It would be hard for most women to hear another woman praised as Hattie had been tonight by all the men present.

What would his mother have thought of Hattie? He believed she would have liked her. After all, his mother could ride and shoot, perhaps not as well as Hattie, but it was only a few years since every western woman needed to learn to shoot to survive. He would never know what they thought since it had been six years since he lost both his parents to Typhoid fever, following the big flood. He paused to stare at their framed portrait. He felt sure his parents would have admired Hattie's 'spunk.'

Rubye was jealous. The more the men bragged about their dinner, the more it got her goat. She'd been in a real lather all evening. Almost as bad as the day Hattie had commented about how dirty the windows were and then spent the day cleaning them.

It might have passed if the men hadn't come in, not knowing, and bragged about how bright and wonderful everything looked. Rubye had been furious.

Hattie was clueless to the woman's resentment. If she had not been, then she would never have offered to mop the floors real good and maybe wax them for Rubye. He had been afraid that Rubye would go up in flames.

For a girl who had been orphaned so young, she knew a heck of a lot about housework, gardening, and cooking. When you added in what she knew about animals and ranching, well, she might not be a lady but she was special. Donna knew when to curtsy and simper, how to use a compliment to insult, was up-to-date on proper clothes, and who and what was acceptable. He was glad Hattie didn't know all that. She was still a remarkable woman.

His actions today had been wrong. But the thought of her being confronted by those trashy low-lifes had panicked him. He'd been furious when Rubye finally told him about the last encounter in the barn. The fact that the grisly trophy had sat on the mantle for two months before Rubye mentioned it didn't help. She had seemed proud of Hattie for sticking up for herself, but he knew if the housekeeper hadn't backed her with her shotgun, they might have…

His mind closed down on what could have happened. Today when he heard those shots, his only thought was to reach her in time. Maybe he had grabbed her too quickly, held her too tightly. But she had looked so smug and satisfied, with her coyote tails and her prize hen and rabbit, while he was distraught and terrified. He had wanted her to feel the fear that was running through him.

For some women being manhandled and kissed might be a fantasy. For an eighteen year old girl who had already experienced rape, it could only be a terrifying reminder. Her terror, her panic, had made him regret his action as soon as he'd started it. The kiss had changed from threatening to comforting. But when he had finally stopped that wonderful kiss, had he imagined she was kissing him back? Donna, Donna, what was he doing?

He had promised Hattie she would always feel safe when she was here, that he would protect her. He realized before he could go to sleep, he needed to apologize to her. Galvanized, he moved swiftly to her door, raising his hand to knock. No, if he knocked he might wake the baby and Rubye, and then reap hellfire and damnation from the already upset housekeeper.

Gently he held the knob, then slowly turned it. Inside, he was surprised to hear Hattie talking to the baby. The sweet coos coming from the boy sounded like he was talking back. Jackson stood mesmerized at the sight of her snuggled against the baby, crooning a fairy tale to him, while he smiled and crooned back at her. J.D.

startled first, turning his head to stare at his Daddy. Hattie half rose in bed next. Before she could say anything, Jackson raised a hand.

"I couldn't go to bed," he whispered.

She stared at him wide-eyed, warily lifting the baby in front of her as a barrier as she listened.

"Today, I was frightened, worried about you. When you seemed so carefree, it made me angry. I had no right to manhandle you that way." He stared at her intently but couldn't tell what she was thinking.

"I'm sorry, it won't happen again." He was aware of the lamplight on her face and her swiftly changing expression. Her blue eyes looked enormous in the dimly lit room, her hair pulled back and tightly braided only emphasized how small and blonde she was. Where the top three buttons of the yellow gown were open, he could glimpse skin, ghostly pale compared to the golden brown of her face and hands. He remembered coming in early one day, seeing her sitting with a cloth soaked in buttermilk across her face, two hands dipped in a bowl of the same liquid. Rubye's attempt to bleach her sun burned features of their 'red Indian' look.

"Thank you."

The words were soft but full in the night. He felt the pull of the woman and the bed. Swallowing hard, he blinked and closed the door.

CHAPTER ELEVEN

Rubye continued to be short-tempered with Jackson and Hattie. There was never a moment when the two were left alone or unobserved, as though it mattered. Jackson avoided her all day, seeing her only with the baby after the men were gone. If Hattie noticed, she didn't let on. She whistled and worked like a dervish to help with cooking, cleaning, and dishes while taking care of the baby, her garden, and her chickens.

Rubye reclaimed her kitchen. She planned meals and did all the cooking, unless it was allowing Hattie to prepare vegetables or meat as directed. One day, Hattie insisted on saving some cream that had soured. To Rubye's horror, she added a little to a small jar, keeping some souring at all times. When she added it to the potatoes one night, all the men were excited about the sweet, tart taste. After that, Rubye let her share some more of her mother's recipes, but made sure to prepare the majority of the meal.

Between Hattie and the cowhands they had the dogs broken from ever chasing chickens. Any time they looked at one, somebody would reprimand them and chuck a clod of loose mud or rock toward them.

The chickens recognized the sound of the screen doors bang and boiled out from the barn, manure pile or pasture to cluck and gather, hoping Hattie would share some fresh kitchen scraps, cracked corn, or stale bread. She now had the dozen surviving hens, plus the thirty young chickens.

◇◇◇

It was a Sunday afternoon, all were relaxing after church and lunch. The cowhands were watching the eight or nine young cocks mock fighting, dusting up into the air over some imaginary insult or scrap of pie crust. The men were joking and placing bets on the winner. Hattie watched too, while she finished stringing and snapping a mess of green beans. She eyed the small warriors to decide who would be her new rooster. When she had him marked, she scattered the bean strings and stems in front of the porch. As the chickens all gathered, she shocked everyone by quietly walking through the flock, grabbing a chicken and twisting his neck. When she had three, she returned to the porch and quickly plucked and singed the pen feathers, then carried the chickens inside to cut them up.

Hattie put her beans on while the meat soaked in salted water. Then she planned out her meal while she worried with the fussy baby. He had complained during church and fussed while nursing today. After a night when she had woken nearly as often as she had when he was new, she was worn out from holding him. As soon as she handed the baby off to Jackson, he cajoled Rubye into helping him entertain J.D. and to leave the cooking to Hattie. He hadn't forgotten the day a month before when she had cooked the entire meal and made Rubye furious.

She came out with a crock of frozen pudding for the hands to crank, then returned to the kitchen. Hattie made buttermilk biscuits and put them in the oven, while she soaked the tender chicken in buttermilk. Then she dredged it in salted and peppered flour before frying it in hot oil. She added bacon crisps and fat to the stewing beans, made thin slices of potato and onion, waiting to fry them when the chicken was done. She made a dish of cold cucumber slices in vinegar and sliced a plate of ripe tomatoes. Finally, she put a dozen eggs on to boil for dressed eggs.

She served the meal, embarrassed by their compliments even before they sat down. By the time the meal was on the table, the boy was once again in full throttle.

She carried her plate and the baby out to the front porch. Overheated and exhausted, Hattie retreated to the porch rocker to feed the baby in the evening breeze while everyone else was inside. First she ate and shared the frozen custard with the baby. Then she parked the happy baby against a pillow in the cradle so he was sitting up like a little sailor in a boat, then shooed the dog away that wanted to lick his face.

She ate, relaxing in the cooling breeze, using one foot to keep the baby rocking. Jackson came out on the porch, patted his tummy, and smiled at her. It was the first time in a month they had found themselves alone. Afraid, he would upset Rubye more or make Hattie uncomfortable the way he did by his actions the day she shot the coyotes, he had kept away. Through the screen door they could hear the satisfied cowboys still talking, arguing about who deserved the ice cream paddle based on who had cranked the longest.

"I would have argued that your chicken and dumplings dinner was the best I ever had, until tonight. That was definitely the finest chicken dinner ever served to anyone."

Hattie looked up from under raised brows. "Well, the next batch will have more meat on them, but the third frying will probably be about the same size. Rooster chicks are cruel, soon many will be frazzled and missing feathers. Of course, in another month there will be the young hens that don't lay, and just before cold weather, we'll probably have to stew one of the older hens that quit laying. You can't keep a strong flock without culling."

"And there we thought we would just get to watch them meandering around and settle for fresh eggs. By the way, everyone loved the dressed eggs."

Hattie sat quietly, blushing at all the praise. He started to step inside, but J.D. was chortling and waving his arms and Jackson laughed as he scooped him up. "Come on son, let's go talk to the other cowboys."

Hattie sat, sucking on the crisp skin on the chicken wing she'd picked up, studying the tall lean lines of the man as he sauntered back inside. J.D. was greeted by all the cowhands. Frustrated by her wandering mind, she focused on the baby. At four months, he was a lively active baby, already trying to roll from side to side. She was proud of how quickly he was growing, but had given up leaving him in bed beside her. The first time he almost completed a roll he had slipped between the bed and crib, crying frantically and waking her before he fell all the way to the floor. Now she would cuddle and play with him until he went to sleep, but return him to spend the night in the crib, at least four hours at a time.

According to Dr. Padgett, she was in danger of being an overprotective mother, the type who never let her child take any risks or explore on his own. She shook her head. He wasn't her child, but Donna's, and she had promised to take care of him. She didn't want to think of J.D. getting hurt until he grew bigger and stronger.

When the first cowboy came out onto the porch to thank her, Hattie quit wool-gathering and hurried to slip inside. The man doffed his hat and stopped her with the words, "Miss Stoddard, I don't know how such a pretty gal can be such a great cook, but you're the prettiest and best I've ever seen."

Hattie blushed, startled by the attention. Looking down she curtsied as she'd seen Irene Dawson do at church to a compliment and slipped past and around into the kitchen. Several of the men were telling her "thanks for the fine meal" but Hattie stayed hidden until the last man was gone. She noticed that Jackson looked after her, wondering what the man on the porch had said to send her hiding.

Rubye glared at her. "You'd think those men had never had fried chicken or fried potatoes the way they went on."

Hattie cleared the table and made herself busy washing dishes while Rubye sat with the cranky baby. She could not help the pride she felt as she carried empty plates to the dish pan, every bite of everything was gone. She had finished washing up and grabbed a dishtowel to dry when Rubye came in with a wet and crying baby and traded him for the dishtowel. Hattie took the baby, hurt that there were no words being exchanged. Well, if Rubye wanted to be angry and jealous, so be it. Nothing Hattie could say would change things.

◇◇◇

"Boss, there are cows missing on the south range."

Jackson stared at Cliff. "What do you mean cows are missing?"

"Seven or eight head in that little clump that had two sets of twins. We rode out like you said, to brand everything, not just count heads, and they were gone. We checked that part of the range, compared what we'd seen when we were heading back to the bunkhouse. Nobody saw them. They're gone.

"All right, but is there any sign where they might have gone?"

"No, but it rained the night before. No tracks."

He sat there, waiting, knowing Cliff would have more to say.

In a minute he started again. "At church, I heard a few of the squatters talking. One had a prairie fire, and you know it's not that dry and we haven't had a lot of lightning with the rain that's fallen. It took his silage field. Most have been losing animals, a handful at a time."

"Yeah, I heard the same talk."

"Tony did what you said when he was in town, nosed around. There was nothing with the Stoddard brand in the feed lots or in back of Thompson's. He even looked through the hides while Mr. Thompson got his order ready."

"Anything with our brand?"

"Only the ones at the bottom of the back stack. Hides were from the ones you sold Dawson last fall."

"Well, if they haven't sold them, they're holding them someplace. With everybody watching, I don't see how they're able to take the animals."

"Hank and I were talking about that, boss. We figure they're doing it on Sundays, you know, everybody goes to church, takes the day off. It rained last Sunday night, too."

"Sounds right. Guess I'll have to get a backache and beg off church next week."

"Hank and I can backslide with you."

"Yeah, if we can keep Tony from 'cowboying it up' Saturday night, Tony can take the North quarter. I hardly see him at church anyway. We can go talk to them now."

◇◇◇

Hattie stared at the men still talking on the porch. She wished they would move off for the evening so she could go back outside again before J.D. started calling for her. She realized it was probably too late as Rubye held him, trying to keep him from getting a finger in his hard gums. He had become a drool monster these last few days, gnawing and slobbering on everything. "He needs a toy, doesn't he?"

"Yeah, something hard to bite on," Rubye turned her hand and gave a mock yell of 'ow.' J.D. looked up and grinned, then bent, hunting for another knuckle or finger to gnaw on

"James might whittle something if you asked?"

"Might if you did the asking. I'm not asking favors of no man." Rubye shook her head. "Maybe you could sew him a doll."

Hattie shook her head. "Momma didn't like to sew. All I can do is mend and sew on buttons."

"There you go. That's all you need to make a doll."

Hattie picked up the old sackcloth diaper, one of J.D.'s burp cloths, that she had handy for after feeding him. Examining the clean cloth, she noted the writing was almost faded, and only faint red checks of the pattern remained. She went to the bedroom and came back with Donna's sewing basket. Inside were scissors, ribbons, needle and thread and at the bottom of the box, a wire held ten brass jingle bells.

She found the short kitchen pencil, then traced a horse on the folded towel. Carefully she cut out the pattern.

Rubye came over and stared down at her. "I never heard of a horse for a doll. But if you sew it like that, he'll only have two legs."

Hattie looked down at it. Then she went to the bedroom and came back with another flour-sack cloth. Opening out the horse, she traced the legs and left a long rectangle between them, shaping the rectangle to a vee in the front and back.

"Humph, that makes no sense, and you're wasting all his burp cloths."

Before Rubye could persuade her to stop wasting her time, she had it cut out. She held it up to show Rubye the design.

"It might work, but the fabric is pretty nasty looking to make a toy."

Hattie went out to the kitchen and found the jar of beets she had pickled a week ago. The beets were already gone but she had saved the liquid to pickle eggs. Instead, she stuffed the pattern pieces into the jar.

"There. It should be a pretty red color when I take it out in the morning. The vinegar will make the color set."

Rubye snorted. "Doubt it, it'll just bleed out in the wash water."

Hattie reached out to take the fussing baby, surprised at how heavy he had grown. He leaned forward, snagging her braid and pulling it into his slobbery mouth."

"Yuck," she tugged at the braid but he held to it determinedly. "All right slobber man, hold on, but we're going to bed."

She watched as Rubye rolled the scrap cloth and tucked it and the scissors into the box, then carried it to set where it had been since Donna used it last. Then she turned back to move the jar of beet juice into the kitchen. In minutes, the house was dark, it seemed that all life was gone with the light. In the silence, all she heard was the baby breathing soft and fast, then she felt an imaginary arm go around her. "Thank you, keep trying, keep him safe," she felt the words through her bones.

With a shiver and a smile she carried the wiggling boy to bed.

<><><>

When chores were done and the men were back out working the next day, Hattie carried the dried clothes inside to fold. She placed a quilt on the floor and laid J.D. on it to kick and play while she worked, settled on the settee with the sewing box on the end table. Taking the soft red cloth, she threaded a needle and fought the fabric until she had the main pieces sewn together. Then she wrapped a jingle bell in scrap cloth and then forced one into each hoof. She then rolled scraps of faded sack toweling into tight tubes and forced them down each leg. Satisfied, she sewed the edges, leaving only a small opening, through which she forced and molded the extra toweling to make the body as hard and tight as possible. When she finished fastening the opening, she tied a snug knot and bit the thread loose.

The red pony was solid and firm, more bitable she hoped then knuckles or braids.

"Are you going to embroider the face and body?" Rubye asked over her shoulder, as Hattie shook it, watching the legs ring.

"Wish I could. Think I'll draw them on."

Rubye blew loudly in disgust as usual. "With what, coffee?"

Hattie went inside the bedroom, not surprised to hear Jackie crying as soon as she disappeared from sight. She came back with her ink pot and pen. Carefully, she painted eyes, nostrils and mouth, and then painted all four little hoofs black. J.D. chortled and grabbed for it, while Hattie held it over him, blowing on the cloth to dry the ink.

Hattie laughed down at the baby. "Almost ready, big cowboy. We need to get a mane and tail fastened on."

Rubye lifted him up, while he kicked and grabbed at the pony. "Goodness, he's getting to be a handful."

"Eighteen pounds, according to Thompson's vegetable scale. Of course he was wiggling on the scale.

"Feels more like forty, don't you bucko?"

"He's nice and solid though, no fat folds and wrinkles."

"That's why Mrs. Dawson keeps complaining. No double chins or dumpling arms."

"He weighs what Dr. Padgett predicts. That should be good enough for anyone."

Hattie sealed the ink bottle, cleaned her quill. Then she hunted through the thread, yarn, ribbon and lace in the sewing basket until she settled on the thin blue ribbon. Making loops around her finger, she cut the end after making ten loops. She sewed the end of the ribbon to the top of the horse's head, then fastened each loop carefully as she worked down the neck. Finally, she made six loops about twice as long, fastened the top of all of them at the end of his rump, and then cut the loops to make strands for his tail.

Watching the eager boy, Hattie carefully walked the pony across the seat of the horsehair stuffed sofa, making each hoof ring and the ribbon mane and tail flutter. Finally, she raised it high and kissed its little painted nose.

She held it out to J.D. and he clapped his hands and squealed in delight. As soon as he grabbed it, he bit it hard.

"Dr. Padgett says babies grow teeth after six months, though some get one as early as three months or as late as nine months. I'm sure he's getting his first tooth."

While Rubye was content to hold the baby, Hattie got up and folded all the clean clothes and hurried to put them away. She held the full basket when she heard a familiar buggy pulling into the yard.

Hattie sighed, glad that Rubye was outside with the baby. She waved to the couple, then sped around clearing up the quilt, the sewing basket and scraps. She also stopped in front of the mirror to comb and neaten her hair and check that she was buttoned straight and neat.

As Hattie hurried to the porch she saw Irene Dawson reach for the baby and saw him drop his new toy as she lifted him. Immediately he began to howl and tried to grab for it.

"What on earth is the matter with him?" she asked Rubye as the boy twisted around in her arms, almost toppling to the ground.

Charles Dawson stepped forward and grabbed the toy and put an arm around the squirming boy. He held out the toy, "Is this what you need, boy?"

J.D. swallowed the tears that had filled his eyes and chortled as he grabbed the toy, clutching it against his belly.

"Good Lord," Irene Dawson fumed. "So much fuss over nothing."

They swept into the house, settling in the two leather chairs by the fire. Rubye excused herself. "I've got to fix some food, the men will be in soon, please excuse me."

For a few minutes, all were quiet. Hattie folded her hands, self-conscious of her pricked and dyed fingers. Finally Irene Dawson broke the silence when she tried to take the stuffed horse to examine it. J.D. howled in outrage.

Hattie watched the contest until Irene finally gave up and released the little horse. J.D.'s triumph rang out as he shook the horse, making the mane and tail wave. When Charles Dawson tapped one of the little black hoofs, the pony jingled and the baby laughed.

"Why is he drooling so much?" Irene demanded.

Hattie hesitated, never having been spoken to directly before. "Dr. Padgett lists it as a sign that he's teething."

"Nonsense, he's much too young for that."

"Dr. Padgett says they can cut teeth as young as three months. He's nearly four and a half months and he's been fussier than usual, just like the book says."

"Well," she rose, clearly annoyed. "At least you can read. Where did he get this disgusting toy?"

Hattie bit her tongue, breathed deep until she could control her anger. "I made it."

"Of course you did. Here, take him, he needs changing."

"He's getting stronger," the banker added as he tugged at the horse and J.D. pulled it in closer.

Hattie swept forward, again curtsied and took the baby, wrinkling her nose. "I'll change him and bring him back in a few minutes."

"Did you ever get his weight?" Irene called after her.

"Eighteen pounds, last week at Thompson's store."

"So little," she complained.

"I'll bring you the baby diary and the book so you can check the charts in the back.

Hattie laid the baby in the crib, then carried out the books for them to read. Without a word, she returned to the baby, cleaned and dressed him, then nursed him a little before walking back to the grandparents, the baby riding on her hip.

Charles Dawson smiled up and took the baby, letting him stand on his legs while his wife studied the baby advice book.

"Very well," she declared primly.

Hattie knew he was two pounds more than Padgett predicted, strong and plump, but not fat. He grew stronger every day, playing with the cowhands and his Daddy every evening. She knew the woman would be bragging about his teething so soon. Donna's child was more than perfect, even if Irene didn't like to think he could have messy pants like a normal baby.

At the sound of the men arriving, Hattie walked out to the kitchen, shrugging when Rubye raised her eyebrows at her. She took the bowls Rubye handed her, then counted out spoons and returned to the dining room to set the table.

Rubye carried out the big pot of chili and Hattie scurried behind her with the cornbread and onions. Rubye invited the Dawsons to join them for supper as usual.

Hattie didn't wait for the refusal, just hurried back for the pitchers of cold water and sweet milk as Rubye hurried back for two more bowls and spoons. No sooner was the table set, then the men began to file in, faces still dripping from being dunked and splashed by cold well water to remove the worst of the dust from their hands and faces.

Hattie added the crock of butter and the bowl of pickle relish and retreated toward the bedroom.

Jackson took the baby from Charlie Dawson, smiling at the boy. "What you got there big fella?"

Hattie turned and stared, trapped by curiosity, as J.D. raised his little horse up to his Daddy. Jackson held it, turning it around, studying the blue ribbon mane and tail, the little painted face. When he tilted it, he heard a bell, and J.D. reached out to pat it, making another hoof ring. When Jackson shook it, the baby chortled and the cowhands laughed.

"That's a pretty pony, fella." J.D. pushed it back at him and Jackson raised his eyebrows.

"He's waiting for you to kiss it," Hattie called. The Dawsons stared at her sternly. Jackson blushed, and then kissed the nose of the pony.

Everyone laughed. J.D. took his pony back and bit it hard on the nose. The cowboys clapped.

Rubye bustled about filling bowls and glasses, even as Hattie disappeared into the bedroom. When Rubye reached James Boyd's chair, she paused. "He needs some toys. Maybe someone could whittle something for him, too."

James looked up at her. "Sure, I reckon I could, if you're asking Miss White?"

Rubye bustled on, ignoring the looks between the cowhands.

◇◇◇

Finally, the company was gone, and Hattie emerged to clear the table and sit down to her own bowl of chili and wedge of corn bread.

She had heard all the talk as she glimpsed the table through her open door. The talk about rustlers and lean times for the settlers was hard to ignore. Dawson had confided that more than usual were coming in, asking for loans. She noticed that he didn't say whether he granted any to the desperate men.

Most of all, she was surprised to see Irene Dawson seated at a table of cowhands. She didn't eat, merely took turns holding J.D., studying the boy and how much he was enjoying his toy. Hattie wondered what it must feel like to lose a daughter and only be able to touch her when you saw or held your grandson. So what if the woman was conceited and full of airs. She loved J.D. Even the stuffy banker came because he loved the little boy. If anything ever happened to Jackson, heaven forbid, at least she knew the couple would make sure J.D. grew up well cared for and loved.

CHAPTER TWELVE

It was Saturday night when she first felt a wave of cramps. The first time in months, but she knew the morning would bring the return of her monthly flow. J.D. was so fussy, even the pony and the hand-carved lamb that James had made for the baby did nothing to soothe him. Hattie could see a little blister near the center of his lower gum. Instead of providing comfort, nursing irritated him.

She had spooned some warm oatmeal in him that morning, to help fill his tummy, but he had wanted to nurse, at least until she gave him her breast. He would nurse a minute, give her a hard bite, and then cry in frustration. She had been near tears as well from the sharp little bites and the need to empty her full and achy breasts.

Finally, she pumped some milk into a bottle and tried to feed him that way. But he bit the rubber nipple savagely and the milk dribbled out of his mouth, then came too fast and made him cough. Finally, only when they were both exhausted, had he relaxed and nursed briefly, wincing and stopping when his gum hurt too badly, but unwilling to give up long enough to cry. Eventually they both slept.

Sunday morning, Hattie rose to cook some apples into sauce for the fussy baby. Balancing him on her lap, she alternated feeding his thin gruel and the still warm applesauce. Hungry, he ate it all as quickly as she could spoon it in, rake it off his chin, and spoon it in again.

Rubye came in, tying an apron around her waist, stopping to enjoy the spectacle of J.D. eating. When he gave an 'hmm' sound, both women laughed.

"Rubye, the baby is fussy, and I just started my monthly. J.D. and I will have to stay home."

◇◇◇

The older woman stared at them both. It was true that the baby was eating and at the moment looked content, but there had been lots of tantrums the last few days, (something totally out of character for J.D.) with lots of crying and complaining. Rubye couldn't imagine the preacher or congregation would be happy to have a squalling baby at the service. As for Hattie using her flow as an excuse, well it was a first since she had come to the ranch.

"I thought your Dr. Padgett said you wouldn't have a flow while you were breast-feeding the baby?" Rubye barked.

Without realizing it, Hattie lowered her voice to a whisper. "He said most mothers wouldn't. He said it was possible, just not likely to be regular and monthly. Mainly, it was advice that a woman was unlikely to be fertile and conceive again as long as she was still nursing the last baby. None of that relates to me."

She snorted, "Well I reckon everyone will understand, especially if they've heard all the fussing and hollering the last day or two. And they only have to look at you to know how bad you're feeling." She flung the last words as she pranced into the kitchen to prepare Sunday breakfast.

◇◇◇

Hattie wiped J.D.'s face and rose, shocked to see Jackson standing at the door to the study, staring across at them.

Her face flushed, just at the thought of what he might have heard, praying their voices had been too low for him to hear the last of the conversation. Flustered, she grabbed J.D. and hurried into the kitchen." I can finish dinner if you want so it's ready to serve when you get home."

Rubye blew angrily, "Don't worry yourself. I'll put on that big rump roast before we leave. If you add potatoes and some vegetables to the big pot about ten, it should all be ready to eat when we get back." Hattie nodded and took off for her bedroom, juggling J.D. on her hip again, a toy clutched in both hands.

As she entered the room, she heard a loud wail. Frightened, she sank down into a chair and turned the baby so she could see his face, searching for blood or any sign of injury. When she checked his mouth, she could see the little blister had popped, probably when he bit down on the hard edge of his little carved lamb. When she stared in his eyes she saw him grin, then he turned to nuzzle her breast.

She felt the milk start to flow from her heavy, swollen breasts, soaking her shirt before she could even open the buttons. As the baby relaxed against her, suckling contentedly, she felt so relieved. The tight pressure in her throbbing breast eased along with the frustration that had built the last two days when she had not been able to meet his needs. Almost in tears, she smiled down at the sweet baby in her arms. She looked up in shock to see Jackson standing there, staring and smiling down at them both.

Horrified, she realized how exposed she was, and raised her hand to hide herself.

Jackson continued to smile and walked over to the crib for a blanket to hand her.

Hattie took it, blushing as she became aware she had revealed herself again in reaching for it.

He looked sheepish. "I heard the baby scream, I was worried about him."

"The blister on his gum broke. He's finally able to nurse again."

"Does that mean the tooth has come through? Will he ..." He swallowed in embarrassment, had almost asked if the boy would bite her.

Rubye came in with a plate of eggs and bacon, plopping it down on the dresser. "Eat it!" She turned and stared at Jackson. "What are you doing in here?"

"I heard the baby scream."

"He heard the baby scream."

They answered at the same time.

"Harrumph!" she snorted. "Are you ready for a plate of breakfast?" Rubye asked Jackson, but looked pointedly at Hattie, "Do you want coffee, or just milk?"

"Both please."

"All right."

Jackson started to tell Rubye about having a backache, but it was Sunday and he couldn't start the day with a lie. "Can I have coffee too?"

Rubye headed out and as soon as she turned, Hattie looked up at him. "You were about to say?"

He shook his head. He managed not to say anything, but then thought, what would it matter if she knew. "Some of the hands are staying home from church with me. We want to prepare for the rustlers, try to catch them if we can."

"Do you think you have a chance?"

He shrugged. "They rustled a few head last week while folks were at church. We want to be ready in case they come again."

Rubye set coffee and milk on the dresser, handed Jackson a mug. "Your breakfast is getting cold. Get out of here."

As she herded him out, she asked. "You might what?"

He repeated what he had told Hattie. "Some two-legged coyotes are dodging the cows with calves in the south pasture. Plan to keep a few of the boy's home this morning to help exterminate them."

"So you're staying home on a Sunday morning, not going to church?"

He glared at her tone. "I just told you we are. I'll have James Boyd drive you and the other men into church."

Men began filing in for breakfast and Rubye stormed back into the kitchen, banging pans in case Jackson didn't know what she thought of his plans.

Rubye left to get ready for church before the men finished eating and left James Boyd to clean up. The two of them and the newer hands finally left for church.

Rubye cast a suspicious glance back at the house. It felt strange to be leaving so many behind. Especially since that girl had stayed home the same morning as Jackson. But even as they wheeled onto the track toward church, she saw Jackson and four of the men ride off south from the ranch. Satisfied she turned back around, wondering how she would satisfy Irene Dawson when her bundle of joy didn't arrive.

◇◇◇

As soon as they were out of sight of the ranch, Jackson had the men split up to head for the four quadrants and look for signs of any intruders.

Coming over a rise, Jackson saw the fleeting shadows of a rider and spurred his horse forward. To his left he heard the loud braying of a mule, quickly joined by another. Henry and Pepper for sure. He unsheathed his rifle and cocked it while riding along the ridge, reining at the end of it.

He sighted at the end of the draw, holding his breath. The first to emerge were the two mules and Hattie's old horse, Nugget. Alongside appeared two riders, who were both hazing the lead mules and a dozen cattle. Calmly Jackson took aim and fired. The lead rider dropped the reins and sagged forward but managed to grab the mane and pommel of the saddle to hang on. Jackson changed his aim, ejecting the shell and cocking as he swung to the left. The other rider screamed and pulled to the left, cursing as he whipped his horse into the woods. As he disappeared, Jackson fired, levered in another shell and fired again. He grinned as he heard a loud scream.

Jackson shoved in more shells, yelled 'whoa,' and watched as Henry stopped on a dime. Pepper followed and the cows bunched up behind them and stopped. From behind, Jackson heard riders and waited, hoping it was Cliff or Hank. He breathed a deep sigh as he saw Cliff's tan hat and buckskin pony.

"Careful partner, I hit one, he rode off down the trail, but I only winged the one that rode into that brush thicket."

Cliff drew his rifle and gingerly rode around the cows.

"Reckon we better get these animals back," Jackson said as he rode around the other side of the herd.

He reined up and stared around, the hair on the back of his neck bristling. He reached out and grabbed Cliff, pulling him down between their horses as shots rang out. They stood trapped between their horses, the cattle bawling. Jackson swept off his hat and slapped the flank of the nearest cow, yelling giddy-up in a loud voice.

Henry spun around and charged back up the draw, the cattle following, the two men crouched down between their horses, hanging onto the stirrup as they ran. Two more shots snapped branches overhead and pinged off the rocks of the cliff.

"Must be a third one. I thought I saw a rider before I came out on the ridge."

"Do you need to go after him?"

Jackson climbed back in the saddle, Cliff looked around, then mounted too.

"Let's wait until the other men get back, then we'll trail them. Let's get these animals back to the ranch, first. I want to get the sheriff out and a couple of the neighbors."

"Damn rustlers. Why'd they take the mules?"

"They couldn't get the cows to move without them. Hey, where's the horse?"

Cliff pulled rein, waited until all the animals were past, then wheeled his horse back the way they'd come. A gun barked, and Cliff spun around again.

"Let's cut a blaze, boss."

Jackson rode, moving the cattle ahead of them.

"I figure if we catch them, we've got enough evidence to string 'em up. I want witnesses though."

"Sure, when we get back, I'll send Tony to town, Hank to church, see who's still there that might want to ride on the hunt."

Jackson had the stock back in the paddock and the rest of the men sent to neighboring ranches for more men to form a posse. He knew he had wounded two of the rustlers, maybe worse. Although all he could see were a dozen cows that should never have been hazed from their pasture, somewhere there were more missing Harper Creek cattle. Only when he found them and the rest of Hattie's rustled animals, would he be satisfied. Seeing the men hung for it would be some comfort.

◇◇◇

The adrenaline from the fight left him all at once, even as he walked toward the house. He washed up, knocked the dust off his boots and pants, and then stepped into the cool shadows of the house, only to hold up short. Hattie had spread a quilt on the waxed planks of the floor.

Now she lay on it smiling and playing with a naked J.D.. He lay in the beams of sunlight, cooing and making little noises as she tried to catch his wiggling body to diaper. The edge of her skirt had been kicked up to show the lace of her petticoat and reveal one stocking-clad slim ankle. Her blouse was wet and two buttons were open. It was plain she had just bathed the baby.

Jackson poked his hat back with one finger and grinned. As usual, J.D. noticed him first and waved his arms even more excitedly. Hattie quickly sat up, self-consciously buttoning the blouse and pulling her skirt down over her shoeless feet, before turning back to the giggling baby.

Unable to resist his command, Jackson sank to the edge of the quilt, leaning down to blow bubbles on the tender neck and belly. J.D. went wild, wiggling and laughing. Jackson leaned back laughing too. Hattie used the breather both were taking to get a diaper on the baby.

"Why the quilt?"

Hattie blushed again and Jackson enjoyed the sight of her pink face, startled blue eyes, and the way her hand rested tenderly on the baby's chest.

"Dr. Padgett says he should be able to roll-over, and he hasn't done it yet? He has just rolled onto his side, not from front to back, or back to front yet. I thought on a firmer flat surface, he might be able to roll all the way over."

Jackson laughed and J.D. made a gasping sound and opened his eyes wide to stare at his Daddy. Hattie laughed at his look of astonishment and J.D. rolled in her direction, grabbing at his foot as he rolled. Jackson chuckled at her delight and J.D. rolled back over toward him. Hattie sagged down on the quilt and Jackie flipped over, raising up on his arms to look at her like a little shell-less turtle, then rolled over to face her. Hattie clapped her hands. "You did it. Did you see that, daddy? He made a 360-degree-turn."

They smiled at each other, each touching the laughing baby between them.

CHAPTER THIRTEEN

"What the hell is going on?"

Hattie got up, but Jackson lay back on the quilt watching as J.D.'s face puckered up, ready for a cry. Wordlessly he lifted the baby against his chest, kissing the soft, scrunched face. The baby pushed a fist into his mouth and Jackson nibbled it.

On her feet, straightening her clothes, Hattie spoke defensively. "We were playing with the baby, teaching him to roll over."

"Sure you were. I knew something was up when you both came up with excuses to miss church. When I think of the faces of the Dawsons, missing seeing that boy."

Hattie sputtered. "We've done nothing wrong."

Rubye looked like she would slap the girl, and Jackson sprang to his feet.

"Miss White, I think you'd better apologize to Miss Stoddard."

"Apologize, to that lying minx. That baby is no more teething then the man in the moon. I doubt it's her monthly either, but you'd know more about that than me?"

"Stop!" the voice was fierce. "Stop before you say things you'll regret."

"The only thing I regret is believing two liars. I'm leaving this house of sin."

Hattie started to say something more in protest, but Jackson reached out and put a hand on her arm, then moved that arm behind her. This let J.D. reach out to grab her and change arms. Hattie felt a huge ache grow in her chest. She wanted to crumple from the angry scorn of a woman whom she had taken for a friend.

The baby's lower lip was quivering at the tension in the air and Jackson placed a hand on the soft little back, letting his hand stroke the velvety skin. J.D. curled into Hattie's arms. She felt comforted by Jackson's arm bracing her back and the baby clinging to them both. At the slam of Rubye's door, she pulled free, but as she turned to carry the boy to the bedroom, her eyes pooled with tears of disappointment and she clenched her jaw to keep from shedding them. Was she never going to be free of suspicion and accusation?

<><><>

Rubye hurriedly packed and quickly left for town, driven and comforted by James Boyd. The Dawsons had long ago offered her a place if she ever found living with 'that woman' too difficult. Even after all these months, Irene Dawson had stayed angry that Jackson had dared to bring the woman into his house, into his wife's bed, and given her the care of her precious grandchild. Irene Dawson would be only too eager to welcome Rubye and listen to her accusations and stories about that 'white trash.'

<><><>

Hattie rushed into the kitchen as soon as J.D. was asleep in his crib. Upset with Rubye's reaction, she was relieved that the food was ready as the men should arrive any minute for dinner. She rushed to dish up the roast and vegetables, sliced a bowl of ripe tomatoes and the large wheel of cornbread. She had dishes and silverware on the table, then stepped back in shock as strange men began to ride up. Already nervous since James and Rubye would not be there to serve, she started to shake.

Frightened, she called for the one man who could make her feel safe. "Jackson?"

He came into the kitchen from his study. Hattie felt her heart sink when she noticed the guns strapped to his hips. She had never seen any of the hands on the ranch walk around armed before. They kept rifles in their saddle scabbards but they were mostly for shooting varmints. Handguns, like her father's pistol, were for shooting men. More than the strange men continuing to file into the yard, the sight of this armed man left her stunned.

Jackson shook his head. "Sorry I didn't warn you in time. There will be a lot of men coming to form a posse. I had a run-in with rustlers this morning, and I plan to catch them and see them strung up this time. Dinner looks good, but we don't have time to sit down and eat."

Hattie knew her confusion and disappointment showed.

He gave her shoulder a pat in consolation as he asked, "Can you get a couple of pails of water for these riders and clear this table, but leave the bread? Then stay out of the way while we talk." He stepped down the stairs into the cold cellar only to emerge in minutes with a bag of deer jerky and several strings of beef jerky that had hung from the ceiling below.

Hattie awoke to her surroundings at his touch, quickly carrying the food back to the kitchen stove and returning dishes and silverware to the pantry shelves. She started through the door to the porch, then stepped back behind the screen at all the staring eyes. Jackson walked up behind her and told her curtly. "Never mind, stay with J.D."

Hattie knew if she were stronger she would snort like Rubye at the request that she just fade into the background. Instead, she felt grateful for the reprieve and quickly disappeared into the back room.

Hattie kept the door cracked a little so she could hear, wanting to know the reason for the guns, the men arriving, the details of the animals taken, the shots fired. It was an hour later, when the men were finally gathered, that Jackson addressed them all. She heard about the exchange of gun fire, felt surprisingly elated on hearing that two of the rustlers were wounded and all the cattle and two mules were back. Maybe it was the Sweat brothers and Rafe Hogue. It was un-Christian she knew, but she prayed it was the three rapist. She was afraid, since they were going to chase after the rustlers. But she felt optimistic that they would catch up with them soon and this time Jackson would have all these men as backup.

It surprised her that so many of the local ranchers had also had cattle rustled. They were as angry as she felt. There was agreement that it was time to go after them.

◇◇◇

Tony rode in spraying dust. "The sheriff's on his way; he wants everyone to wait until he arrives."

There were already over twenty men ready to ride and Jackson burned with irritation at the needless wait. He had already shared all the details of the shoot-out this morning, and he didn't want to repeat it. His irritation spilled over when James Boyd pulled in with the empty buckboard, minutes before the sheriff finally arrived. The reminder of the scene with Rubye White and her abrupt departure fueled his anger. Now what had been settled would need to be worked out again. He would need to make more arrangements just to keep his household running smoothly.

It was nearly three o'clock by the time everyone was gathered and Sheriff Tate finally rode onto the ranch in his high-wheeled buggy. Again, pacing and talking loudly, Jackson explained what happened, why they needed to hurry and ride after the rustlers.

Hattie paced inside the house, echoing his anger and excitement, bouncing the wide- awake and fussy boy. She knew from Jackson's description, that at least one man was hurt badly enough they should at least catch him. She crossed her fingers, making a selfish wish. Let it be Rafe Hogue, not Able or Silas Sweat. Please let it be Hogue, the leader, the instigator, the brutal animal. Let him be wounded, dead, or about to be hung as a rustler. Her name might never be cleared, but her father's beating and death would be avenged.

The sheriff stood in his buggy, interrupting her thoughts with his speech. "I will tolerate no vigilantes. We will catch these men, but they are to go to Star to be held, to wait on the circuit judge and a fair trial."

His words were greeted with angry arguments. "What about our animals?"

"If the brands are there or you can offer proof that they are your cattle, then you can hold them until the trial. We'll make a tally of all animals recovered and who takes each, in case of future disputes."

Jackson pointed to the back paddock. "We recovered Miss Stoddard's mules and a dozen of my cows and calves. Cows are branded; I reckon each calf will identify its own momma. Range law says it belongs to the owner of the cow."

"True about the calves. How do I know those mules are Stoddard animals?"

Jackson was tempted to say, just ask them.

Hattie piped up through the screen door, softly so Jackson could hear her. "They wear Stoddard brands."

Jackson repeated the answer though the sheriff had heard it. The sheriff stared at the shadow, deliberately making no nod or tip of his hat. Instead he wrinkled his nose as though from a bad smell and Jackson felt the insult burn up the back of his neck. He still felt the rage of Rubye's casting them in the role of sinners. He could not, nor ever would, slug a woman. But if the sheriff dared a similar comment, he would reconsider those words sitting in the dust.

His housing arrangements would be the first issue Jackson would have to resolve when they returned. Hattie already did most of the laundry, more than her share of cleaning, and often helped with the meals. Even taking care of J.D. full-time, she could probably take on the chore of feeding the men. However, with the housekeeper moved out, even Jackson would not dare sleep under the same roof with her. Hell, he had problems.

Finally, all agreed. As quickly as the house and yard had filled, it emptied.

◇◇◇

It was Cliff, who picked up the blood trail, the other half of the party headed northwest, keeping each other in sight as the line spread out over the range. The rest of the men, including Jackson, Hank and the sheriff, fanned out southeast, doing the same thing.

When Jackson crossed the boundary onto the Stoddard ranch, he heard the bellow of a large bull. Excited, he spurred his horse down the valley toward the seeps and the mud puddles where Hattie had sent his men months ago in search of eighteen cows and a black, trick horned bull.

The area was fenced with logs, animals crowded into the space. Along with the Stoddard animals were his eight missing cows and their twin calves and most of the animals that had been pilfered during the last months, including several saddle horses. He was disappointed not to see Hattie's old gelding, but the excitement of the ranchers on finding their missing animals was palpable. He looked, but the first fifty cattle the Stoddard's had lost were gone.

Maybe they had rustled and sold animals quicker before the Stoddard place became available? Now they could hide out and keep the animals until they had enough to trail north. Something about the arrangement didn't add up. Where were they getting the feed? When they'd moved Hattie, they'd moved all the food stored here, though there hadn't been that much. Where did outlaws get the food to keep the stolen cattle penned up and fed?

He held the men up. "It looks like they're holed up at Tom Stoddard's place. We'd better go in slow and cautious." He grinned as he looked from face to face, "All this crowd, they might know we're here, so keep your guns ready and try to find and use all the cover you can find."

They crept in, inching from the cover of the trees to the protection of the barn, all the time expecting to hear shots. Jackson and Cliff rode into the barn with one of the farmers holding the door open. As he suspected, the loft was full of hay, and there were two barrels of oats for the horses. There were wheel marks clearly showing where a wagon had sat, probably moving no farther than a foot from where the oats were unloaded. He toed the ground, noticing a bright fleck of red. "Hey, look at this."

Men who had approached the house, called in complaint. "They're gone."

Entering the house, Jackson put his hands on his hips, resting them near the guns. The place was filthy, food dropped on the floor, everything rough. He noticed there was a new table, four good chairs where the broken table and two busted chairs had sat before. In each bedroom, there were two cots, just like the ones he had been sleeping on in the study. Not just feed in the barn, but somebody had provided furniture for these owl hoots. Someone with money was behind the rustlers. In a town like Star, there were only a few men who had that kind of money.

Sheriff Tate looked around the cabin and Jackson felt his suspicion rise. This was the man who told Hattie he would arrest her for indecency for wearing pants, but told her he believed low-life saloon trash, not her. Jackson felt his jaw clench and he let his hand rest on the butt of his revolver before calming enough to speak.

"Ben, you and your deputy rode in from town. Clearly one of these rustlers was wounded badly. They doubled back here for a wagon, because the wagon that was in the barn is gone. Did you pass them on the way into town heading to Doc Jenkins?"

The sheriff rolled his eyes at him. "Damn, Harper, I know you think you're the big dog, having a shoot-out with the rustlers and finding their hidey-hole and the rustled cattle, but I am the sheriff. You think if I rode past a bunch of bloody men, I wouldn't have noticed and stopped them? Especially, when Tony rode in and told me to ride out and arrest some rustlers?"

Jackson wasn't the only one who gave the sheriff hard looks. He wanted to say, yeah, if you're being paid not to see them. He just stared and didn't answer.

"All right, let's drive these animals back to the ranch, make a tally, and then get people home. Those of you who live in town, you can look for wagon tracks; see if you can find a lead. Hank, you can try to trail the wagon while it's still light, maybe they went across the prairie."

Everyone wanted to comment, but none of them did. Later, when the sheriff was gone, Jackson knew there'd be plenty said.

"Why drive them to your place? Take the tally here, divide them up. Save these men a little of their Sunday." Tate said as though he were already running for reelection.

"Anyone know who's been staying here at the Stoddard place?" The sheriff bellowed.

No one answered. "Don't worry. If they're as shot up as Jackson claims, they'll be easy to spot," the sheriff laughed.

"They're shot up, or do you think I painted the blood trail here and out in the barn?"

The sheriff's face changed from smiling campaigner to man in charge.

"Come on, let's get these animals tallied and moved home," he barked.

◇◇◇

As Jackson hazed forty animals home, most with Stoddard brands he was relieved not to have to ride guard tonight. He'd probably move his cot out to the porch. He'd left Tony behind since he and his horse were spent, but also because he didn't want to leave Hattie and the baby unguarded.

James Boyd was back from town. Maybe the chuck wagon cook could be persuaded to move into the house and take over Rubye's job. If he did, that might be the best solution. Then Jackson wouldn't have to fight off the hounds and mosquitoes to sleep on the porch.

As they approached the ranch, Jackson sent his men to move the animals into the large front paddock with the other recovered animals. "Cut out the horses, see if you can get them stabled and grained"

Tony came out into the yard to greet them. "See you found our cows, boss. What about the rustlers?"

"Not yet, but Cliff and Hank are still on their trail." Jackson looked up at the darkening sky, "Although I expect they'll have to give it up soon. James inside?"

"Yeah, he's been back a couple of hours. He's inside, helping Miss Stoddard rustle up some grub."

Jackson slid from the saddle, patted his horse's neck. He knew the animal was as relieved as he was to be home and done for the night. He loosened the cinch and swung the saddle over the rail, pulled off the bridle and turned the big bay into the barn. The animal swished into his stall and snorted, already demanding his food and rub down.

Tony smiled at Jackson. "I'll take care of Red for you, boss. Reckon they've been holding supper awhile."

CHAPTER FOURTEEN

Jackson nodded. He stopped at the well, drew a pail of water and washed up first. Then, untying his gun, he uncinched the gun belt and carried the belt with its dangling guns and his long rifle toward the house.

He was surprised to see James Boyd in an apron, waiting on the porch. So much for a peaceful home-coming.

"James, I'm glad to see you. Appreciate your helping Hattie get supper."

"Yeah, I need to talk, boss."

Jackson sank wearily into the rocker, motioned James to the porch rail. When the older man was settled, he asked, "You got Miss Rubye settled in town."

"Oh, yeah, them Dawsons welcomed her in like company. She was pretty hot still boss, had a lot to say."

"Yeah, I figured she would."

The older cowboy looked bashfully beyond the screen into the house. "She's old-fashioned, you know, boss, and was awful fond of Miz Donna."

"I know, James, we all loved Donna."

"She had heard a lot of gossip, boss, we all had, about Tom's daughter. Reckon we all had made up our minds about her not being the right kind of woman for our baby."

Jackson felt his face flush with anger, then took a breath and forced himself to stay calm. "I had my own reservations."

Boyd shifted uncomfortably. "I tried to talk Rubye into coming back and apologizing, but she…"

Jackson nodded, "I know, she can be mulish."

James laughed softly, "Mulish is right."

"What do you think, James, about Miss Hattie?"

James stared at the porch floor and looked uncomfortable. "She's not what the gossips said."

"No," Jackson sighed, "no she's not. She'll need our help now, to do all the work."

"I was thinking, I could move in, maybe put a cot in the living room, and do most of the cooking."

Jackson extended a hand and rose taking the older man's arm. Feeling happy he patted him on the shoulder. "Thank you, pardner. Why don't you just take my cot in the study? I'll sleep in Rubye's room. It's been too long since I've slept in a real bed."

James nodded. "Good, it puts you a little farther from the missy."

"There's nothing going on between me and Miss Stoddard," he bristled.

"That's too bad boss, I was wishing there was," he added and left a shocked Jackson on the porch.

◇◇◇

Jackson wanted to talk with Hattie, but she was in her room. James set food out and let the men help themselves to rewarmed sliced roast and vegetables, sliced and stewed tomatoes, and fresh buttered cornbread. He knew she was listening, but the men were too tired and hungry and stayed unusually quiet.

◇◇◇

It was morning, when she rose to fire the stove and put on coffee and porridge before she got her first inkling of how things would go. She held the egg basket in one hand, the six eggs inside in her apron.

"I forgot to gather the eggs yesterday, or feed the hens." James added sheepishly. "They may go on strike and quit laying if I forget them again."

"They do a pretty good job of finding plenty to eat. The only danger of not gathering the eggs is that the older hens will go broody and see it as their job to start nesting."

"Maybe the boss will let me and a couple of the boys get a coop built. They all sure like eggs for breakfast."

Jackson came out of Rubye's room, "I'll have the new hands help do it today. Now, how about a couple of those eggs for our breakfast?" Hattie started to cook them, when he added, "James."

James smiled, "Okay, boss. But it's going to be hoecakes for the rest of them. Let me get some bacon going first." He took the basket of eggs from Hattie, set it down next to the stove and headed down to the cellar for a slab of bacon.

◇◇◇

Jackson motioned for her to sit down, and then carried out coffee for them both.

"I should help James while J.D. is still asleep," but even as she said it, they both heard a half-hearted cry. Together they walked to the door and watched the baby, rear in the air, stretching and getting ready to fuss. Hattie picked up a clean diaper before reaching him. She removed the wet gown as the baby stood upright, holding shakily to his daddy. She pulled the wet gown over his head while Jackson passed her a dry smock and she expertly changed and dressed the standing baby.

She walked into the kitchen, and dipped half a ladle of hot oatmeal into the bottom of the bowl. When James emerged up the stairs again he carried a jug of cold milk. He poured a dollop over her hot porridge. She sat down at her place, blowing to cool the cereal in the spoon before offering it to J.D. Jackson sat down, watching as the baby leaned forward, his mouth pursed in imitation of Hattie's. When the boy opened his mouth like a little bird, Jackson began to talk while she was feeding him.

"As you heard yesterday, I shot two of the rustlers. We trailed them back to your ranch, but they'd cleared out ahead of us."

"They were living in our house? How?"

"Somehow they had four cots in the bedrooms, a new table and chairs out front."

"Dad and my beds?"

"Not sure what they did with them. Just know they had four beds, four chairs, and a table that didn't have broken legs."

"So you believe there are four rustlers? I always felt it would be the Sweat brothers and Rafe Hogue."

"I've figured the same. But we didn't catch them. There could be more than four. Cliff and Hank came back when it grew too dark to read sign. They said the wagon tracks turned onto the main road and were lost by other tracks, mainly by those from the sheriff's horse and other men coming from town. I still don't see how he would have missed seeing them on that road."

"You think he or one of his deputies could be the fourth man?"

"It just seems suspicious to me. I planned to talk to the other ranchers, but the sheriff stayed until we'd made a tally of the animals and sent them home with their owners. Didn't get a chance to talk it out, but you could tell everybody thought something was odd there."

She wiped J.D.'s face, kissed his cheek, leaning him back in her arms to smile at his sweet face. He reached out a hand to touch her breast and her hand paused at the top buttons. Before, it had become routine to feed him his porridge, then let him nurse a while before getting up to help Rubye feed the men. Now with two men present, that wouldn't be possible.

She heard bacon sizzling in the kitchen, heard James singing a soft song as he stirred up pancake batter. Jackson smiled at her as the baby butted against her chest and started to complain. Hattie blushed.

"I'll get the blanket."

Grateful, she began to unbutton her blouse and as soon as Jackson dropped the blanket over her shoulder, J.D. began to nurse.

He refilled his coffee cup and sat down. Hattie started to thank him when J.D. suddenly tugged the blanket down. Gasping, she grabbed a corner and hid herself, but this time he pushed it away with his fist. Embarrassed, Hattie lifted baby and blanket and fled the room.

◇◇◇

Jackson laughed at her red face and James came out of the kitchen with two plates. "What did you say to run her off?"

"Not me. Something J.D. did."

"Well, no sense letting eggs go to waste." He sat down across from Jackson and started to eat.

"I thought you were the new cook."

"Might be the cook, but I ain't new. Ladies ate before the hands filled up the place. Seems like a good notion to me. If a cook eats last, he either goes hungry, or has to eat a lot of really bad cooking."

◇◇◇

Hattie put a happy J. D. in the porch cradle and set it to rocking. She carried both wash tubs to the yard beside the well. To one she added a washboard and a cake of onyx soap before filling it with water. Next she carried out and added the dirty clothes, turning the empty basket upside down and once again rocking the cradle. Quickly, she washed out and scrubbed the clothes. She called to James to watch the baby for a few minutes before hanging them.

The sun was almost up and the house empty. She stepped into the barn, scooped up grain then walked outside calling to wake the sleepy chickens. She heard three or four half attempts at crows, but her favorite, the little red rooster, leaped to a rail and gave a full throated cock-a-doodle-do. She could already see darkening colors among his short tail feathers, definitely her little rooster.

Quickly, she sprinkled a handful of grain below the rail and cooed. "Come on down, cock robin, eat the pretty grain." He cocked his head, eyed her suspiciously, and then stretched for a second crow. Satisfied that he wasn't headed for the skillet, he hopped down to gobble his special share of grain.

Hattie laughed, feeling free and happy. In the barn, it took several minutes to find all the nests and gather the eggs, most with two eggs in them. She even had one of the older hens who was trying to set. Hattie looked at her but left no feed. The foolish hen might set another day, but hunger would draw her off. Even foolish hens recognized cold eggs were never going to hatch, of course, neither were infertile eggs.

She stopped in surprise when one of the horses nickered at her from the back stall. She slipped back and set her full basket down to grab the nose poked over the stall rails. "Oh Rose," she climbed on the stall gate and hugged the tall neck of her roan mare. It had been a year since those men had taken her and her father's saddle horse. She looked over and saw the wide white blaze of her dad's gelding. "Hey, Buddy," she patted the nose tentatively leaning closer.

"They were part of the rustled animals we recovered last night. You want to see the rest?"

She wiped her eyes and turned toward the deep voice behind her. It didn't help. She let go of the rail and turned into his arms.

For a moment he held her, while she fought for self-control. Then despite his better judgment, he leaned closer, catching the scent of the horse she'd just hugged, the chickens she'd just fed, the scent of laundry soap, even the sweet scents of milk and baby. But underneath it all was the warm musky smell of woman. His body reacted instantly.

Alarmed, he pushed her away.

"They're still in the front paddock," he growled. He almost made the mistake of grabbing her hand, but instead, he touched her elbow to guide her in the right direction.

Hattie gasped, totally confused. She couldn't believe she'd turned into his arms so easily. Recalling herself, she stopped and turned to walk back for the egg basket. As they passed, she set the basket on the porch, watching as James sat peeling potatoes while J.D. clutched and chewed on his pony.

She gave the old cowhand a watery smile. "Did you know about the horses?"

He gave her a grin, "Wait till you see the front paddock."

The scene there made her worry that she might tear up again. A big angry bull stood, snorting, amid a herd of fifty plus cows and calves. She turned in wonder and delight toward Jackson. "Those aren't all mine?"

"No," he laughed, "there are thirty that are ours. But almost all of yours are pregnant or have calves. We couldn't find your first fifty that were rustled, figure those were sold off. But the rest are all accounted for and their calves. You've still got over sixty head, come fall you'll probably have over eighty.

Hattie clapped her hands, then dipped her head. "Thank you, thank you, Lord." Beaming she smiled at him. "Thank you Jackson."

Then he forgot what Rubye would think was proper. He reached out and pulled her in, an arm around her shoulder. "It's all right girl, it's all right. We'll get those rustlers yet, won't we men?"

"That's right, Miss Stoddard. We'll get them."

Hattie raised her head, stared at the cowboys who had answered as one. They met her eyes, delighted with her smiling face. To a man, they accepted her for who and what she was, not what the gossips in town accused her of. It was too much. Hattie raised a hand to cover her mouth, nodded and turned to rush back toward the house.

◇◇◇

Jackson felt a tightness in his chest that he hadn't felt since the night J.D. was born. He cleared his throat, looked toward his men, then asked. "Now, what are we going to do with a second bull?"

"You mean three, don't you, boss. That little black ones cut him out a herd to practice on," Tony called.

Cliff looked around, "Move this one and these cows to the north range with the other Stoddard cows. Let that long spotted bull have the south grass, and let junior duck and dodge the way he's been doing. Looks like the Stoddard bull does pretty good at getting the job done."

"No, I think Hattie's bull will head back south, to his own range. Might as well move them to that sector to begin with, leave the north grass to our cows and bull. I think your plan for Junior is a good one. All right, maybe we can keep them apart for a while. But somehow, they'll work it out to fight," Jackson added.

"Yep, but then the best bull will win. In the meantime, we can get some fine calves," Cliff said.

"Maybe, but I'm thinking someone around here might want to buy a good bull. Or even a young bull with potential," Jackson said.

"Junior may not be as deep chested or heavy as this bruiser, but he'll do," Tony said.

"I'll ask Hattie what she wants to do." Jackson looked nervously back up the yard, watching as Hattie quickly hung clothes. She could work faster and harder than two other women. Even as he thought it, he saw her set the basket down and begin working through the huge garden. She carried the basket on her hip from row to row as it grew heavier with tomatoes, greens and the last of the green beans.

While he watched, she walked to the corral and stripped the beans from the plants she had pulled from the hard soil, tossing the brown edged plants before her mules as a treat.

Whatever needed doing, she did it as soon as she thought of it, which was part of the secret. She patted Henry lovingly, pulling his long ears, and then hurried to the house, putting the green beans down beside the washtub.

She used the pail, quickly carrying the dirty water to water the garden while the air was still cool, then rinsed the washtubs, filling one with clean water and taking the time to wash the vegetables, before putting them back in the clean laundry basket. Emptying the rinse water in the garden, she stacked the tubs on the end of the porch, passed James the clean vegetables and took the fussing boy from him.

He noticed how she turned the rocker before sitting down, so her back was to the rail and the rest of her was blocked from view of the kitchen window. She was always thinking and planning.

Donna had been smart and a good wife, but she only did what she thought she was expected to do. Hattie acted as though she had it all to do by herself, and she tried her best to do as much work as efficiently as possible.

One of the men yelled at him, and Jackson swung around to open the gate, embarrassed to be caught mooning over the girl. The black bull wheeled out of the paddock as though fired from a gun.

He motioned to the men to indicate he was ready and one by one, the cows were hazed out after the bull. Finally they were left with a pen full of calves. It seemed cruel to brand such little ones, but with rustlers, they didn't have the choice. Mavericks could and would be branded by whoever found them first.

The first branded were Harper calves. By lunch, all the calves had been tended to and released to join the cows. The hands carefully separated the stock, hazing Harper cows North and Stoddard cattle toward the south pasture.

Minutes later, they were all washing up for lunch.

CHAPTER FIFTEEN

Jackson walked toward the house. "Hattie?"

She looked over her shoulder, rapidly buttoning her blouse. She felt guilty, dozing in the sun just like the contented baby.

As he walked onto the porch, he had to smile at the sleepy eyed couple. Hattie stretched and extended the baby to place in the cradle. Jackson noticed with satisfaction that the baby had out-grown it, his head nearly touching the top, his little feet near the bottom. The air was hot, the day becoming steamy. He felt sweaty and sticky from the work with the cattle. He noticed Hattie had left the boy naked, except for his diaper; a little circle of damp sweat lay underneath his chin. He knew Rubye would have scolded her, but the baby looked comfortable. Hattie spread out one of the thin diapers over the cradle to screen the sleeping baby

James stepped out onto the porch and handed both of them glasses of cool water. Jackson swallowed his in two gulps, Hattie sipped hers slowly. Jackson nodded toward the two young hands who had stayed behind to help Boyd build a chicken coup. They were taking turns dunking themselves with gourds of water from the well.

"All set?" Jackson set his empty glass on the rail.

"Yeah, everything cleared and put away. Reckon I got three or four hours before they need fed again."

They walked out into the yard and watched the chickens scratching through the garden where Hattie had pulled the tired beans, busy gobbling any worms or insects that had been exposed.

"Where did you two have in mind?" Jackson asked.

Hattie raised her head, letting the hot summer breeze dry her throat. She wished it wasn't deemed necessary to keep her whole body covered in this hot weather. She felt damp under the arms, under her heavy, full breasts, and in a line down her back. It would be so wonderful to be J.D., innocently open to the air.

James scratched his chin, rubbed a hand across his thinning hair. "Miss, where do you figure is best?"

Hattie sighed and looked around. The well, garden and clothesline took up a good part of the yard on this side of the house. Downhill, the path narrowed toward the privies. The barn and corrals were within a brisk walk from the house, but on this warm day, she was glad the familiar barn odors were blowing away from the house. A chicken coop would add to the odors.

She considered the options, and then pointed to the barn. "I think leaning against the back side of the barn. You can put up a double ledge for nesting boxes – keep them out of reach of possums and coyotes so they can sleep. Save on materials since you'll just need posts and the chicken wire you already bought. Of course you'll need some planks or tin for the roof."

When she said tin, the men exchanged a glance.

"Would tin be too expensive?"

"No, we have a house worth," Jackson answered. "Donna hated the sound of rain on the metal roof. So we redid it with shingles. There's a layer of tin in the attic, over the rafters. But you'll need more than chicken wire to keep the wind off them come winter, otherwise they'll just move back into the barn."

"How many of those double long rails do we still have?" He turned to ask James.

"Over twenty, I used four when we extended the garden.

"All right, how big do you think it needs to be?"

She froze, swiveling her head toward the house. "It needs to be at least big enough for fifty chickens to spread out on the ground. A big need is a door so I can let them out in the day, coop them up at night."

She was already heading back to the house, bending to scoop up J.D. who was complaining and trying to pull himself up by the cradle side. She lifted the baby and balanced him on her hip as she stepped to the rail.

"Jackson."

He raised a brow at the summons, and then smiled as J.D. chortled and waved his plump naked arms at him. He reached for him and Hattie apologized, "he's wet."

"Cleaner than any of those cows I handled this morning." Jackson laughed and took him, bending to kiss the soft neck. The laugh made the other men laugh as well.

Hattie disappeared into the house. She moved the pot of beans that had boiled over to the back eye, tilted the pot lid. She took a minute to check the roast that was already starting to brown in the oven. As the wood burned down, the oven would still be hot enough to cook the meat to the brown outside, red inside that the men preferred. Satisfied that she could leave everything, she grabbed a dry diaper, long sleeved gown, and bonnet for J.D..

When she came out, she was surprised to only find Jackson sitting in the rocker, a naked J.D. standing on his knees, his little bare bottom bouncing up and down as he squealed in laughter. She laughed at the two.

"Your Daddy is a brave man."

J.D. laughed and Jackson patted the little bottom. "You wouldn't pee on daddy, would you pardner?"

As though he understood the word, J.D. started to pee but Jackson laughed and just held him out so the spray hit the porch, not him. When the stream stopped he lifted the laughing baby back on his lap. "Why fight a good system?"

"Good for who? He just made two messes instead of one. I was wondering, if you could, well I was thinking, maybe you would like to fence in this porch as well."

Jackson scowled at her and she kept talking while struggling to get the long sleeved lawn gown over the baby's head despite his protest and wiggles. "Why smother him in all that?"

"If I don't, he'll cook in the sun." She managed the last sleeve, and then held up the bonnet she had carried outside. "I can make a little mattress and cover it and if the porch was changed, so the bottom has another rail so he can't get through and the top were screened, then when he gets a little bigger and ready to crawl, he would have a safe place to play in."

"And you brought it up, because?"

She finished dressing the baby and pulled him back onto her hip. "No, Jackie, leave it on." She sighed as he pulled off the bonnet and pulled it into his mouth. "I thought while you had the men ready to work, they might tackle this as their next project."

He rose towering over her, and Hattie forced herself not to give way and crouch by the rail. "One thing at a time. You got any more suggestions; you better come out to the barn and show us." Ignoring her, he took the baby back in his arms, letting him ride on his arm as though he were weightless instead of nearly twenty pounds.

Hattie hurried ahead, eager to get through and back to her jobs in the kitchen. If she worked quickly, she might have time to make a batch of yeast bread after sweeping the floor and mopping the kitchen area and the porch.

The afternoon flew by. Jackson had kept the baby with him, saying, "No, we've got work to do, don't we boy?" She had nearly an hour with her hands free, time to make bread and prepare the other vegetables as well as managing to sweep and mop inside and out. When J.D. grew tired, and curled into his daddy's neck, he had carried him back inside and given him to Hattie.

He was pink from the sun and she wanted to scold them both, but the baby looked so sleepy and content that she took him without protest, only taking time to wipe his face and neck before feeding him and putting him down for a long nap.

When she had the table set, meat and bread sliced, she came out on the porch to ring the cow bell Rubye used to call the gathering men into dinner.

The room quickly filled up with hot sweaty cowboys and Hattie would have left to hide, but after this morning and the sympathetic looks from the men, she felt safe to finish serving the food. She added the cooked green beans and wilted garden greens drizzled with bacon fat and crumbled bacon. The real draw was the ice cold tea she had cooled in the cellar and the fresh baked sliced loaf bread. James Boyd asked if she needed help. When she shook her head he wearily settled into her place at the table and let her wait table, refilling glasses of tea and milk as quickly as they drank it.

When J. D. woke, it was Jackson who went and fetched him. He seemed happy to be passed around from man to man, each one playing and joking with him, letting him sip their tea or milk, eat their potatoes. They laughed when he made faces at the wilted greens, shaking his head at the sour, sweet taste, and then leaning forward to taste it again. He tried to eat bread when he reached James' chair, but Hattie had to use a finger to rake it out of his mouth when he started to cough.

He made a face and bit her.

"Ow," she pulled her finger out. "Hey you, is there a tooth in there?"

Jackson reached over, holding out a finger, then gave a loud "ouch! That's a sharp little milk tooth."

He smiled at Hattie, "You'll be in troub…," the words faded away and he blushed scarlet, swallowing hard as the men looked away at Hattie's gasp and florid face.

J. D. started at the look on her face, and then began to wail. She stiffened, set the pitcher of tea down, and took the baby from James lap. Holding him close, she fled from the room.

As she closed the door, she heard one of the cowboys say. "I don't see how it has anything to do with it, calves, kittens and puppies all come with teeth and their mommas manage just fine."

"Hush, Tony," James scolded, and then stood up to take over the chore of waiting on table and cleaning up.

◇◇◇

By noon the next day, the chicken coop was started and Jackson and the cowboy carpenters had moved to the porch to work out how to change it into a playpen for the boy, but still look and work as a porch.

Hattie had laid out a simple lunch. Leftover roast beef, sliced thin, served with thick sliced bread. The table was loaded with plates of sliced ripe tomatoes, big onions, and fresh cucumbers, and a big platter of dressed eggs. Pitchers of water and milk sat at either end of the table and the huge pot of black coffee sat on the back of the stove. She slipped outside, leaving the men to serve themselves when Jackson called her name.

"The foods on the table," Jackson called names and some of the men went on inside while the young men and James stood waiting.

Jackson stood with his hand as a visible marker for where he wanted rails to be added. Ben and Tony were arguing that they were too close. "How close do they need to be to keep him in?"

She disappeared and reappeared with the boy bouncing on her hip. While she stood there, Jackson measured with his hand the correct width needed to keep the boy from wiggling through the rails. The last two men rode up. Neither spoke nor looked her way. Hattie felt the old shame wash over her. Had they stopped, talked to someone, heard some new rumor that reminded them she was a scarlet woman?

They removed their hats as they walked past quickly into the house, not making eye contact. Jackson stepped up onto the porch, his face expressionless as he walked into the house. Tony and Ben made excuses and walked past her into the house. Hattie heard frantic whispers, hushed "oh no's," then more muffled voices.

A few minutes later, the men began to stream out, tipping their hats but quietly drifting away until the two late-comers came out, carrying plates loaded with food and mugs of coffee. Even James tiptoed past, "I'll clean up later," he said softly.

Hattie folded her arms around Jackie and pulled him close to her chest and rocked back and forth on her heels, upset, but unsure of why? Such a small thing, a snub by some of the men. But it brought all her old insecurities rushing forth. She felt a tightness in her chest. J.D. reached out a hand to touch her face and she gave a choked laugh, kissing the little nose and intent face. "Jackie, my love, thank you." She brought him even closer to kiss, accepting all the unconditional love.

◇◇◇

Jackson stepped out on the porch and she turned her back to him, hiding against the baby. He waited, giving her a chance to face him but she didn't, just stood looking sadly out into the distance. He sank into the rocker, reached into the cradle to pick up J.D.'s pony and gave it a shake.

When the boy reached for his favorite toy, Hattie surrendered him to his daddy. Jackson took the boy, nuzzled him, and then set him into the cradle beside him. Talking softly he began.

"Hank and Cliff saw some buzzards when they were out."

Hattie looked up, surprising him with her sudden jump to the conclusion. "They found one of the rustlers dead?"

He shook his head, looking around at the deserted yard. All the men clearly didn't want to hear or see her reaction. "It was your horse, Nugget."

Hattie felt her lip quiver and her emotions switch again. "He was getting old."

"No, he got shot, Sunday when we had the shootout with the outlaws. We'd looked for him, surprised he wasn't still with the mules and your herd."

"I don't understand."

"It was a shot to his chest. He must have run a long time. They found him, up in the north sector. It looks like it pierced a lung. Eventually, he wore down. Once he went down, his other lung would have collapsed."

Hattie pictured her fat old horse, gold coat flecked with blood, frightened, hurt, and alone to suffer such a long death.

The tears that she had held back for weeks were flowing, soft and quiet down her cheeks. Jackson held out a hand and pulled her toward him and she started crying for real. He pulled her onto his lap, lifted her legs to rest on the arm of the chair so that she was draped against him. J. D. looked up, his face puckering up in sympathy at the sound of her sobs. Without hesitation, he pulled the boy up into his arms and together, he and Hattie held the baby between them. Without thinking, Jackson nuzzled her, kissing the top of her head, then turned to nuzzle and kiss the frightened baby.

They heard a wagon pull into the yard. Hattie started to pull away, but he held her closer, confused about what he was feeling, just knowing he didn't want to release her until she stopped crying.

◇◇◇

"My word, it's worse than she said."

Hattie pushed against the rock hard chest, though she wanted nothing more than to sit and feel safe a little longer.

She lifted her apron and wiped her eyes, blew her nose. In horror, she looked out from where she sat to see her preacher and two of the deacons. They were staring at her like she was some kind of monster. She realized her petticoat was flipped up and her ankles were exposed, worse, she was sitting in a man's lap in plain sight. Together, they were holding a nearly naked baby.

From the thunderous look in her pastor's eyes, Hattie wondered how much worse things could get. She rose shakily, holding the baby in her arms, trying to keep him from wiggling down to her breasts.

"Brother Harper," the preacher thundered. "You must put this woman out of your home at once. You are offending God and the people of this community with your sinful ways."

Jackson stood up, prepared to argue, but Hattie moved behind him and he felt a compelling urge to protect her from their thunderous condemnation. "Never, my son needs her."

"If you are not going to put her out, then you must marry her," the preacher stated. Both deacons shouted agreement.

"A man cannot have a woman sleeping alone in his house, unless they are married."

"She's not alone in the house with me. James Boyd sleeps in the house too."

The deacons shook their heads and the preacher again spoke for them all. "Sleeping with two men is not better than sleeping with one."

"We've done nothing wrong. There's no reason for us to get married. If people want to talk, let them talk. I'll marry again, when I feel there's a need, not when a bunch of busybodies order me to."

◇◇◇

Hattie turned, crying so hard, she could barely find the door handle. She managed to reach the bedroom, tumbling onto the bed with the crying baby. Minutes later, she was lying there nursing him.

She couldn't stop crying. He didn't want to marry her. Why did his saying those words, hurt so much? She felt like the world had ended. J. D. patted her face and whimpered and she leaned down to kiss him, raised him to hug close, and then changed breasts to continue feeding him.

The reason she realized was obvious. She loved him. But clearly he didn't love her.

CHAPTER SIXTEEN

There was a knock on the door. "Miss Stoddard?"

Hattie stirred; surprised she had fallen asleep beside the baby. How had all her wretchedness changed into slumber?

"Just a few minutes, please?"

It was ten minutes before Hattie opened the door. J.D. was asleep in the crib, once more properly gowned. She had cleaned her face and changed from the sweat soaked blouse to a fresh unstained one. Her hair was once again neatly combed and pinned. Except for the pink puffiness of her eyes, she felt almost presentable.

She opened the door and Pastor Goodwin stepped inside, cautiously leaving the door half open. "Miss Stoddard, we're waiting on you outside."

Hattie turned with a frown, "What are you saying?"

"Mr. Harper is ready to do the right thing. He has agreed to marry you."

"Really, how noble of him. What makes you think I'm willing to marry him?"

"My dear girl, if you are ever to regain any shred of respectability, this is your only choice."

"And what, Pastor Goodwin, would a woman of my reported morals care about respectability and community opinion?" Hattie stiffened her spine and put her hands on her hips, trying to look like a woman of ill repute.

Pastor Goodwin stepped around her and stared down at the baby.

Hattie moved protectively closer to the baby, in case this pompous fool should start insulting Donna's baby, the way he had her.

His soft voice shocked her. "My dear, if you don't marry him, you'll have no choice but to leave." He opened his arms wide, his hand an open palm above the boy. "Can you leave this beautiful baby?"

"He won't ask me to leave. He knows J.D. needs me."

"Maybe not now; but when the boy is weaned, when the year is up, will you be able to go back to your ranch – alone?"

Hattie swallowed, involuntarily reaching over the side of the crib to grasp the small hand, the one that had patted her so lovingly while she cried.

In his sleep, J.D. clamped on her fingers and it might as well have been her heart.

Hattie raised her glance toward the preacher and saw Jackson standing in the doorway, staring at her.

"Excuse us pastor, we need to talk."

The pastor stepped to the door, and Jackson pulled it closed behind him.

Hattie raised her head. "I know you don't want to marry me. I don't want to trap you. If you were there long enough, you know I'm used to being 'a woman-of-ill-repute.' It's not your responsibility to salvage my reputation."

Jackson stared at the girl, eyes glittery from hurt pride. She was so young, so fierce. Holding her gaze, he crossed the room to stand in front of her.

"Shh. It wasn't you I wanted to reject. I just don't appreciate having someone tell me I have to do anything."

She looked confused. "I don't know what to say?"

"Hattie, I don't know what the answer should be, but I know everything the pastor said is true." He stepped even closer, put a hand under her chin and tilted her face up. "Donna made me promise to find someone. I know it sounds strange, but sometimes I imagine what she would say, as though she's still here."

Hattie nodded, "Yes, sometimes I feel her, sense what she wants me to do."

"She told me to go get you, to save J.D."

Hattie was having trouble swallowing. "Marriage is forever, it requires love. I don't know if loving the same little boy is enough for forever."

"I don't want a marriage in name only, Hattie. If you say yes, I'm moving back into my bed."

She backed up, her eyes filling with terror.

He stepped closer. "Don't be afraid. I'll never force you to do anything you don't want to do, ever."

She tried to breathe, but couldn't find the room.

He held out his hand. "Trust me, Hattie. Marry me and J.D."

She was afraid, but she could feel a pair of hands pushing her forward.

She gave him a quivery smile. Then extended her hand to take his and let herself be pulled toward the closed door.

When they came out, Hattie was surprised to see their three visitors seated at the table. James was pouring tea for them and Cliff was waiting at the door. Apparently there would be no need to put away leftovers.

James came over, drying his hands. "Cliff and I will be witnesses. I'll be mighty proud, to act in your father's stead and give you away, Miss Harriett."

For just a moment, Hattie thought of protesting but at his hopeful smile she nodded and curtsied. Everyone she knew was married in church, her parents had been married there. It had been a long time since she had thought of a church wedding for herself. But she wondered if one in a house would be considered legal by people like the Dawsons. She giggled nervously. No matter what they did, the Dawsons would not accept her as Jackson's new wife.

Jackson stood stiff and straight, nervously he released her hand, touched her elbow, and then touched her hand again.

Of course he had married Donna in church. She remembered the elaborate ceremony. Everyone in town was present to watch the bride in her beautiful bustled white satin gown and the handsome rancher in his new black suit.

Now he was dusty from working on the chicken coop and porch, and unlike her, he hadn't changed. But she reminded herself, he had held his nearly naked son in that dusty outfit. He had swept her into his arms and onto his lap to comfort her when she cried. What did it matter if she wore her mourning black and he was in dusty work clothes? Their witnesses, the deacons and the cowhands, could testify to the marriage. The preacher would say the usual words, the same as he would in church.

Perhaps the nerves knotting in her stomach would disappear if she had a veil, or wore a white dress. Would her hands feel like ice if she had a woman to fix her hair, friends to giggle and joke with while she waited to walk down an aisle? Would her heart be happier if there were music and dancing and a big feast waiting to celebrate the event?

No. A woman with no reputation did not deserve a white dress, veil or a church wedding. She should be grateful that she would have a husband, even if he was being forced into it. They had been accused of doing things neither of them had done. What had he said, 'he didn't want to be told he had to do something?'

She had no family or friends to celebrate with anyway. She had had parents who loved her. Both were dead. This tall man and his son, they would be her family from this day forward. For the first time, she felt joy at the prospect.

James Boyd walked over toward her and she gratefully hooked her arm over his elbow. One of the deacons moved the Bible table in front of the fireplace and the preacher walked behind it.

Cliff said, "I guess I'm the best man, boss."

Jackson looked as at sea as she felt, but he let the red-headed cowboy herd him over toward the fireplace to stand to the left of the preacher. The deacons rose and stood at the right.

James leaned toward her and whispered, "Guess they're the bridesmaids. "

Hattie giggled again, trying to control her shaking knees. She gripped his arm tighter. There would be no organ music to tell them when to begin.

James placed a hand on her arm, giving her a pat, just as they heard a waking cry from J.D. "Let's get down there, then I'll go get the baby."

Somehow she managed to walk to her place in front of the preacher and the tall slender oak table on which rested the Harper's family Bible. She shivered, icy fear sweeping down her spine.

Jackson turned woodenly to face her. If only he would look directly at her, give her a smile. Was he remembering his first wedding, his perfect marriage to Donna? There was still time. She could break and run, go back to the family ranch, alone.

Suddenly she heard someone humming. She and Jackson glanced back to watch James Boyd walking down the makeshift aisle, humming, then singing the wedding march to the fussing baby. As he sang the baby quieted, then raised his hands to smile, showing the tiny white tooth.

Jackson stepped closer and took her arm, smiling down at her as she smiled up at him.

The preacher called them back to the moment as he asked. "Do you Jackson Harper take this woman, to love, honor, and protect, in sickness and in health, as long as you both shall live?"

She could only stare up in disbelief when he loudly said, "I do."

"Harriett Stoddard do you take this man, to love, honor and obey, in sickness and in health, as long as you both shall live?"

All she could feel was joy, deep, and compelling as she softly whispered, "I do."

"I now pronounce you man and wife. Whom God has joined together, let no man put asunder. Amen."

"Amen," echoed the deacons, "amen" echoed the cowhands. Then outside, she heard yet another wave of "Amens."

J.D.'s squeal was the final amen.

She was married. She stared at Jackson, holding her breath, waiting for a ring, a kiss, another word to release her.

He must have felt the same way. Slowly he reached out, lifted one hand, then the other and pulled her closer.

Her head felt light as he leaned near. As soon as she felt his lips on hers, her knees buckled, and she fainted.

Jackson felt her crumpling and swung her into his arms.

James Boyd was holding J.D., his gown bunched around his waist, his face red in complaint. "That's some kiss, make a gal swoon."

"Water, somebody bring cold water to her room," Jackson barked.

◇◇◇

He laid her on the bed, then lifted one of her feet, grabbing a buttonhook to undo the tightly buttoned shoe, then repeated it on the other.

James Boyd was in the room, still holding the crying baby.

Jackson removed her shoes, and then moved to unbutton the stiff high collar, stopping halfway down and unbuttoning each cuff. Without hesitation, he lifted beneath her and unhooked the snug band of her skirt.

"That boy is pretty unhappy," James said.

"He'll keep a minute." Jackson said as he tugged the blouse free of the skirt and then unbuttoned the bottom half, making sure it still covered her front.

James came on in the room, putting the baby in the crib, setting the pitcher down. "I'd think you could wait for that at least until after the preacher and deacons are gone."

"Go to hell. You know it's not that. Did you see her eat anything today? Hand me a damp cloth and pour some water in her glass."

James scratched his chin, "No, nary a bite, and that's a fact. You think that's all that ails her?"

"That, the heat, and marrying on command. She was upset about her pony before they even showed up and then she had to go through all this."

He laid the damp cloth on her forehead and reached over to rub the downy hair on the baby's head to comfort him too. "See if you can find something for her to eat. Send the preacher off and put some beans on for supper."

He pulled the crying baby up into his arms, then kissed him and put him back in the crib. The boy stared at him, then began to whimper. "I've got these two."

He sat on the edge of the bed and gently washed at her flushed face. Hattie's eyes flew open, dark with shock and confusion. She started to sit up and Jackson moved between her and the curious cook.

"Tell Pastor Goodwin and the deacons we'll see them Sunday. Put Cliff in charge of the men and get them back to work. My wife needs a rest."

"Yes, sir, boss."

"Oh, Boyd."

"Yes, boss…"

"Knock before you bring in the food."

The cook looked confused, then grinned and backed out the door.

Hattie's eyes were huge and dark blue. Jackson smiled at her, and then held the glass of water for her to drink. Hattie would have taken it, but he had a firm grip on it. She swallowed, wondering how she'd gotten here. He took a moment and lifted her into a sitting position, propping both pillows behind her before releasing the glass into her hands. While she watched in confusion, he walked over and used the damp rag to clean and change the smelly baby, leaving him bare and hanging onto the sides of the crib.

He held the dirty diaper and gown up and she pointed to the covered pail beside the dresser.

"Why did you tell James to knock?" she asked, her voice squeaking.

He grinned at her mischievously, then peeled down one sock, then the other. When she gasped and leaned forward to protest he stripped off the black striped blouse and hung it over the bed post, then tugged her skirt off and hung it on the foot post.

Hattie curved into a crouch, folding her arms in front of her body, tucking her bare feet beneath the ruffles of her petticoat. "I thought you promised not to …,"she couldn't find breath enough to say more.

A breeze fluttered the curtains, dispelling a little of the heat. He lifted the naked boy over the rails and handed him to her.

"Best feed him before James brings you your dinner." He walked to the door, staring at her as he walked. "I'm going to check to make sure everyone is gone and the men are back at work. See you later, Mrs. Harper."

Hattie sagged against the pillows as soon as the door closed. She raised back up, and removed the hairpins. Holding the hard bun she shook her hair loose. J.D. crowed in delight, climbing against her. She had to admit the breeze felt good on her bare arms. The baby curved against her, as delighted by her bare skin as she was in his.

"Okay, young master Harper, just because you and Mr. Harper have some strange notions about proper attire." She kissed all along the soft curve of his back and J.D. laughed and made little kissing bites along her shoulder.

She felt tears sting her eyes, the joy was so blinding and strong. "Son, my son, I love you so much, till death do us part. I know your mother Donna still loves you. I feel her here all around. But now I can love you and your daddy the same way, without fear." She kissed his cheek, nuzzling him as he was nuzzling her, and then fed him.

◇◇◇

Jackson was disappointed to find the preacher still in the sitting room, his hand on the open Bible.

"Is Mrs. Harper all right?"

Jackson nodded, "She just didn't get around to eating today, got a little light headed."

"I took the liberty of opening to the family page here. I thought you might like me to sign it, too."

Jackson stared at the gold trimmed page, with its list for marriages, births and deaths. Beneath his parents' names, with their wedding date, were his and Donna's names and the date of their marriage.

He noted that all the entries for his parents, their marriage, birth of their children, their deaths, were complete. He felt a wave of sadness when he realized it was true for Donna as well, date of marriage, birth of child, and death. Would he always feel a little guilty that it wasn't over for him?

Soberly he took the pen the preacher offered, filled in names and date of marriage, and then turned it for the preacher's signature. Now, maybe the man would leave without another sermon.

His pastor didn't disappoint him. "I know you may still feel resentful, the decision being taken from you. But a man needs a wife and a boy needs a mother."

Jackson stared at him hard. "Don't you have other people you can visit and set straight?"

The pastor stared at him. "It's customary for the groom to offer a token, beyond gratitude, to the man who marries him."

Jackson laughed. "Well, when a man asks for a preacher, maybe so. But you could walk around meddling all over town, working up business. No, I figure your reward is in the satisfaction of doing a good deed. I'll let you know when I feel it's worthy of some other token."

The pastor eyed him coldly, then put his hat on his head and stormed out.

James stood at the dining table with a plate of scrambled eggs and a small dish of potato salad. "Them church vultures didn't ask for no invite to supper neither, hardly left a bite for your new missus."

"Thanks, James, I'll carry it in. Do we have any milk left?"

"Sure, sure."

A minute later Jackson turned the knob and smiled as he held the food and stared at the lovely vision inside. Hattie was half-asleep, the breeze blowing the lace curtains on both windows, stirring her loose blonde hair around her shoulders. She had one brown hand curved under the baby's bare bottom; an arm curved around his back holding him to her beautiful naked breast, the skin snow white against his rosy cheeks. Her small white feet and slender ankles were brazenly bare to his gaze, as were her firm white arms and shoulders.

Whenever he watched her working, he was always aware of how slim and graceful she was yet how supple and strong. But sprawled, half asleep with the baby at her breast, he realized how perfectly formed she was and how desirable.

Quietly he crossed the room and set the plate and glass of milk on the dresser. Before when he had caught glimpses of her feeding the baby she had blushed and hurriedly hidden herself. Now he was aware of her watching him through lowered lashes. Shocked, he watched as she flung an arm above her head on the pillow, the white of her underarm vivid against the brown of her burnished face. He felt a heavy wave of desire.

Drawn irresistibly, he sank down on the edge of the bed. He leaned forward, kissing first the underside of her arm and as she turned to face him, he softly kissed her mouth, breathing deeply to control the urge to kiss her deeper. Using all his control, he raised up and smiled at her.

"You need to eat. I'll see you both later," but before he could rise she shocked him again.

Using the white arm he had just kissed, she reached up to pull his face back down. "Thank you." Tenderly she kissed his cheek and leaned her forehead against his.

CHAPTER SEVENTEEN

All afternoon as he supervised the men and helped finish the chicken coop, he remembered her gentle touch and soft kiss. He wondered why she thanked him. The food, cleaning the baby, the wedding, the kiss? The possibilities in each answer tormented him.

At dusk of the hot day, the men walked on down to the creek and bathed in the deep pool, splashing and joking. All gave him a hard time about the night stretching before him. He let it go on a few minutes before raising a hand.

"It's not that kind of night. Preacher kind of got ahead of his place. We are married, but we've got a lot of things to work through before the marriage part really gets started. Not that it's any of your business – but I don't want you teasing my wife with all this nonsense, the way you've been riding me."

Cliff stared at him, and then looked as disappointed as Jackson felt. "Real sorry it ain't boss, real sorry. She's a sweet, pretty girl. Never did believe that nonsense we heard in town. Never did."

All the men nodded and Jackson went cold. It went without saying that a woman who'd had a baby wasn't an inexperienced virgin. But hadn't he believed the gossip when he heard it? Harriet Stoddard wouldn't be the first woman known to have fancied the boys and enjoyed sex too much, only to end up in disgrace. Thelma's place was full of good-time girls.

Even his Donna hadn't been a virgin. She was plain spoken and clear about what she wanted from him. But when she became pregnant and they'd married, they found ways to make it work. He had been proud of his wife and they had a loving relationship and a happy home together.

He wanted the same with Hattie. Then he shook his head. He would need to know, to understand before they could build a relationship. For now, it was enough to give her the protection of his name and provide J.D. with more than breast milk. Hattie loved that boy and he loved her. She was the only mother he knew. When he started talking, he wanted J.D. to call her momma. He didn't doubt she loved the child and he loved her in return. What he wasn't sure of, was if there was room in her heart for him? Would her fear of men ever allow them any relationship more than what they had now?

He was one of the last to leave the pool, waiting until the cool water cooled down the ardor he felt every time he imagined sharing her bed. Dressed, he followed the men to the house, watched as the chickens fussed their way into the coop, establishing pecking order and choosing roosts. Hattie would love it when she saw it tomorrow. He felt surprised at how much it mattered to him, what his new wife thought or wanted.

<><><>

Hattie and J.D. dozed through the warm afternoon until his accident woke them. She quickly diapered the baby and put him in the crib while she drank the remaining water in the pitcher, and then asked James to bring her a pail of water. The air coming through the windows was cooler and she removed the window jambs to close both windows. The trouble with Texas was the drop in temperature as soon as the sun went down.

When the water came, she lit the lamp, quickly stripped and took a sponge bath by using a bar of soap and basin of the cold water. It was hard not to miss Rubye and the luxury of a hot tub bath in the pantry. By the time she finished, she could hear the men entering the dining room. Quickly dressing in a gown and wrapper, she moved the dirty clothes and bedding to the corner of the room. Gently she slipped a soft gown on the still sleepy baby, and made up the bed in clean sheets and quilt.

It was Jackson who brought her a bowl of chili, taking the restless and playful J.D. out with him. She could hear the men, laughing and playing with him as they fed him crumbled cornmeal in a glass of buttermilk. She had tried it once before, and he had made such a terrible face, she laughed to think of it. She hadn't tried it again. Apparently, everyone wanted to see the face for themselves and from the sound of things, J.D. was eating the mess this time.

Hattie sat at the dresser, braiding her hair and worrying her lower lip. Despite their agreement, would Jackson wait to claim his rights? She could hear the words from this morning, he intended to return to his bed once they wed. Nervously she paced the room, full of pent up energy.

Finally, she sat on the edge of the bed, updating her diary on J.D.'s progress. She included the new tooth, the cowboys playing with him and his eating cornmeal mush. She hesitated, and then added the fact that Jackson and she were married; now she was his mother.

She put the diary and pen up and picked up Dr. Padgett's book, eager to discover how old J.D. would be when he could call her momma. Pulling back the quilt and sheets, she slid into the bed, propped up with the pillow to read.

By the time Jackson and the boy entered, she had discarded the book and was making mental lists of chores for the next day. On the list was laundry, it had been two days since she had last done laundry and it was piling up. With a baby, one needed to wash something every day. At the end of the list was to try and make a cowboy doll. She had seen a beautiful china doll last week at the Thompson's store, with a lovely dress and old-fashioned pantalets. She wanted to make a doll for a little boy, with a lace-up vest and pull-on pants.

"Who's that, J.D.? Is that Momma?"

At the words Hattie held out her arms to the baby, tears pooling in her eyes. Donna was his momma, but now she was his momma too. Instead of crying she managed to say, "He won't be able to say it for another five or six months."

She gave the excited baby a big hug, and then sat him back against the pillows. He promptly rolled over and laughing she sat him back up. "Yeah, you can roll over, can't you Jackie." He cooed back at her and Hattie laughed and gave him a kiss.

Jackson watched for a minute, then without hesitating, began to remove his shirt. "Scoot on over you two – this is my side of the bed."

Alarmed, Hattie scooted over and lifted J.D. up.

"Do you need to get, get your clothes, so you'll have things to wear in the morning?"

He stared at her and she saw the little twitch in his jaw, the one that told her how he resented being bossed. But instead of yelling at her, he nodded.

"Good idea. I need to get it all, since I'm moving back in. Will there be room in the dresser for my stuff?"

"I have my things in one drawer, I'll get them out."

"Right, and add them to the wardrobe."

"But the wardrobe has Donna's things in it."

"They're all your things now."

Hattie put J. D. in the crib. He was so roly-poly, she never left him on the bed alone. She knew he would fuss if she left him lying down, so she stood him up, holding onto the crib side. He pulled against the rails and squealed in excitement as it made a rattling noise.

◇◇◇

Jackson brought in the laundry basket and emptied the clean clothes, mostly unfolded onto the bed. "Grabbed these for you."

"Thanks." Hattie smiled at his retreating back. Now the bed was covered with what she'd taken out of the dresser and the new clothes.

She opened the wardrobe and each of the dresser drawers on the left. Slowly she added her coarse cotton drawers and chemises to Donna's silky, embroidered ones. She hung her black blouse and skirt on a padded hanger, amid the brightly colored and ruffled clothes. When she'd finished, she folded the new clothes, mostly underwear and denim jeans, and hurriedly stowed them away in the dresser before he returned.

◇◇◇

She heard raised voices in the hall. Stealthily, she cracked the door to listen.

"Reckon if that's how you feel, I'll just move back to the bunkhouse."

"James, you know there's no reason for you to do that, but suit yourself."

"I think you need to let me go get Rubye, now her objections have been taken care of."

"No. She's the one who left. Let her ask us if she wants to come back. Hattie may not want her back, after the harsh things she had to say. Besides, between the two of you, the work all seems to be getting done."

"Yeah, well I didn't sign on to be cook and bottle washer. I'd rather wrangle cows."

Jackson gave him a hard look, "Yes, you did."

James ducked his head as though he'd hit him.

Hattie closed the door quietly, embarrassed to see James yield. She'd learned more than enough. Not only was Jackson going to sleep in her bed, but they would be alone in the house.

◇◇◇

Gratefully, she stared at J.D. "Stay awake, will you partner."

It was several minutes before Jackson came in, this time carrying another laundry basket and a set of saddlebags as well as an armful of shirts on hangers. He handed Hattie the hangers and nodded toward the wardrobe. She sprang to her feet and squeezed them in among the ruffled clothes.

She watched as he unloaded the saddlebags, setting his shaving mug/soap and razor blade beside the washbowl and pitcher.

For the first time she absorbed the fact that he was always clean shaven. She also noted the dark hair, curling a little long on his neck. She had always assumed J.D. had his mother's coloring, but she realized that both his parents had the same dark brown hair and blue eyes. When he turned toward her, she felt her mouth grow dry as he again removed his shirt, this time his eyes locked on hers.

"Where is your sleep shirt?"she croaked.

Jackson hung the shirt on the post, and then reached for the top button of his Levis.

"I don't wear one."

As he unbuttoned the second button, she realized he wasn't wearing long johns either. Panicked, she scooted across the bed and backed up against the wardrobe.

"You promised…"

"I plan on keeping it. It might help you a lot if you could turn your head while I get undressed and into bed."

Hattie turned around and stared down at her bare feet peeking from under the edge of the gown. She commanded her eyes to behave, but even terrified, she wanted to look at him. From his handsome face to the heavy muscles in his arms and bare chest, he was beautiful. She shivered from the effort.

Staring at his bride, Jackson tried not to laugh. The small figure in the big gown made him think of a startled rabbit. Frozen and quivering in the mistake that standing still would render her invisible.

He flipped back the comforter, settled in and grinned at J.D., who was watching both with complete fascination. When Jackson grinned, the baby laughed. "It's safe," he called, and Hattie moved gingerly to the bed, barely lifting the covers to slip inside. She lay back rigidly, her eyes focused on the ceiling, her hands folded on the edge of the cover.

He hesitated, and then smiled. "Ready for me to blow out the light?"

She gripped the edge of the quilt tightly, pulling it up under her chin, then nodded.

Jackson rolled to sit up and blow out the lamp. There was complete darkness and quiet for a minute, and then J.D. let out an ear-piercing scream.

Jackson hauled him out of his crib as Hattie sat forward. He tucked the baby against him and for a moment, J.D. was happy, just feeling his naked chest and shoulders.

Hattie lay back, relaxing for the moment, glad that J.D. lay between them. She relaxed even more as she heard Jackson crooning to the baby, nuzzling the soft curls on his head and along his neck. J.D. was thrilled, grabbing at hair and nose, trying to hold onto his daddy in every possible way. It was several minutes before he began his downward squirm, searching for a full breast and milk.

"Ouch," Jackson called out and Hattie laughed.

J.D. made a little whine of protest and Hattie rolled onto her side to take the fussy baby. Jackson turned to face her as she slipped the gown off her shoulder in the dark room and began to nurse the baby.

"Does he bite you?" It was the same question that had embarrassed them the other night in front of the men. This time she surprised him with her quick answer.

"He's only tried a couple of times; he's usually too busy nursing."

He extended a hand to play with the soft curls of brown hair on the sweet smelling head and J.D. batted him away. When he touched him again, the baby latched onto the brown hand and pulled it lower. Jackson lay, smiling, totally relaxed and happy. At the end of his knuckles he could feel the cotton of the gown, a soft thin barrier between his fingers and her warm skin. Slowly he let his eyes close, lulled by the rhythmic sounds of suckling and relaxed breathing.

◇◇◇

He came awake quicker than he went to sleep. A growing warmth against his leg let him know he was not alone on his cot in the study or on Rubye's hard bed in the narrow room at the end of the house. He opened his eyes to see his beautiful son still asleep, his little mouth pursed and making sucking motions at the air.

Hattie had rolled over on her back and her open gown revealed the vee of her breastbone, not the breasts he had hoped to glimpse. The even rise of her chest let him know she was asleep – but he figured there were only minutes before the cooling diaper would wake J.D. who would wake her.

He wondered if he could reach a diaper and change him first, then decided it would be easier to just remove the one he wore.

Slowly he went to work, tugging the soggy diaper off and dropping it in the pail beside the bed.

◇◇◇

Amazingly, they both remained asleep. Later, he awakened again, this time when he heard the young rooster proudly saluting the morning with one final cock-a-doodle do. Hattie opened her eyes and J.D. made a little face and gave a single high-pitched wail.

Instead of rolling toward him, Hattie lifted the sleepy baby, kissed his face, and then rolled so her back was to Jackson before moving her gown enough to let the baby nurse.

Feeling cheated, Jackson rolled to curve around them both, and then he realized his mistake. One touch against her slim hips and he was fully aroused. Even worse, Hattie was instantly aware of his presence and his condition. He knew it, because she slipped from the bed, J.D. held before her chest. The boy looked over his shoulder and gave Jackson a dirty look for spoiling his morning meal and cuddles.

"It's not what you think ... it is ... but I didn't mean anything by it."

She looked more irate than J.D.

Jackson realized it was time for him to make a retreat but he had a very large problem.

"Hattie, I'm sorry. Its morning ..." At her angry scowl, he shrugged. "You'll need to spin around."

She lifted the complaining baby to her shoulder and a humiliated Jackson climbed out of bed, quickly pulling on jeans and shirt. Carrying his boots and hat, he padded out of the room, holding his pants up with one hand.

◇◇◇

In the quiet room he dressed and rubbed his chin. Donna had hated for him to go unshaven. If Hattie felt the same, she'd need to allow him back in the bedroom. Fat chance of that. He headed into the kitchen and started the fire. He put coffee on and took the empty pails and headed to the barn.

James Boyd was already on the job, one pail full of milk beside him.

"I thought you quit."

"Nope, not until I'm replaced. You know me better than that."

Jackson stared at the old cowhand. Forty-two or three, some old man. But ranching did that to a person. A rough season, an injury or two, suddenly you found yourself on the chuck wagon instead of heading up the crew chasing the cows.

"How long have I known you, boss?"

"Since I was a sprout, about like J.D.. About as long as I've known anyone."

"That's our first real fight."

Jackson laughed, rubbed his chin, and laughed again. The startled cow moved away and James barely caught the pail. Jackson moved the other pail out of reach.

"Now look, I can remember the time you nearly broke my jaw, the time you did break my arm."

"I don't mean physical fight, I mean hurting words fight."

Jackson stared at him a long time. "Women?"

James nodded, "Women."

"Yeah, that's always what comes between good friends. I'm sorry. It's just Rubye is so bossy, like us, and she spent a good deal of time keeping Hattie in her place. I just think if she is the one asking to come back, it might let them establish a better relationship."

"I was afraid you wouldn't let her come back. I know how she was, not fair to the girl at all. I just, well, she's got no real home."

Jackson looked around at the horses, all leaning over their stalls, ears perked forward as though intently listening. "None of my business …but why haven't you ever proposed to Rubye? Everyone knows you love her."

James surprised him by offering no denials. "What have I got to offer a wife, a broken down saddle tramp like me? Naw, it wouldn't be fair to a fine woman like her."

"We'll see her Sunday at church. We'll go from there." Jackson switched the pail to his left, then held out his right hand and waited. James set down his bucket and shook.

◇◇◇

When he came back to the kitchen, Hattie was dressed in the same outfit as yesterday. J.D. lay on a folded quilt on the floor, playing with his pony and carved wooden cow, the little lamb nearby. He could smell bacon frying and biscuits baking and was astonished to see the table already set. He set the bucket of eggs on the counter.

She pointed at the eggs, "Count seems a little low."

"Oh, guess it could be the new surroundings, put 'em off a little in their laying."

"They finished the chicken coop?" She gave a little clap of excitement.

"Sure did, you'll have to inspect it soon. Boys are pretty proud of the job, but we'll make changes if you have any suggestions."

She grabbed a trivet and the handle of the oatmeal but he took both and carried them out to the table, along with the molasses. Hattie added grease to the skillet, then cracked the first four eggs into the pan, waited, then when the edges started to curl, raised the pan to flip all four. In minutes the men were piling in, each taking time to check the baby. He raised both legs in the air, then settled on one to twist so he could chew on his toes.

"Pretty slick trick," Cliff said. "Bet you can't do that Hank."

"Bet you're right, but my bones aren't still stretchy like his."

James bustled in with the fresh milk, hurrying into the kitchen to filter it into the churn, then going down to bring cold milk and butter up.

J.D. seemed to realize he was his last chance. He rolled onto his belly, arched up and made demands that someone come back to lift him up.

Jackson grinned and went to pull him up into his arms, twirling around like a big bird for a second. J.D. squealed in pleasure.

Hattie handed James the platters of bacon and biscuits, carried the plate of eggs herself. She served two or three to each man, then put the platter down in front of Jackson. He took a biscuit, buttered it and poured a puddle of molasses on his plate to dunk the bread in.

"Mighty fine, Mrs. Harper, mighty fine vittles," Cliff said, as Hattie settled in the chair beside Jackson and took J.D. into her own lap, smiling at the compliment, aware of her new position in the house.

"You know," Hank said, "I purely do like ranching chickens, except for that scrawny going-to-be-rooster."

Tony laughed. "He sure was cock-of the-roost last night. Soon as they all went in he set about sorting them out and claiming top perch."

When everyone had been assigned tasks and sent off to work, Jackson held Cliff back. "You ever find any leads in town about our vanishing rustlers?"

"Nary a sign."

"I figure someone got them on a stage."

"Yeah, James, Hank and I were talking about that, how to find out. I told them the station master's daughter might be able to find out, if she had the right incentive. She's an old, buck-tooth gal, looks like her papa, but she's mighty sweet on Tony. She's always trying to block him in the aisle at church, main reason he doesn't like to go, according to Hank."

"What did Tony say?"

"I can't repeat it in mixed company, but it boiled down to, no."

Jackson grinned. "I can telegraph the marshal, have him make inquiries in Abilene, tell him what we suspect. But pretty much everything sent gets seen by the sheriff and Charlie Dawson. I hate to muddy the waters in my own drinking hole."

"Know what you mean. Maybe I could ride on into Waco, send a wire from there, and maybe check on their owl-hoots while I'm in town. It would take a day or two away and maybe a little pocket money."

Jackson smiled, drew out a gold eagle and told him to fill his saddle bags with biscuits and jerky.

James Boyd came out from the kitchen. "You know Rubye's being at Dawson's house, she might be able to learn something, that is, if I could get away a little. Wouldn't need no gold piece to go calling, neither."

Jackson nodded. "Take the wagon, pick up supplies and mail while you're in town. I'll see if Hattie needs anything, make sure she can handle lunch alone."

CHAPTER EIGHTEEN

When he found Hattie, she was in the side yard washing clothes. He noticed she had J.D. out on a quilt on the porch, with one of the cow dogs standing guard duty. When the baby would start to roll, the dog would move so the boy ended up alongside him, where J.D. would lustily grab fur and ears until the dog would nudge him and the baby would roll in a different direction.

It wasn't the best solution, but he noticed the slight bruise on the boy's forehead where he'd already taken a tumble this morning. With her keeping watch, he guessed the big yellow dog was the best choice.

He walked to where she was rinsing and wringing clothes. "Hattie?"

She turned to eye him coolly and looked past him to the dog. "He always seemed to be watching him anyway, so I put him to work when Jackie tilted the cradle over. I know it looks bad, but he only cried a minute and I don't think it's going to raise a knot.

"Sam, the dog's name is Sam."

At his name, the dog sat up, his mouth open in a grin. Hattie smiled, for the first time this strange morning. J. D. squealed and the big dog flopped back down, still grinning, to let the baby curl into him.

"What did you think of the chicken coop?"

"I haven't seen it yet."

He growled. He and three hands had spent two days working in the heat to get that job done, just to please her. "Leave that and come take a look."

"I'm almost done. If I leave it, something might spill the clothes out and I'd have to start again."

He picked up the basket, surprising her, and began hanging the clothes, checking to see how she had hung the others.

She wrung out her dark blouse and followed the basket and Jackson to the line. "Here, I have to hurry before Jackie starts crying." Snapping the blouse out sharply, then quickly pinning it to overlap the corner of the shirt he had already pinned, she shook the tail of his shirt out without pulling it loose from the pin.

He laughed and handed her the next piece, moving to keep up with her as she made quick work of hanging their clothes side by side on the line. Jackson felt a sudden tightness in his chest as he stared at the dog, the baby, and the slim blonde beside him. She tugged at the last piece in his hands, feeling her breath catch at the tender look in his eyes as he stared down at her.

"Jackie?"

"I'm used to calling J.D., Jackie, when it's just the two of us. J.D. seems so grown up for such a little boy."

He shrugged in acknowledgement. "I don't know if you should trust Sam that much, with Jackie. He's great at herding reluctant heifers and surly bulls, I've seen him back down wolves, but I'm not sure if he might not snap at the baby."

She left the washtubs to empty later and hurried to the porch, squatting to rub the head and ears of the rough yellow dog, before picking up the happy baby. The dog whined and raised his head to lick the bare foot of the boy, making him giggle and squirm, trying to reach the dog.

Jackson shook his head. "Well, I've seen it all."

Happy at the light sound of his voice, Hattie laughed. "Well, I haven't. We need to see this fantastic chicken coop, don't we

Jackie?" She leaned to kiss the bruised spot. "Poor little noggin." J.D. lifted a hand to capture her face and she nibbled at his thumb as they walked.

When Jackson set down the basket, she passed him the baby. With the boy held in the crook of his arm, he managed to loop an arm around her waist and tug her forward. He relaxed when she didn't pull away or struggle to remove his arm. Not willing to tempt fate, he let the arm slip, but captured her hand as he did so.

He noticed her glance at the washtub and the garden wistfully as they walked past. "I'll help with that when we get back."

Once again, Hattie felt the warmth of their connection. She smiled up at him.

At the barn, she started for feed but he stopped her. "Taken care of when we turned them out and collected eggs."

Another fleeting smile, then the dazzling one he'd been hoping for when she saw the finished coop.

It rose like a wing against the regular barn. She was surprised to see the stack of the roof panels against the barn. At her puzzled look, Jackson handed her back the baby.

"Let me show you." He lifted and slipped a panel in place between the upright poles. "Comes a blow or blizzard, we can close it all in. We figured why rebuild it when its winter."

"Clever," she nodded, "very clever, Mr. Harper."

Smiling, he gave her a mock bow, delighting J.D. with the quick motion.

She laughed and suddenly the worry from the morning was gone. If he could just keep her happy, the world would be a fine place.

"If you had a ramp up to the first plank, then they could run up and go to roost at night."

"We debated it, but Cliff said foxes or coyotes might follow them in and destroy the flock. Better if someone is around at night to close the door."

She shrugged, I'm sure he's right. "It's wonderful, thank you."

"You'll need to thank the hands, Cliff and Tony worked really hard on it." He stared at her, read the gratitude in her eyes. He wanted to fall into the sweet blue clarity of her gaze. Slowly he moved closer and leaned down to kiss her softly. Hattie surprised them both by leaning in and kissing him back. J.D. squirmed between them and they pulled apart.

"Hey, boss."

Surprised, Jackson turned to see James standing at the barn door.

"What was the decision?"

Hattie looked up at Jackson in confusion. He shook his head. "I came out to ask you a couple of questions. Do you think you can handle the meals, if James drives into town?"

"I'll try."

James shook his head and disappeared inside.

She stared up at Jackson, regretting the interruption by the older cowhand. "What was the other question?" Her voice quavered as she focused on his mouth, remembering how amazingly soft and warm his lips had felt.

Jackson put out a hand to touch her shoulder and J.D. reached out a small hand to touch his face. At the baby's squeal of delight, Hattie raised a hand to feel his stubbly jaw. She raised her eyebrows at him.

"I was chased out before I shaved. I'll go back and do it."

"I'm sorry, but I was afraid you were going to take advantage of the situation."

"No, ma'am. I'm waiting on your permission."

"Then why were you …." She blushed so prettily, he wished they were back in the bedroom.

"Aroused?" he growled the word and she turned her back on him, ready to walk back to the house. Quickly he stepped closer, an arm around her waist, clutching J.D.'s legs gently as he whispered near her ear. "You keep me this way. Looking at you, hearing you talk, smelling you," he growled.

He waited for her protest of terror, but all he felt was the quiver of her as she inhaled quickly against his body.

James emerged from the barn, riding in the buckboard behind a pair of big red horses. "I have your missus' list. Did you think of anything else you need?"

"Yeah. I need a nightshirt, maybe a couple of pairs of summer drawers."

James Boyd whistled, blushed red to his ears, and snapped the buckboard into motion.

Hattie pushed out of his arms and stomped back to the kitchen, J.D. craning his neck to watch his laughing daddy.

◇◇◇

While Hattie put the elk shoulder in the oven to roast, Jackson emptied the wash tubs on the garden and stacked the tubs on the end of the porch. Next he grabbed the hammer and nails and picked up the sawed rails to get to work.

When Hattie came out, ready to hoe the garden, she deposited J.D. back in the porch cradle, setting it to rocking with the sleepy baby drowsing beneath a clean diaper for shade.

She stared at Jackson, noting his shirt was already damp from the heat. Stepping down, she examined the corner of the porch, where the closely spaced rails were tacked into place to close in the lower half. "I didn't expect it to be done instantly."

He put down the hammer and straightened. "It's not nailed or screened, but at least you won't have to rely on a dog to let him down on it."

"Sam was doing a good job," but even as she spoke, J.D. awoke and tried to pull up on the side of the cradle, tilting it to one side. Before he could spill out they both raced to catch him. Jackson swung the baby up, crying "whoa, boy." And Hattie wrapped an arm around the baby and him. He stared down at her smiling face for the second time in an hour. Again he felt the urge to kiss her but knew if he did he would only push for more, so he shook his head to clear it. "Do you think it will be all right if I put him down in the corner that's fenced?"

"You can if Sam can block the open end." She spread the quilt again and laid the happy baby on his back. In a minute he was ready to roll over and Jackson slapped his thigh and called "Sam." The big yellow dog was instantly back on the job.

◇◇◇

An hour later, she set the washed basket full of cucumbers and green tomatoes, along with one big cabbage and a pail of water on top of the step. She then opened the new gate so she could step up onto the porch and slide the basket forward. She stared down at the sleeping baby, "He's asleep?"

"Yeah," he finished pounding the last rail and grinned at her. "He watched a while, but I guess it was too boring. As soon as Sam yawned and plopped over J.D. yawned and went back to sleep."

"But you've been hammering, look at all you've done."

She sank into the rocker, staring around at the nearly enclosed porch. "Is it finished?"

"Almost." He wiped his face and neck with a hankie from his back pocket. "I'm planning to ride out to your old ranch to look around. Is there anything you want me to look for? Anything you've been missing?"

She clapped her hands. "Yes, I need crocks, the little one for pickles and the large one to make sauerkraut. James is supposed to be bringing me jars, pickling spice, and two gallons of vinegar, but I like sour pickles too and they require the crock."

He stared at her. "Is there anything you can't make or cook?"

She blushed at the compliment and laughed. "Cake. Rubye was teaching me, but I'm still not sure I can. And sewing, embroidery, all the beautiful things your Donna made for Jackie. I can't do any of that."

"You made his pretty pony."

She smiled sadly. "I felt like Donna was there, you know, helping me have the courage to try it."

He nodded, "Yeah, I'm not a carpenter, but I felt her say, Jackson go on, try it."

Hattie shivered despite the heat and he felt the same chill sweep through him.

"I still feel sad, that she was robbed of all this, his coos and laughs and little bumps," she said.

"I think she's watching over him. That's why we feel her so much." The words left his mouth dry. He lifted the pail and drank the cold water from the dripping bucket. "Well, I've got to go. Tony is staying close by. You need him, just give a shout and he'll come running."

She looked around, but didn't see any sign of the young hand. She shivered again. "You think the rustlers might show up? I thought they were gone."

"I'd rather be too careful, then sorry. Stay close until I'm back. Keep a gun handy."

She had just finished moving the cradle and vegetables inside when he rode up beside her. "You sure that's all you want, two crocks?"

"No, I need Momma's meat mill. It should be under the floor in the kitchen, too. I could make some sausage if you brought it."

"Sausage? I don't see any hogs here. Besides it's the wrong time of year."

"Dad and I made sausage out of deer, antelope, whatever he shot. Ground well and seasoned right, it's a nice change from roast or stewed meat. I could have used more of the elk, if I'd saved the gut and ground the scrap meat for sausage. But I can use some of what's left to make mincemeat if I have my mill."

"All right, I'll look for it."

She opened the gate and stood on the top step. Before she would never have had the courage, but now she dared, reaching out to him as she asked. "Why are you going?"

"They were hiding there before. Maybe they went back."

Then she moved into him, wrapping her arms tight around his neck. "If you think they're there, don't go alone. It's too dangerous."

He smiled, gave her a tight hug back and a light kiss on the forehead. "I'll pick up one of the men along the way. Stay inside with the baby. Be careful." It almost slipped out, I love you too, but he firmly removed her arms and gently pushed her back onto the porch before he let the emotion swelling in his chest burst out.

◇◇◇

She stood still as she watched him ride away. Why didn't she tell him what she felt? Grabbing up Jackie, she hurried into the house, closing the door behind her. As soon as she put the baby down, he started crying. Several minutes later she had him changed and happily playing with his toys while she made yeast rolls, her father's pistol on the counter beside her.

She was lucky to have so much work to do. Thinking about Jackson and what he had said this morning left her too fluttery. Minutes later, she was busy shredding cabbage for coleslaw. She pushed washed greens in a pot to wilt down.

Finally she poured molasses into a small pan, added the sliced tomatoes and peppers and some ground cayenne and added a generous splash of cider vinegar. She stirred it, adding black pepper and paprika, tasting until it was right, then left it over the other back-eye to finish stewing down into a barbecue sauce.

Since Jackie was still playing quietly, she went to the bedroom for her cloth and scissors. This time she used a flour-sack gown and another of her homemade diapers to cut a pattern for a little cowboy. Working quickly and with far more confidence then she had on the pony, she had him sewn and stuffed before the baby woke. She cleared the scraps and put everything away before rescuing the hungry baby.

◇◇◇

She had J.D. cared for and playing with his toes on the folded quilt when the men began to arrive for supper. The table was set with the spicy meat, pulled and seasoned in a big bowl. The rolls were split and the slaw lightly seasoned. Fresh tomatoes were sliced on a big plate and there was a bowl of sliced cucumbers in vinegar. The men drank cold water and hot coffee, and ate quickly, the fresh greens disappearing first. No matter how hungry, they would leave enough for the men still to eat. But something rare, like the greens, was always first come, first served.

Hattie waited on table, missing the conversation that flowed so easily when Jackson and James Boyd were present. Mostly, she missed Rubye. Even though they had seldom gotten along, she was always a little frightened and edgy being in the house alone with only men.

As soon as she could, she moved to the settee and took J.D. onto her lap, prancing the pony for him. As quickly and almost as quietly as they arrived, the men rose to leave, each stopping to thank her for the great meal. Clearing the table, she covered all the remaining food with a cloth, then carried plates to the kitchen to wash. The house was silent, the baby playing with his pony and carved toys.

Hattie shook her head. When would the fear go away? She could feel her hands shake as she stacked the dirty plates. She knew these men; they were all respectful to her and had been nothing but kind. But just being in the house alone with them made her heart beat faster, her knees quake with fear. Even Jackson, her own husband, whom she respected and felt far more for, had filled her with terror this morning in bed.

Yet, outside, in the morning sun, when he'd held his son and smiled at her, her heart had beat with joy, not fear. He was so kind to her, why couldn't she be a real wife to him? Finished, she sat and talked to J.D. while she went back to work on the doll.

She made loops around her hand with reddish orange yarn. Stopping, she stitched the middle of the loops onto the doll's head. The double row of stitches formed the part in his hair and she added a row of stitches along the bottom of each strand to keep his hair combed, and then clipped the ends of the loops to leave the doll with a mop of red hair.

This time while she worked, she imagined the abandoned ranch and her new husband riding in to look for trouble. She went to the room for ink and pen, then as carefully as possible, drew eyes, nose and a smiling mouth on the doll. Not satisfied with the mouth, she made a smaller series of loops and tacked on a mustache, the ends caught with thread and stitched down to give him a funny, red handlebar mustache.

She shook the doll, laughing at the silly face and hair. J. D. reached for it and she held him lower for the baby to look at closer. When he squealed in delight, she handed him the doll. Next she would have to make the little naked cowboy some clothes. She wondered if she could make a pair of boots and vest from the rabbit skin, still tacked to the rail on the porch.

◇◇◇

As soon as she stepped out onto the porch, she saw the wagon headed toward the house. She started to run inside, but then recognized James. For the first time since Jackson left, she relaxed.

That was a mistake. The old cowboy dismounted and almost fell over the gate. Hattie managed to catch the bottle of vinegar but Boyd let out a string of curse words. The air still blue, he unloaded the buckboard, then drove it to the barn to unhitch the horses.

Hattie wondered if he was upset about the gate or if he was mad for other reasons. Once he was inside, she invited him to eat while she put things away.

"Done took supper with Miss White, over at the Dawson's. Where's the boss?"

The nervousness that had shadowed her all day returned. "He rode out to our ranch this afternoon, promised to take another hand with him. Cliff and Hank haven't come in to eat either."

"Cliff will be gone a couple of days. He had to go into Waco."

She smiled sadly, shaking her head. "How is Rubye doing?"

"Ha, we ate in the kitchen, since she's just help. The Dawsons set a little higher than other people."

Hattie knew without asking what Rubye would think of that. While they talked, James carried the dry goods inside the pantry, helped to store them. When J.D. sounded off about being abandoned, it was James who went back to pick him up.

She carried out her mother's spice jars to the table where she had left the small bags, stored the new spices, then carried the canning jars into the kitchen to wash and stand to drain.

◇◇◇

They heard horses in the yard and Hattie couldn't hide her excitement. She ran, stood at the door and felt like crying when Jackson swung down and handed his reins to Hank. Brushing at her eyes, she stepped onto the shadowed porch. "You're home safe," she cried.

Before she could move, he opened the porch gate and swept her into his arms. This time, in the dark, he kissed her and she clung to him, fighting back the tears that had shadowed her all afternoon.

When he finally released her and they moved apart she whispered guiltily. "James is just back from town."

"Good, I've got a lot of questions for him." He smiled down at her, his teeth flashing in the shadows. "Hattie, that's the kind of welcome that makes a man glad to be married," he whispered, his hand reaching out to stroke down her cheek and lift her chin so he could see her nervous smile.

She reached up to grab his hand, confused by all the conflicting emotions sweeping through her and tugged him inside.

James Boyd stood in the kitchen, holding an excited J.D. Jackson smiled and leaned over to kiss the baby who gave him an open-mouthed kiss in return. He held his new toy up for Jackson to kiss in turn.

He looked at the funny red-headed doll and turned to grin at her.

"It's a cowboy for his pony. I need to make some clothes. I was going to try to use the rabbit skin for boots and a vest but James came and I haven't had time."

James still held the bouncing baby, even though J.D. was trying to get his daddy to take him.

"Sorry bucko, but I need to wash up first," Jackson said, handing back the doll.

While Jackson stepped into the kitchen, James said to Hattie. "There's a bag of rags in the bunkhouse, old shirts and ripped jeans. I'll bring them over in the morning before church. As for boots and a vest, you might have better luck sewing kid-leather then rabbit skin. There's probably some of that in the barn in the leather patching kit, I'll check for you."

"Thank you James. I guess he's a silly looking doll, I just thought he might like having another toy."

"Naw, I think he could make a tough little cowboy, especially with that big mustache."

She blushed, glad again for the compliment. Jackson smiled at the exchange, and then moved the cloths covering the food. "Looks good. Everybody else ate?"

"Nearly an hour ago. James ate in town, but there should be enough left for you and Hank."

"You ate?" The question was pointed and Hattie realized she hadn't and remembered what had happened the last time she skipped a meal. She shook her head and sank into a chair. Obediently she filled her plate, making a sandwich of the pulled elk and sliced tomatoes, taking a few cucumber slices to eat with it, leaving the rest of the coleslaw for them. James brought up milk and poured some for her, leaving the pitcher beside her just as Rubye would have done.

Hank came in and James sat down with the others, sipping at a cup of coffee.

"Tastes mighty good for elk," Hank said over a mouth full of the barbecue.

"I'm sure it was better hot. I probably should have heated it up for you."

Jackson shook his head, turned to James. "How's Rubye doing?"

He repeated what he had told her before they arrived.

"Any talk about the rustlers in town?"

"None, and when I asked, people gave me the 'what-you-talking-about' look. Rubye said it was the same at the Dawsons. The one time she asked Mr. Dawson, he gave her a look like she was making up a fairy tale – like he didn't know rustlers even existed."

Jackson took the news, chewed on it while he finished one sandwich and then made another. Hank did the same, spooning extra sauce over his meat before forking up the last ragged slices of tomato. Hattie wished she had made dessert. Tomorrow, maybe she would try baking a cake.

"Does she want to come back?" Hattie asked.

"You mean you're willing for her to live here again?" James asked.

"Of course, why wouldn't I be?"

"Well, you seem to have things under control. Handling it all alone, it looks like you even have time for sewing and canning."

Hattie smiled wearily. "You and Jackson did my chores before breakfast and the roast was already cooked. Without the help, I could barely have cooked for the men. Jackson helped me by emptying my wash water and helped me hang clothes. Then he fenced the porch and built the gate so I could make sure Jackie was safe while I worked outside, or I couldn't have picked and washed the vegetables. He even helped watch the baby for me so I could cook supper. I need help."

"Rubye said some mighty mean things."

Hattie looked down at the table, and then raised her eyes. "She would have to apologize to both of us, of course. Do you think she would be willing to do that?"

"It's hard to say with Rubye. She can be mighty stiff-necked sometimes."

"Forget all that for now. I've got your crocks outside and that meat mill," Jackson interrupted. "But I want a hot bath. So, let's get some water on to boil. James, can you help?"

CHAPTER NINETEEN

The old cowhand rose and left to get the water and Hattie went back to the kitchen to fire up the stove again. When the tub was filled in the pantry, the men left the house so Hattie could take the first bath. Jackson stood on the porch and stared down at James. The sleeping baby was cradled against him, his head on his broad shoulder, the new toy wedged between them,

"What was the reaction to the news that we're married?" Jackson asked.

"I didn't get a chance to tell Rubye before the preacher dropped by and gave the Dawsons and her the low-down. You don't want to know what they all had to say. Reckon he'll have the word spread around town before church tomorrow."

"I was hoping that it would remove Rubye's objections and she would want to come home. I knew the Dawsons would be upset."

"Upset, don't begin to cover what Irene Dawson was. She started ranting like a crazy woman."

"I don't want Hattie to have to put up with any more nonsense. We're married, she's my legal wife, and I won't tolerate any slurs about my wife. Maybe I should wear a gun, maybe we should just stay home again this Sunday."

"Ain't that what started all the uproar the first time? You want people to quit talking, you'll need to face them down, both of you," James said.

Jackson nodded. "You're right, as usual. Did you get a chance to talk to Rubye alone?"

The way the older man hesitated, Jackson knew he was grateful to be on the dark porch too.

Hank must have felt his discomfort. "I'm going to turn in guys, talk some more in the morning."

◇◇◇

When he was gone, James finally answered. "She's unhappy, mighty unhappy. She feels guilty for what she said, for leaping to conclusions and saying what she did. She felt even worse because she went to the preacher with her concerns."

"She ought to feel ashamed. She's known me my whole life. Hell, after being with Hattie all this time, she had to know there was nothing secret going on."

Jackson wished they were inside, so he could see the other man's eyes.

"She could see what the rest of us could see. You two are crazy in love, and not just with that baby. Hell, your eyes never leave each other. Since you're both too stupid to admit it, she pointed it out. You have to understand that she loved Donna, she wants to protect her interests."

"Donna is dead. J. D. and I are still alive. That baby is her interest and I'm doing my best to take care of him."

"Rubye broke down and cried, that's how sorry she feels. After that preacher came into that house, telling how he married you guys, she's afraid she's the only reason it happened. The way he's telling the story, he shamed you two into giving up your sinful ways and into getting married."

For several minutes, there was nothing but a blue cloud of profanity. Finally, a shaken Jackson stopped as J.D. woke, crying in terror. He reined in his temper, cooing and trying to soothe the baby, but J.D. was having none of it.

James beat a retreat without any more arguments.

◇◇◇

She was nearly asleep in the cooling water when the door opened and Jackson burst in with a frantically crying J.D. She held her arms up, and Jackson lowered the squirming, squalling baby to her. "What's wrong with him?" she gasped, half-rising from the tub.

She felt beneath the gown, surprised to find a dry diaper. His kicking feet hit the water and as quickly as he had begun to cry, he gasped and stopped. She pulled the gown, carefully working his arms loose and handed it to the silent Jackson. Then she removed the diaper and slowly let the baby into the tub with her. Using his body to hide her own from Jackson's gaze, she gently lapped the water over him. Jackie laughed and kicked playfully and for a minute they were all content to just enjoy the moment.

Jackson knelt down, careful not to block the lamplight, and using soap and washcloth, gently soaped and bathed the giggling baby. With Hattie's help, he lathered and rinsed his hair. As the boy changed from playing to wanting to nurse, Hattie raised up, ready to get up.

Instead, Jackson continued to soap the washcloth, and then gently and thoroughly, he soaped her back and tugged her left arm loose so he could soap it as well. He soaped and washed the arm cradling the baby, gently washing under her arm, the curve of her breast and down along her side. Hattie knew she should protest, but he made sure to cradle and raise the baby as he did it, and the rough gentleness of it made her relax even more. J.D. continued to suckle, even as Jackson lifted her hair, and proceeded to shampoo it. His firm fingers against her scalp, made Hattie lean her head back. He rinsed her hair with the bucket she had beside the tub. The splattering water only made J.D. stretch, but not give up his nipple.

When he tugged her foot up to soap she initially tugged it back, but he persisted, rubbing between each toe, and moving the washcloth up her leg, even under the water. She swallowed nervously, her eyes all pupil as she stared up at him. He carefully changed legs and repeated the process. When the baby finally relaxed, releasing the nipple, Jackson smiled, hung the washcloth on the side of the tub and lifted the warm, relaxed baby up, motioned her to stay still, and left the room.

It was five minutes later before he returned. Hattie watched as the shirtless man grinned down at her. "It was wet," he answered the unspoken question. He picked up the washcloth and she sighed, started to get up, but he stopped her, gently soaping her chest, fondling each breast lovingly, and then trailing the washcloth down beneath the water over her flat stomach. When she didn't protest, he moved the cloth down between her legs and ended in the nest of curls. She gasped and stared up at him. Startled, she grabbed his arm but did not pull away, instead trembled in pleasure beneath his touch. Minutes later he rinsed her and lifted his sleepy wife, wrapping her in a towel and carrying her to the bed.

"My hair is wet," she murmured.

He sat her there on the edge of the bed, toweling her hair gently, grabbing her gown to pull her arms through, much as he had the baby minutes ago. She lolled under his rough touch, and once again he lifted her in order to tuck her beneath the covers. Leaving her damp hair in a dry towel wrapped around her head, he kissed her cheek and disappeared.

Jackson scooped out a bucket of the lukewarm water, and carried it outside to dump. Then he lifted the hot water from the stove and carried it back to sit beside the tub. He worked quickly, stripping the rest of the way, making sure to wash thoroughly from head to toe, and enjoy the hot water shampoo and rinse. But fear of what might happen or not happen kept him in the water until it had grown cold. Toweling roughly he donned the silly looking nightshirt and short underpants that James had brought him from town. Thus armored, he entered the bedroom.

◇◇◇

Inside the dark room, he stood by the door, waiting until his eyes adjusted and listened to the even breathing of the baby and the woman who was now his wife. His own breathing quickened as he tiptoed to the bed, lifted the cover and slowly crawled inside. As he leaned back stiffly, he was surprised to see her eyes were open and she was staring at him.

He waited for the terror of the previous night but she surprised him by smiling. He raised his arm and she accepted the invitation and moved against him, resting her head on his shoulder.

Restlessly, she stirred against him, trying to nestle comfortably then pushing away. He waited, holding his breath. She sat up, pushing the towel away, revealing her tangled hair. He sat up too, reaching for the hairbrush on the dresser.

"Here," he whispered. "Turn around and let me brush it." Like bathing her, these were intimacies he had never shared with Donna, but then Donna hadn't been terrified of men. Gently he worked the brush through the long tangles, holding the hair above so it wouldn't pull. Finally he had it all brushed, letting it fall in silken waves over her shoulders, working the hair with his fingers to brush it back from her face. She leaned her head back and sighed. Gently he leaned closer and kissed her cheek, nuzzling her ear.

This time she turned into him and he was kissing her as he had dreamed of doing. Gently he rubbed her ear, cupped her neck, slipped his tongue into her softly opening mouth, and then dropped his hand to move in tantalizing strokes until her nipples peaked against the soft fabric. As she moaned, he took a minute to tug at one sleeve, then the other, removing the gown as gently as he had slipped her into it.

As soon as he tugged the gown free, the moon escaped the cloud cover and bathed her in a shimmer of moonbeams. As lovingly as he had touched her, the light followed. It caught in her golden hair, caressed her strong cheekbones and big eyes, and slipped over the full, ripe breasts and slim body. Shyly, she tried to lift the covers and he pushed it away and stood beside the bed to stare at his moonlit goddess.

Frantically he removed the starched nightshirt and short underpants, but Hattie put out a hand to stop him from climbing back in bed. Just as he had studied her, now she stared at him. Jackson straightened, stood motionless while he tried not to smile at the changes in her face, very aware of everywhere her eyes were focused on his body.

Suddenly, even as he watched, her eyes pooled with tears, her lip trembled, and her body shook. Jackson sank onto the edge of the bed and gently folded her into his arms. "Shh," he whispered, rocking her like the baby. Automatically Hattie turned to squirm into his lap, pressing her body close to him. Carefully, using all the control he had left, he pulled the covers between his body and hers.

He kissed her cheeks, used the cover to wipe her nose and tear streaked cheeks. "Sweetheart, don't cry. I promise we won't do anything you don't want to do. I'm sorry, I thought it was what you wanted, too. Here, we can put the nightclothes back on."

Hattie pulled away, sat up in bed and blew her nose on the hem of the gown he handed her. "You don't understand. It is what I want. I'm just so afraid..." Her voice faded to a whisper.

"Damn those worthless bastards. I promise I'll make them pay."

She shook her head, the words coming out in gulps, "No, today I was so afraid they might be hiding at our ranch. I was so afraid something might happen to you. I couldn't bear it if they hurt you."

Jackson shook out the sheet and coverlet, covering both of them, settling her back into his arms. He heard the baby whimper in his sleep and lowered his voice. "I was afraid for you too when I left you alone. I kept thinking of the finger on the mantle, the day you and Rubye chased them away."

Without realizing she was doing it, she kissed his throat and then his chin. "I kept thinking of the shootout, when you brought the cattle back. It seemed worse, the fear, since I thought it was finally over, that they'd been forced away. But when you left, I knew it wasn't true and the fear came rushing back."

"You were afraid for me? Why?"

She leaned back so she could see him, her head on his arm, suddenly aware of being completely naked in his arms. As her awareness grew, she felt his body's answer.

Smiling he leaned closer and whispered. "I love you too, Harriett Stoddard Harper."

She smiled and leaned in to kiss him. "I love you," but her voice still held the tears of earlier.

When he started to fold her body beneath him, again she put a hand on his shoulder in panic and he paused. Sighing, he collapsed back on the bed and stared up at the shadows of the ceiling. Rolling his head to stare at her he whispered. "Touch me Hattie, however and where ever you want."

Timidly she reached out, her hand following the smooth, hard muscle of his shoulder, down the corded arm to touch the inside of his wrist, then on to the callused palm, letting her own fingers tangle with his.

Jackson breathed deeply, forcing himself to relax, even as she pulled her hand free of his fingers, gently traced a hand across his chest, boldly over the rows of muscles in his stomach, and then lower. He sucked in a deep breath, praying she would touch him where his throbbing need waited, but she trailed down along his hair roughened leg, feeling the strong muscles there. Bending forward, she traced down one leg, then up the other, letting her taunting fingers circle his nipple as he had done hers when he bathed her. But slowly as she did, she moved closer, her body brushing against him, her breathing growing more rapid.

When she drew closer, her mouth pressed against his shoulder, her leg raised to rub against his, he dared to ask, "Tell me what to do, when and how you want me to touch you," he growled. She reached out and lifted his hand to her breast. He teased her until she was moaning, then he raised his head to kiss her temple, her nose and then her mouth, enjoying her response. Her body glided over his as she moved into the kiss and he felt her dampness and knew he would die if she pulled away again. When she tugged his hand down her stomach, he knew exactly where she needed to be touched. Minutes later, he lifted her and slid inside her slick entrance, grateful for the power of her need, the urgency they both felt. In minutes, she was arching backward, then falling forward and he felt the release he had needed so long.

They lay together, their body's one, finally united as man and wife. He rolled to his side, holding her in place, so he could stare into her face. "Sweet Hattie, I love you. Did I hurt you darling?"

She leaned back, feeling a huge swell of love at the tender question. She raised glowing eyes to smile at him. "Will it always be so wonderful?"

He laughed, hugging her closer. "God willing, sweetheart, God willing." When he drew back he arched an eyebrow and her eyes widened in surprise as he stirred inside her. "Want to try again?"

They did, this time facing side-by-side, slower and gentler until she frantically wrapped her leg over his hip and grabbed his shoulder and he rolled her beneath him. This time she was so focused on the sensations inside that she merely gripped him with both her legs and hung on as the motions became more frenzied and they both cried out in satisfaction. Moments later he rolled off and lay back with her head once again cradled on his shoulder.

In the dark, they heard J.D. whimper and stir and both held their breath until he sighed back into sleep. Totally relaxed, they both slept.

◇◇◇

A knock on the door awakened all three. "You want grub and to get to church on time, you sleepy heads better get a move on." James called through the door.

Jackson lay back, listening to a couple of the hands laugh in the distance.

He shook Hattie's shoulder, rousing her and then he rose, rushing to shave and dress. Hattie tended the crying baby, changing, then feeding him, finally giving him a quick sponge bath and handing him off to Jackson to finish dressing. Frantically she brushed her long hair, blushing as she saw his eyes in the mirror and remembered the magic of his brushing her hair earlier. Intently, she twisted her hair, winding it and pinning it into place on top of her head in a snug bun. She bent to open the bottom drawer.

"No, not today," Jackson said, putting the fully dressed baby into the crib. He crossed to the wardrobe and opened the top drawer and removed silk underwear and stockings. He then opened the other side and removed an extravagantly ruffled and lace covered blouse and skirt that had a matching bonnet which he removed from the top shelf.

Hattie stared in dismay at the lovely garments, but Jackson was already on her side of the bed. "Wear this today, for me."

Helplessly, she trembled as he removed the wrapper, leaving her standing nude before him. She swallowed hard as his eyes lovingly swept over her until she blushed from head to toe. He held the pantaloons and she stepped in, feeling her legs buckle at the warm sweep of his hand as he pulled them up and tied the bow at her waist. When he dropped the silky chemise over her breasts they stood at attention. As he pulled her arms through the sleeves of the wonderful blouse she leaned into him, shocked at how much she wanted him. He leaned down, kissing her savagely, then gently pushed her back to quickly button the blouse. "Later," he growled.

He held out the skirt and petticoat and she shook her head as she held them up in front of her. "I'll need to hem the skirts."

She pulled on her plain cotton slip and the black skirt that was already faded to a soft charcoal gray. Finally, she tied a wide black grosgrain ribbon around her waist, unwilling to leave the house without any black on.

She tied a large side bow on the lovely white bonnet he handed her, delighted when she tied the matching one on J.D. and he didn't protest.

Jackson hustled her through the door, even as she tried to delay to make the bed. The other men were already waiting by the buggy. James handed Jackson a large mug of coffee and a napkin with biscuits and salt pork inside as they quickly climbed into place on the buckboard.

Hank leaned forward. "I can hold J.D. while you two eat. You sure look pretty, Mrs. Harper."

Hattie smiled and blushed, hiding beneath the brim of her bonnet as she turned and let the baby go into the waiting arms. Jackson opened the napkin and took a large bite out of the biscuit loaded with fried pork, then held it out for her to take a bite. He enjoyed her hesitation, but hunger won out and she leaned forward, placing her hand over his as she bit the biscuit. He noticed the exchange of knowing grins between the cowboys behind them. Surprisingly, he didn't feel angry but strangely proud. He stared down at his pretty wife.

Although the blouse had been one of Donna's favorites, it looked entirely different on Hattie. The high collar and lace edged sleeves helped to hide the rosy skin where his whiskered chin had scratched her delicate skin. Even J.D. bore rosy scratches on his tender cheek.

Hattie leaned forward to swallow tepid coffee, and then accepted a second bite of biscuit. They ate, trading bites and sips until J.D. protested, and Jackson reached back to pull him forward. By the time they were finished, they were pulling into the church yard. Hattie brushed crumbs from the dark skirt, then when Jackson brushed her blouse, rubbed her mouth, she tilted her face up for his kiss. Instead of a kiss, Jackson sprang down, then held a hand to steady her as she stepped down. He handed her the baby, nodded at the men, then took her arm and walked up the stairs to the church. They were late.

CHAPTER TWENTY

They were late, but services hadn't started. Hattie thought he would drop her arm and leave her at the back pew where she had always sat with Rubye. But he didn't leave her. Instead he kept her arm firmly locked with his. Hattie carried the baby, aware that his flowing lace trimmed gown and bonnet was mirrored by her own blouse and full bonnet. Her legs trembled as she heard the shocked whispers as people reacted to their passing.

When they were at the front of the church, he indicated the center aisle. Hattie slid in, grateful for the feel of the solid oak pew at the back of her legs. When they were all in she sank down, and Jackson raised an arm to rest on the back of the pew behind her back.

There were more angry whispers. From under the edge of the bonnet, Hattie glanced over at the Dawsons. They both faced forward as though unaware of the commotion around them. Hattie wondered what they must feel, having Jackson bring her in like this and set her in their daughter's place. It must be horrible for them.

J.D. tugged irritably at his bonnet. Jackson leaned forward to tug the ribbon loose and remove the bonnet to reveal the soft brown curls of hair. The boy leaned forward and cooed at his grandparents.

Both grandparents half-turned as the baby stretched to stand on his daddy's legs, the bonnet hanging from a chubby fist. Hattie watched as they turned his way and smiled. She tried to see anger or resentment, but all she saw was the joy they felt in seeing their grandson. Maybe they were happy about the wedding, about her sitting here with Jackson. She smiled in their direction and both faces suddenly became rigid. Just as quickly, they changed back to smiles.

Irene pulled a small red object from her drawstring bag and shook it lightly. J.D. bounced up and down and chortled, reaching out for it. Jackson passed the baby over to Charlie Dawson and Hattie relaxed as the grandparents held the happy boy.

When the sermon began, J.D. stopped babbling and listened. Minutes later, every time the pastor paused, he would babble in the same sing-song pattern as the preacher. When Irene shook the rattle to distract him, he squealed with delight and tried to pull it into his mouth.

Half-way through the sermon, J.D. had finished preaching and was busy teething on the gourd rattle when Irene Dawson blurted out, "Look Charlie, he has a tooth." Unfortunately it was during a pause, and Irene covered her mouth in embarrassment as several people giggled.

Before the closing prayer, the preacher paused meaningfully and everyone became still and quiet. "I would like to present to you for your congratulations, our newest couple. Please rise, Mrs. Harriet Stoddard Harper and Mr. Jackson Davis Harper." The whispers intensified.

When the murmurs died down, the preacher continued. "Congratulations too, to the young Reverend J.D. Harper, on his first tooth." This time the response was laughter. "Now, bow your heads for the closing prayer," the preacher added, sternly.

Hattie managed to refasten J.D.'s bonnet on the way out, but there was no way he was going to release his new rattle. To her surprise, several people waited outside to congratulate them, mainly the small ranchers. She noticed the Dawsons, Thompsons, and other town's people were avoiding them. A couple of the town ladies made a point of standing and waiting, only to turn away as they approached, in case they might miss the snub.

But Jackson kept his arm around her and the baby and she held her head up, wanting him to be as proud of her as she was of him. He had presented her as his wife to the entire congregation, to all the people in town who mattered. If he could stand the whispers and snubs and still look proud and happy, then she could do it too. J.D. loved the attention. Used to being passed around at the ranch, he expected everyone to be eager to talk to him and want to play.

She heard and savored the comments as people moved toward their buggies. "Such a beautiful baby, such a lovely family." Each kind word buoyed her up and with Jackson as armor, she smiled and chatted and let the snubs and slurs bounce off.

The only one she wanted to see was Rubye, who she realized was missing for some reason. Had the Dawsons told her to stay home, had she wanted to avoid them, was she sick?

"I had expected to see Rubye."

"We'll need to give her time to accept us. I'm sure if you can spare him, James can go by and find out why she's not here. In the meantime," he leaned closer and whispered, "Our little Bronco needs a change."

Hattie smiled and carrying the baby, walked to the buckboard. On the lowered tailgate, she changed him, then took the lacy blanket and baby and let James Boyd lift her up onto the seat. Jackson pulled James aside and after tipping his hat, the older cowhand took a horse from one of the men and rode into town.

In minutes they were all loaded, Jackson climbing onto the seat beside Hattie who had covered the nursing baby with his lacy blanket, his bonnet once more hanging from his hand. In minutes, Jackson was able to snag the bonnet from the limp fingers of the sleeping boy.

As they drove out of the church yard, she saw Charles and Irene finally emerge from the church. It was obvious the couple had not wanted to leave and have to talk to them. Hattie again wondered what Donna would have wanted them to do. How could her parents feel differently when she sat beside their daughter's husband, held Donna's baby, wore her blouse and bonnet, even sat in her place at church? She knew it had to hurt them.

◇◇◇

The next morning it was nearly dawn when the baby finally woke. Jackson took the time to change him before carrying him to slip into the bed between them. He couldn't remember being so happy, ever. His son was busily nursing, keeping one hand on Hattie's breast, the other pushing Jackson away. Jackson laughed, nuzzling him and kissing his shoulder. "She's all yours, is she partner." J. D. lifted his defending hand to push at his jaw, moving away at the prickle of whiskers on his soft fingers.

Jackson kissed his cheek, then kissed Hattie, tasting her joy on her lips.

When J. D. finished and lay there cooing and laughing between them, they spent time, enjoying and playing with him. When Jackson smiled at his relaxed bride, he reached out to caress her cheek, wanting to capture her smile. J.D. reached up to grab his hand and keep him away. "I think he's telling me you're all his."

Hattie yawned sleepily, tired from the long day of cooking alone and feeding the hands. James had stayed in town. She reached across to touch Jackson's face, cradling his jaw. "I thought you shaved."

"Hours ago," he growled, leaning closer in to rub his jaw against her sensitive neck.

J.D. kicked and Jackson reeled back, moaning. "Uh-oh, got me bronco!"

Hattie surprised him by leaning down and kissing his hurt. Instantly, he rose to attention and she sat up and stared at him, her eyes widening. "Did I do that?"

"Yeah, let's see if the boy can go play in the crib so we can play in bed. Where's his pretty pony when you need him?"

Minutes later, the baby was contentedly playing with his favorite toys and Jackson and Hattie were quietly playing under the covers.

◇◇◇

Monday morning, she heard James talking to Jackson after breakfast. "The Dawsons asked her to stay home, they were afraid she would rush over and apologize and make an embarrassing scene."

"Does she plan to come back to us?"

"Yeah," he hesitated and Hattie strained to hear what was said, but when she saw and heard Jackson laugh she blushed and stayed busy in the kitchen washing dishes. Did everyone know what they were doing? It made her remember the night before and blush even more. No, that laugh had to mean something else.

The big pot of water boiled over on the stove and she scooped some of the water out into the dishpan. James stood in the kitchen door. "I never pickled or seen it done – et a few at the store. Do you need help?"

"Yes, I forgot to ask for a jar lifter. I just thought Rubye would have one. Do you think you can figure out something we can use? I need to dip the jars and lids first in the boiling water, pack and fill them with brine, then boil them filled for a few minutes. When the vinegar inside starts to boil, I have to fish the jars out to cool, and pray they seal.

"What do you do if they don't seal?"

"Eat a lot of pickles for a few days."

He nodded. "I got just the tool."

While he was gone, she checked her fresh picked cucumbers and dill, carefully added the zinc lids and glass jars into the boiling water. Then she prepared the pot of brine of salt and vinegar and waiting for the second pot to reach a boil.

James came in with a strange device, but when he looped it around a jar and tightened, he lifted the jar easily from the water. Hattie took the jar in a towel and set it at the end of the counter, while James fished the remaining jars out and added more jars. She dropped garlic, dill, and pepper into the jar, and then packed it with fresh cucumbers.

J.D. started to fuss, and she hurried in to make sure he was all right, then came back to finish the jars. She cleaned her hands before topping the first jars with the boiling brine. Then positioning the heavy zinc lids on the wiped mouth of the jars, she twisted to tighten them. James had removed the last of the clean jars and put the filled jars into the hot water bath while she packed the remaining jars.

By the time the last jar was done, she was soaked with sweat, but the counter was filled with gleaming blue jars of pickles. Hattie smiled at James who was seated out at the dining room table, telling stories to a happy J.D.

"I'll take him for a while."

"What do you want me to do with the boiling water?"

"As soon as I get this little man fed, I need to do the laundry. When it's safe, I guess add it to the washtub. We'll be out in minutes."

◇◇◇

She burped the full baby, but J.D. was not in a mood to nap. Hattie was delighted with the fenced porch and put him down where he could watch and talk to her as she worked. Now he could sit up with only an occasional roll, it was possible to leave him propped up by pillows on his usual quilt. It seemed to take forever to finish the pile of clothes, bedding, and baby things, but finally she was able to sit down on the porch and hold the happy boy.

When the first hands rode up, she realized she hadn't made lunch and how messy she must look. James stepped out on the porch with a pitcher of cold water and a damp towel and Hattie stared up at him. "Thank you, but what are we going to feed them?"

"Made beans and corn bread, won't be as good as your feed, but they won't starve."

"Bless you James. Let me get in and wash up before Jackson gets home. I know I must look a fright."

The older cowhand stared at her pretty flushed face and grinned. "Scare the man to death."

She bolted up and James took the full baby, just as Jackson rode into the yard and she raced into the house and the bedroom. Jackson dismounted at the porch and opened the gate, dropping the reins and bounding into the house after her. "Something wrong?" he asked James.

The cowboy shrugged and J.D. squealed after his daddy. Hank stepped onto the porch and said, "Hey cowboy," and the baby happily swung into his arms instead.

"Where's the calf?" Hank asked. "I see you got the castrator in here."

◇◇◇

Jackson didn't wait for an answer but crossed the house, pulling open the bedroom door, concerned only with making sure that Hattie was all right.

Hattie stood by the dresser, her face flushed and her hair uncombed. The bowl full of cold water and her sweat-stained unbuttoned blouse revealed her intent. Hattie blushed even redder.

Grinning, Jackson closed the door.

As soon as he grinned her knees buckled and she sank to the floor, cowering, clutching her blouse together.

He rushed to her side, knelt down, eager to pull her into his arms. But he froze as he saw her shaking with tears running down her face. "Hattie," he whispered, his voice soft and low as he balanced on the balls of his feet, his arms open, but afraid of what might happen if he touched her. "Sweetheart, look at me."

Finally she raised her head and stared at him. Groaning, she raised her arms to him and he pulled her into an embrace, kissing her cheek and tasting the salt of her tears. She shook her head. "I'm sorry, I just suddenly…"

"Hush, no explanation needed. Let me get you something to eat while you finish what you were doing."

Outside, he hurried. In minutes, he dished up two bowls of beans, buttered two slabs of cornbread and set it atop the bowls, only adding onion to the top of one. He let James hand him a full glass of milk and tuck the pitcher of additional milk under his arm.

Without a word of explanation and only a quick wink at J.D., he disappeared back inside.

Hattie finished the second braid and let if fall over her shoulder. She tucked and buttoned the throat button of the stained blouse.

Jackson set both bowls on the dresser while she took the glass of milk and then rescued the pitcher from under his arm. "You want to have a different blouse?"

"I don't have anything ironed; they're both on the line."

He opened the closet and rummaged through, pulling out a red checked shirt and skirt. Then opened the other side and pulled out a chemise and petticoat. He walked around to where she was perched on the side of the bed, noting the glass was half empty and she was eating the beans that had the slice of onion on top. He set the clothes down and sat in the rocker to eat his beans while they were still warm.

She set her bowl down, shed the dirty clothes with her back to him, and quickly donned the chemise and blouse, turning around only when she had it nearly buttoned up. Smiling, she held up the petticoat and skirt. Both drug along the ground.

"You need more clothes. The closet's full. Sooner or later you'll have to hem them all."

She sat there, primly eating cornbread and beans, only pausing to wash it down with the milk. Jackson refilled her glass, then took a deep drink.

She shook out the skirt again, noticing the wide ruffle at the hem. There was a similar ruffle on the bottom of the slip. She rolled across the bed and rooted through the sewing basket until she found a small pair of scissors. Carefully she used the tip to snip a thread on the petticoat, then slowly and carefully worked to detach the ruffle. This time she didn't turn her back, but dropped the skirt and slip quickly before donning the clean petticoat. Standing up, she lifted a foot for his inspection.

Jackson nodded. "Perfect."

She finished the petticoat, and then repeated the procedure on the checked skirt. When she slipped it over her head, she turned neatly so he could fasten the back buttons. He did, slipping an arm around and turning her to face him.

"I'm sorry for frightening you."

"It was the look in your eye, and the voices of the men in the other room," she explained with a shudder.

He tugged her onto his knee, the smile back. "I'll try not to leer again."

She smiled, leaned closer to kiss his cheek, and then stood. "Do you think it's too baggy?"

He rose from the chair, putting the empty dish down inside hers. He tugged at the band of the skirt, pulling away more than six inches of excess fabric. The blouse was equally loose and baggy.

"Maybe I can figure out how to take them up too."

"I'll get Donna's book. She learned all of it from the book, since Irene Dawson never did her own needlework."

She stared at the pretty blouse and skirt noticing the cross-stitch pattern on the skirt pockets for the first time. Jackson pointed at the top and Hattie turned to see the yoke.

When he returned, he had the book and the baby. He handed her the baby first, took the dishes, gave her a wistful look and a soft kiss on the top of her head and left.

◇◇◇

Hattie tended to J.D. first. While he played, she settled down with the book, carefully read and studied the diagrams. Leaving the door to the bedroom cracked a little to draw a breeze from the open windows, she settled down beside the boy and slowly and frustratingly hemmed the skirt. She put the skirt on, then removed and hemmed the petticoat, working faster now that she had the hang of it and knew the stitches would not be seen.

◇◇◇

Hattie carried the last basket of clothes to the house, happy that James and the dog Sam were both on duty while J.D. played on his blanket outside. The clothes that didn't need ironing she had carefully folded as she took them off the line and they were already put away. Unfortunately, that left both clothes baskets full of ones that would need to be starched and ironed. Although, Rubye or Irene Dawson would probably not approve, she had carefully folded sheets and both her and Jackson's underwear instead of putting them in the stack to be starched and ironed. She had no intention of ever starching or ironing either of them again.

She managed the hemming, baked a cake, and put the roast in the oven before the baby woke from his nap. James peeled potatoes and turnips, though he disagreed with cooking them together the way she planned. There was still a pot of soup beans left. Over

James protest, she added three ripe tomatoes, a large dried onion chopped fine, and a generous dollop of molasses to his beans before sticking them in the oven with the roast to bubble and bake.

Sighing, she looked around the room. She was tired, but she needed to boil starch, dip and roll the clothes, ice the cake, and cook the potatoes and turnips. She would wait until tonight when the dishes were done to start the ironing.

◇◇◇

Before it was time for the men to arrive, Hattie was exhausted. She still needed to make starch and roll the clothes. J.D. had to be teething again, since he wanted to bite and slobber on everything. At least this time, he hadn't needed her to sit under him all the time, just most of it. She had held him on her hip while she made caramel icing, then added cream and cracked pepper to the potato/turnip dish. She had left James to set the table and get the finished food dished up while she tried to get Jackie to nurse and stop fussing.

When Jackson rode in, she and the baby were lying on the bed, fast asleep. Carefully, he lifted the bottom of her skirt, noting the precise little stitches in the hem as he removed her shoes. Gently, he eased both over, then hung his gun belt on the headboard and removed his boots before lying down next to them. Slowly, easing into it, he rubbed the narrow shoulders and slim back, picturing it as she had looked earlier, standing bare before him, and trying on Donna's blouse. She had a beautiful back, all lean muscle, smooth, silky white, and perfectly arched.

Despite the awareness of all the people in the next room, he realized he was growing restlessly stirred by her. Even more dangerous, he realized two pair of blue eyes were staring at him. They were now both awake. He sat still, waiting to see the fear flood her face as it had earlier. Instead she surprised him by leaning in, and kissing him warmly until J.D. protested and they broke apart.

"Do you want me to bring supper in here, or do you want to join me and the men to eat?"

"Join everyone. I'm sorry. I didn't mean to fall asleep; it's just been such a long day." She continued to talk, giving him a detailed account, as she rose and pinned her braids to circle her head like a little crown. She stared at the shoes, looking puzzled, but made no move to put them back on. When she realized that he was just smiling, not saying anything, Hattie stopped. "Sorry, I didn't mean to rattle on."

He laughed. "Why? I like hearing about your day." Both in their stocking feet, he opened the door, held J.D. and kept his arm around her back.

The men who were gathering all rose until she was seated beside him at the end of the table. When several complimented her, Jackson took the time to stare at her, all pink from her nap. The color in her cheeks emphasized the angles of her face and the blue of her eyes, the braided hair seemed perfect for the lovely gingham dress. She hadn't taken it in, but he noticed that she had found a belt to take up some of the fullness of both blouse and skirt. If he could keep the terrified girl hidden, Hattie was really a pretty woman.

He listened to his tough hands compliment her, even James bragged about the baked beans. His favorite had been the creamed potatoes and turnips. Hattie smiled shyly, apologizing ahead of time that the cake might not match the quality of Rubye's. Jackson smiled as each of the men had to reassure her it was as good or better than the best cake baker's in the county as they said goodnight.

◇◇◇

While James cleared the table and washed up, Jackson held and played with the baby. They both watched Hattie go through the rag bag James had brought from the bunk house.

Finally she settled on a leg panel from some old Levis and the dark blue sleeve of a shirt that was printed with white stars. He could remember Cliff wearing it when he was Tony's age as his go-to-town shirt. She used a worn yellow bandana to cut out a miniature one for the doll. In minutes she laid the doll down on top and cut the denim, then repeated the process to cut the shirt.

James brought them both another cup of coffee, and sat down, setting the coffee pot and the last quarter of the cake in the middle of the table. Hattie smiled at him in gratitude and leaned back. "Maybe I should just cut a denim barn coat for him, forget about the leather vest."

"Naw," he rose and brought a small handful of leather and laid it on the table. "This should work well for boots, vest, and maybe even a hat."

There was a howdy from the door and Hank stepped back in. "Saw the lamp was still lit. Oh, so that's what happens to leftover cake." He pointed to the cake plate and the waiting saucers.

"Join us," Jackson said and J.D. waved his arms and Hank took him as he sat down.

He laughed when the baby shook the naked doll at him. "I see. Your pretty momma is going to make your naked Jasper some clothes. He nodded at the scraps on the table. Good choice, maybe we ought to call him Cliff, Jr."

James shook his head, divided the cake into four pieces and gave them each a fork.

Hattie positioned the doll's feet on the leather, but rose to get a pencil to trace with before cutting the soft kid skin. She made a wave along the top of the boot leg, and carefully cut out four pieces. She traded J.D. a small blob of icing for the doll and traced a pattern for the vest. She looked across at James. He nodded and she put down the scissors and handed the doll back to the boy. "Okay, but I don't think I can figure out the hat."

Hank nodded at James. "Boyd can make it, can't you James, maybe even a gun belt."

James made a face at him as he finished his small slice of cake.

"Yeah, you can do it, carve him a couple of little tiny pistols, too."

They all laughed. James stood to carry the empty cake plates and fork into the kitchen. "Hank, anything else you want to volunteer me for before you leave, you dang cake thief?"

Hank grinned. "I didn't come back for cake and I'd watch who you go calling a cake thief. Seems you already had plans for it when I came in."

J.D. turned to Hattie and she quickly stacked the cut out pieces and returned the other scraps to the rag bag before standing to take the baby and blow out the lamp.

Jackson rose as well, gathering the coffee cups and pot to carry out to the kitchen. Hank rose, bowing as she passed. "Boss, the reason I came back was I forgot to tell you about the roan mare. Noticed she was getting ready to foal and wondered if you wanted me to bring her in tomorrow."

"Probably best. Goodnight men." He followed Hattie and didn't wait to see if they left or stayed.

◇◇◇

The next morning, Hattie was ironing clothes when the men rode in with the mare on a lead, a tiny strawberry foal behind her. She returned the iron to the hot stove, wiped the sweat from her face and picked up Jackie to follow them over to the main corral. The breeze cooled her and J.D. baby talked all the way over, holding his pony and alternately shaking it and biting on its nose or hooves. Jackson led the mare inside and tied her to the corner of the corral, running a hand down her neck and talking soothingly to her.

Hattie whispered, "J.D., see the baby horse, the pretty little red pony."

He shook his toy and grinned and she pointed to the mare and foal. Jackson walked widely around the mare keeping well out of range of her heels in case the motion spooked her. He smiled as her baby instinctively moved around and leaned against the mare's far side so she was out of sight.

He climbed up and over the corral, talking to his son as well. "It's a filly, Jackie, you see the pretty baby." He took his son and walked down along the rail, stooping so the baby in his arms could peek through the rails. The mare whinnied in fright and the little horse kicked up her heels in a kind of jump. J.D. squealed in delight and Hattie smiled, running a hand along the rail and stopping to take the boy from Jackson. Jackie leaned around her, seeing the little filly, and again squealed in delight.

She and Jackson hugged and together held him up, laughing. "She's so perfect," Hattie whispered, "a perfect little strawberry."

He smiled at the joy on both their faces, and hugged her again. "Almost as pretty as my little strawberry," he gave her a quick hard kiss, and Hattie leaned back in surprise.

Flustered, she forced herself to relax. She was probably as red as the gingham dress she wore. "I was ironing."

He sighed, disappointed again at the quick tension in her body at the sudden kiss. When was he going to remember in time to avoid spooking her? His head knew that with Hattie it would always need to be slow and gentle, but his body hadn't learned yet.

"Glad you stopped to bring the boy out to see them. Here, I can take him if you need to go back to your work."

Hattie wanted to protest, to hold on to the baby and the shared joy from minutes ago, but she couldn't. Once again she had pushed him away. Smiling bravely, she surrendered the baby and turned to walk back to the house.

◇◇◇

That night they lay together, her head cradled on his shoulder. Once again he had listened as she talked about the day, then he had surprised her by talking about the mare and filly. He had spent an hour in the morning and another in the evening with the pair, just stroking and talking to both. He wanted the little filly to be gentle enough for J.D. to pet and ride around the corral by next year, his first real horse.

As she listened, he told her of his plans to raise blooded horses as well as cattle. With the natural spring on their land, he could invest in some brood stock without having to worry about losing it during droughts.

"How was the house when you went there the other day?"

"I wondered when you would ask." It's all right, but it would be better if someone lived there. Now you won't be going back, maybe you'll want to sell it or rent the place out."

"I won't be going home?" she asked, sitting up. "Why not?"

"Because we're married and this is your home now. J.D. and I are your family."

The answer was true, she knew it was true, but she'd always felt she belonged, taking care of the Stoddard ranch.

He sat up beside her, his back braced against the headboard. His voice broke on the question, "Don't you like living in this house with J.D. and me?"

She turned and stared at him, her heart in her eyes. She reached out to touch his face, then leaned in to kiss him softly. "I love it. It's a wonderful house; and you and Jackie, you mean everything in the world to me. I just know Dad would have wanted me to take care of our ranch."

Jackson knew it was probably the time to tell her about the taxes and the deed he had to her ranch, but he held back. He didn't want to risk the trust and intimacy of the moment. Sitting naked in bed with this beautiful woman who was scooting down into him, he wasn't about to reveal secrets that would raise walls between them.

CHAPTER TWENTY-ONE

That Sunday, Hattie wore another blouse and skirt from the cupboard. This time she chose a pale blue blouse and matching skirt, mainly because there was a matching bonnet. It was Jackie who first noticed the blue-birds, one on the shoulder of the blouse, the other on the cap of the bonnet. She changed his gown to the one with the blue-bird and its matching bonnet.

Jackson smiled at them, and then surprised her by changing from his white shirt to a matching blue one. When he stood behind them and they all stared at their reflection in the mirror, J.D. crowed with delight.

They ended up eating at the table, then hurrying to load onto the buckboard. James wheeled past the corral and Hattie pointed to the red filly just to hear Jackie squeal at the sight of her.

The week had been an exhausting one, even with James at hand to help with the cooking and chores. She had made a second batch of pickles, and also had crocks working, one with sour cucumbers and the other with shredded cabbage. They had moved everything down into the cool of the root cellar. J.D. sat on her lap, his little cowboy in one hand, the red pony in the other. At least the little cowboy was properly dressed. Even though in his bright shirt and yellow kerchief he looked more like he was going out on a Saturday night than to church services.

Jackson had volunteered to tool the leather. Using nails heated in a small fire and wearing a leather glove, he used one after the other to make a chain design down the front of the leather vest and a matching design up the sides and along the top of each boot. Even though they were pretty simply made, the dark burned design on the leather made them look like the real thing at first glance.

Not to be outdone, James had whittled and blackened a pair of small guns and cut and made a belt with holsters. J.D. knew his cowboy was special because the cowhands all kept asking to play with him so they could inspect the work on the ten gallon hat, boots, and the little gun belt. But when J.D. almost swallowed one of the toy guns and Hattie had to pick the hat up for the twentieth time in an hour, the holsters and hat had gone to rest on the mantle shelf where the outlaw finger still resided in its little jar of alcohol inside the large match box.

◇◇◇

At church, they were early enough to enter before the Dawsons and most of the congregation arrived. J.D. was fussy but Jackson let him teethe on his fingers, careful to avoid the sharp little tooth that was already through. Hattie helped by rattling the pony's bells when he grew irritated and giving him something to grab for. She had even brought the lamb and the little red rattle and Jackson sat him on the bench between them with all his toys around him where they kept turns distracting him.

Irene and Charles stopped and admired him, but didn't insist on taking him this time. Hattie wondered if they were still embarrassed by his antics the Sunday before.

When the sermon ended, the Dawsons exited quickly, once again giving Hattie a scowl when they noticed she again wore Donna's clothes. Hattie gathered toys while Jackson wrangled the baby. Everyone seemed to be waiting to smile at them and admire J.D.

◇◇◇

Finally, Rubye White stood in front of them and J.D. nearly bounced out of Hattie's arms in excitement. Rubye cried and took him as Hattie released him. She leaned her cheek against the baby's, tears in her eyes. Jackson patted her shoulder. Hattie blinked, surprised at the tears in her own eyes. When Rubye started to speak and couldn't and tried to hand J.D. back, Hattie stepped forward and opened her arms to both of them.

Rubye swiped at her eyes. "I hope you can forgive me ...the tooth. I'm so sorry for all I said, for telling the preacher."

"Hush," Jackson said.

Hattie stared at her. "We owe you so much. If you hadn't said it all, jumped to the wrong conclusion, and forced the issue..."

"We wouldn't be married." Jackson finished. "I will always be grateful for being pushed to do what I secretly wanted to do all along."

Hattie stared up at him, surprised to hear her thoughts coming out of Jackson's mouth.

"Does that mean, you'll let me come home?"

Jackson smiled. "James is ready to quit if you don't."

Hattie looked up at Jackson, "Can we go by and get her things and take her home now."

He left an arm around Hattie and reached for J.D. – then passed him to Hattie. "Nothing makes more sense."

◇◇◇

In front of the Dawson's house, they waited while an elated Rubye raced upstairs, James behind her. Sitting in the buckboard, it became clear that Charles and Irene were not going to emerge to talk to their son-in-law. Hattie had to wonder again what Donna would have wanted them to do. They were her parents, the grandparents to her son. Would she have understood their reaction or expected them to rise above their own feelings to make sure that J.D. received their love?

Jackson looked grim as he sat beside her, then he looked down at the sleepy baby in her arms. J.D. was growing every day, his sturdy little body felt heavier. How must he feel to Hattie? Carefully he took the baby, hoisting his sleepy body upright against his chest until he heard a loud burp. He and Hattie exchanged smiles and he reached down to pat her hand.

For the second time this morning, she knew he had been sharing her thoughts. Rubye and James emerged minutes later with two carpet bags full of belongings and a small memory chest.

Soon Rubye was in the back of the buckboard, seated so her back was to James Boyd. A fact that somehow seemed significant to Hattie as she stared from one smiling face to the other, before they were off on their way home.

James snapped the horses into a trot, and Tony jogged his pony close beside them. "Figured to stay in town, boss, maybe have dinner with Maria."

Jackson nodded, shouting, "Keep your eyes and ears open."

Hattie was busy talking with Rubye her about what to get together for supper and Jackson was talking to Cliff who was riding beside him about possible Sunday chores for the men. Since real work wasn't to be done, Sunday chores were mending harness, sharpening tools, small tasks to while away the afternoon.

Hank who was riding a little ahead was the first to see the vultures as they approached the house. Hank pointed, hollered, and then set off at a gallop. James snapped the reins and guided the buckboard toward the house. But even as they wheeled into sight of the house, Hattie's heart stopped. In the front yard, a vulture floated away from the body of a big yellow dog. She recognized Sam who had been such a help in watching and keeping J.D. safe.

When he pulled to a stop, Hattie grabbed the baby closer as Jackson bounded down. The gate at the top step had been knocked loose and the fence around the porch that Jackson had so carefully nailed in place had been kicked and broken in several places. For a moment she was afraid to get down. It was like the day she had arrived home and found her father beaten and unconscious in the barn. Her heart began to beat in panic and she realized she was gripping the baby too tightly as he started to cry. Rubye climbed over the seat and wrapped an arm around her and got her to loosen her hold.

Panicked, she wanted to climb down, desperate to reach Jackson. When she looked away from the house, she saw vultures being chased away by the mounted cowboys. Behind them she saw two pink mounds in the paddock. The roan mare and her pretty filly were dead. What manner of men would kill them? She knew and her knees felt like jelly.

Minutes later, Jackson appeared on the porch, his revolvers strapped on. "James, get the women and J.D. inside, help them restore some order. I can't tell if someone was searching for something or if they just wanted to make our lives difficult, but they sure have done the latter."

He stared up at Hattie and heard her small gasp as she stared toward the paddock. When he realized what she was looking at and the horror on her face he rushed forward, turning the baby over to Rubye as he swept his terrified wife from the seat and into his arms. Jackson held her for a minute, trying to get her attention. She kept moaning, "No, no, no," in his arms and he quickly hurried into the house and the bedroom, closely followed by James.

The bedroom was bedlam, covers and mattress pulled off, mattress ripped and some of the cotton stuffing pulled out and scattered. Clothes had been torn from hangers and the dresser contents dumped haphazardly about in a snow of linen. Hattie's dark clothes had been shredded, but even Jackson could see it was only hers that had been destroyed. His own were scattered as were Donna's, but none was torn, stomped on or had waste dumped on them like Hattie's. The baby's clothes still rested snuggly in the dresser drawers.

He trembled to think that the demons who did this hated her so much. He held Hattie while James straightened the mattress, poking stuffing back into the slit down the center. Jackson nodded at the sheets and James shook one and they watched it float down onto the ripped mattress that had just been returned to the bed.

Rubye stood in the door, the baby held snugly, while she shook her head. "Well, I never."

Jackson scowled at her. "Rubye, see what you can put up, and carry out the soiled stuff and these torn garments."

Rubye stood, rocking the baby in her arms. "Of course, maybe some of it can be mended or used for patterns to make new garments."

The crib stood untouched, except for the cloud of clothes scattered over it. In minutes it was emptied and J.D. was settled in his bed. Together Rubye and James set about restoring order. She gathered up a simple quilt made of bright squares and as Jackson laid Hattie in the bed, Rubye spread it over her. Then she turned to open one of the bedroom windows.

Tuning out everything and everyone but Hattie, Jackson sat on the edge of the bed, an arm around her, alarmed to see her shivering and curled into a ball of fear. Outside, he could hear his men shouting to one another as they gathered their weapons and traded the wagon for saddled horses. He leaned down to brush her cheek with his own. "I know its hard Hattie, but you need to be strong. I have to go after these men. I need to know you're okay and that you will take care of and protect J.D. while I'm gone."

He heard the deep ragged breath, then saw her force the terror down and turn toward him.

"Where are my guns?"

Jackson leaned forward and kissed her forehead. He turned to the closet behind them. He pushed aside the clothes that Rubye and

James had hastily hung up. He thumped the back panel and it almost opened, blocked by the clothes. He lifted out a thick batch and laid them, hangers and all across the foot of the bed. This time the door swung open. The leather bag of coins Hattie had asked him to hide was gone, along with Donna's jewelry.

Suddenly he was back in the new bedroom, one of the rooms he had added with Dawson's help to accommodate his daughter. His own bed and dresser had been moved into what would become the maid, Rubye White's room. This room, Donna's bedroom with its "cross-ventilation" was furnished by Charles Dawson. Donna had picked out and ordered the furniture and it and the room had been part of her "dowry" as she called it.

He remembered Charles Dawson tapping the back of this wardrobe and saying with pride. "It has a banker's panel, here at the back. Donna, where's your jewelry."

When his blushing bride had handed her father the velvet bag Jackson had watched in fascination as Charles hooked it at the back of the narrow space, then smoothed it flat before tapping the panel back into place. "If you didn't know it was there, you couldn't see or find it. Even the cleverest burglar would miss it," he'd bragged.

Jackson felt around the narrow space but the heavy velvet bag and the small leather pouch holding Hattie's meager coins were both gone. Sinking, he felt around the bottom of the wardrobe, moving around Donna's numerous shoes until he found the guns.

"The money's gone, but here are your guns, let's check that they're loaded." Before doing that, he took the time to tap the panel back in place and rehang the expensive clothes. Sitting beside her, he broke the gun, spun the barrel with her, and then snapped it shut when she nodded. He held it, then slid it under the pillow.

She sniffed, trying to resist the urge to grab the gun back out.

Next, he repeated the steps of checking the rifle with her, and then stood the loaded rifle to rest against the headboard. "James will be here. He has his handguns and rifle and Rubye has her scattergun loaded and ready. We'll ride hard and get back as soon as we can."

She reached out a hand to his cheek, surprising them both that it was still shaking. "I love you. Go, we'll be fine, I'm good now."

He sat there, unable to move. He wanted to pull her into his arms again until the words she said were true. Instead, he kissed her forehead, held her for a moment and then left.

Outside in the yard, Jackson stared at the armed men, each looking as grim as he felt.

"It looks like four riders, boss. I catch them sons-of-bitches, I'm going to make 'em wish they'd stayed low," Cliff barked.

"We're going to ride out in four directions again, maybe we can catch some of the neighbors on their way back from church," Jackson said.

"Did you see what they did to that pretty baby and momma. Shot full of holes like every one of those snakes had to shoot them," one of the young hands added.

"They wrecked our coop, too." Hank added, pulling on the reins to turn his horse in a tight circle to stop its nervous side-stepping. "Pulled one wall down, the sorry S.O.B.'s."

Jackson looked toward the house, torn between chasing the raiders and going back inside to check on Hattie. "We were at the Stoddard's ranch a couple of days ago. I'm pretty sure that's not where they're staying these days."

The men exchanged looks when Jackson continued to stare at the house. "Well, at least this time we know there's no point in going for the sheriff. Pair up, Hank with me. Men let's ride."

Jackson circled the house, then took the road toward town and the Dawson's place. Hank started to argue, but then fell into place beside him. When they crossed the tracks of four horses, Jackson dismounted to study them. The only thing he could tell for sure was that one horse carried a heavier rider, the tracks were deeper and the smaller pony had a nail missing in a shoe. They rode almost up to the front door of the Dawson's house before the tracks veered off.

Cautiously, Jackson rode on into town, following the tracks until they were hidden among dozens of others on the dusty trail. "Hank, do you think you can find Tony, see if he saw or heard anything."

"Looks like you may need a back-up." He nodded toward the horses tied up at the saloon. It was Sunday, but it was customary for the saloon to open after church, since it catered to a different crowd.

"If I do, looks like the sheriff is here to give a hand." He pointed out the sheriff's wall-eyed pinto tied up beside the other four.

"Okay, boss, once I get him, we'll come back, just in case."

Jackson nodded, focused on the saloon door. He dismounted, tying up in front of the Thompson's store. He eased up onto the boardwalk and peered into the dusky quiet of the saloon. At a front table sat Sheriff Tate and a nervous, ugly cowhand, a man Jackson remembered hassling Hattie on the day he brought her home. He couldn't tell anything about the other three, until one lifted his drink and Jackson held his breath. The man clearly was missing his middle finger on his right hand.

So Hogue and Sweat were two of the ones who had shot horses and torn up his place. They were clearly friends of the sheriff and had two new men riding with them. The heavy man could be Silas Sweat, but the man's long black hair and beard gave him no resemblance to the four-fingered drinker.

Jackson eased the gun back into the holster as he realized there was no way to approach them, one against five. Certainly, no reason to see the sheriff to report and complain about the raid. He had probably just heard about it from the raiders. Asking his father-in-law for help was pointless. He had reason to believe it was Charlie

Dawson behind this raid, the earlier rustling, and the harassment of Hattie and her father, as well as the other ranchers. They would pay, but not now, not here in town.

Carefully, he backed off the walkway and mounted up. In minutes, he was waiting beneath an elm tree in the Mexican section of Star. Hank rode up with a rumpled looking Tony. The younger cowhand had the good grace to look embarrassed.

"I did what you asked, boss, checked around for strangers. There are four men who have set up out at the Eastman place."

"Eastman?"

"Yeah, he was one of the small squatters just west of town. He had a really bad run of luck last year. First rustlers, then his barn burned, then he lost his crops to a prairie fire. When he couldn't pay his taxes, the bank foreclosed. Not sure who owns the place, but these four have moved in out there."

"Well, see if you can find out names. I'm pretty sure one is Rafe Hogue, then there's a four-fingered man, pretty sure he was Silas or Able Sweat."

"Missing a middle-finger?"

"The very one. They were drinking with Sheriff Tate." He started to add that their trail lead from the Dawson's place, but he didn't. To accuse a man as powerful as Charlie Dawson, even when he had reason, could be a costly mistake for all of them.

"What's the next move, boss?"

"Tony, you'll stick close, keep an eye on these men on the Eastman's ranch. The rest of us will ride armed. If they cross onto Harper land again, we'll shoot first, then ask questions."

"We could ride in with you, take them on now," Hank said.

Jackson shook his head. "Believe me I want to. But this isn't Deadwood or Tombstone City. Folks don't expect gunfights on the streets of Star and I don't want to be the one to start one, do you?"

Hank shook his head. "No, but I sure want those coyotes dead."

Jackson remembered the terror stricken girl who had touched his cheek and told him she was good, to go ahead. "No one wants them dead more than me. We'll get every one of them. But we'll do it legal. For now, we'll wait."

CHAPTER TWENTY-TWO

When he was once again on Harper land, Jackson fired the two short bursts of rifle fire that was the agreed upon signal. The men poured into the ranch yard as he rode in. He met them at the paddock.

"Some of you will have to drag these horses down to the gully and cover them. We don't want coyotes or wolves this close to the house. Hank and a few of you can tackle getting the chicken coop nailed back together. I'll repair the gate and porch fencing," Jackson said.

"No one saw four horsemen. Don't you want us to go back out scouting?" Cliff asked.

"No need. I found their trail; they're holed up at the Eastman ranch. A place like the Stoddard's that had far too much bad luck, and then got foreclosed on by the bank."

Cliff stared at him hard. "You saw who they were?"

"Yeah, I saw them drinking with our friend the sheriff. Rafe Hogue and one of the Sweats, probably Able, along with two I've never seen. One oversized with long black hair and a black beard, and the other on the runt side."

"I suppose you saw their horses too?"

"A black, seventeen hands at least, probably carrying the fat man. A brown mustang, a dun quarter horse and a small, flea-bitten gray that has a shoe on the right front leg that's missing a nail."

The men exchanged hard looks. "That's a pretty close look, boss."

"Tony is staying in town, keeping an eye on their movements and trying to give us a heads up. I believe it's the best way to handle things."

"Why don't we just ride out, shoot them full of holes like they did those strawberry ponies?" Cliff demanded.

"Nothing would please me more. But with the law on their side, we need to catch them in the act."

"So we just stay home and clean up the mess."

"And, keep an eye on the cattle and the ranch. The priority is the safety of the people here, especially Hattie and J.D."

"You can count on us, boss."

◇◇◇

Supper was a silent affair, the broken furniture in the living room keeping everyone's spirits low. They ate beans, fresh corn, and buttered corn bread with green onions and no one complained. Tired and hungry, they were glad to have a hot meal

Hattie was somber, still wearing the skirt and blue blouse from church, holding J.D. who was frightened by all the tension in the air. He clung to her and rejected all offers of other arms or laps. Hattie no longer appeared frightened, but she appeared sad, hurt by all the destruction and the dead animals. He knew she would normally have changed back into her everyday clothes. Maybe it was knowing that all her clothes were gone, that she would always be wearing Donna's things that gave her face such a down-turned expression.

After supper, the men all got busy with their tasks; Jackson hammered the boards into place and rehung the gate on the porch. Hattie carried the quilt from the bed and the sewing basket into the front room. The tall table had been set upright, the Bible back on top. Although the settee had been slashed on the seat, the back and both arms, its horse hair stuffing still rested firmly inside and none of its wood was broken. It was as though the raiders were going through the motions, but not really expecting to find anything since they hadn't removed the stuffing like they had on the bed.

She began with the encyclopedia of needlework, reading again the section on mending. She chose the denim from the scrap bag, cutting pieces to work beneath the edges of the rips in the upholstery. Then using the curved needle and a red thread to match the fabric, she slowly whip stitched the edges together over the reinforcing cloth.

Her first real difficulty came when she had to make a knot at the end of the seam. J.D. sat beside her on the folded quilt, his back and sitting skills stronger every day. He looked up at her and she had to smile at his studious expression. Knowing it might show, she made the usual double loop, passing the needle through the last loop and then bit off the end of the thread after running it down the length of the seam. At her smile of satisfaction, J.D. laughed out loud.

Hattie stabbed the needle into the slashed sofa nearest her and scooped the laughing baby into her arms. Leaning down to kiss him, she was delighted when he raised up to kiss her back. As she held him in the circle of her arms he stretched up against her. "Big boy, Momma's big boy," she teased and he laughed again.

Jackson stepped into the house staring at the pair on the quilt. The baby stood on wobbly legs, weaving in the arms of his smiling wife. Despite the rage that still rushed through him at the violation of his home and the killing of his stock, he felt his own lips tug into a smile as they both turned to smile at him.

He stopped for a moment to hug and kiss both, then turned to examine the chair. Although its upholstery hadn't been slashed, one leg and the bottom side rails had both been broken. While the boy played between them, both continued to work. Hattie darned one of the arms, just as she had repaired the long rip in the seat.

Then stretching her back, careful not to move her feet, she cut and placed the denim in the tear of the backrest and the remaining arm. J.D. had stopped babbling and lay with his head under her skirt, one hand on her ankle. Jackson finished working the broken leg loose from the chair and the broken rail from the rear leg and smiled at her. "He always figures out what I'd like to do, and then does it for me."

Hattie looked down, moving her skirt just enough to reveal the sleeping baby. "I hope the lord will forgive us for the work this day." She added as she returned needle and thread to the basket.

"I was always taught that no new work was to be done, only cooking and light mending. I'd say that's all that any of us have done." He put down the hammer on the seat of the mended couch, then bent to lift the limp baby.

Rubye stood in the open door of her room. "Did you call me?"

Hattie shook her head, again reaching to stretch her back. "No, I forgot to ask, but was your room all right?"

The older woman nodded. "Can't say the same for the rest of the house. Took forever to clean up the spilled food and grease in the kitchen. The pantry is a real mess. James and I put up some of it, but they dumped your spice jars and we figured you would want to see to that tomorrow."

"Thank you, I will. Did they mess up anything in the cellar?"

"No, I don't believe they knew to look there. Don't worry about rising early, James and I will see to breakfast and the men."

"Thank you, Rubye, goodnight," Hattie and Jackson said, smiling at each other because they had spoken the same words at the same time.

Hattie followed Jackson and J.D., holding the basket to her side as she leaned to blow out the lamp on the dinner table.

◇◇◇

Wordlessly, Jackson blew out the lamp on the dresser and took her hand. In the dark bedroom, they undressed each other, and then soundlessly fell into each other's arms. Afterward, they talked in whispers.

"I'm sorry about how I reacted, when we came home."

"I thought you were going to faint again."

She shook her head. "It was the vultures, the destruction, it reminded me of riding up to our ranch and finding the dog shot..." her voice cracked, "...and Dad bleeding, beaten unconscious. I just couldn't bear reliving all of it."

She realized she was weeping again when he pulled her into his arms, kissing her cheeks as he cooed to her, kissing her eyelids and finally her mouth. She felt as though he were drinking her sorrow with her tears.

Coming up for air, she shook her head. "I'm not usually an emotional or weepy woman. You must think me a real goose." She turned so her back was to him. "I didn't cry, after, after … I just couldn't let go. I guess I knew if I fell apart, there would be no one to care for Dad, look after the animals that were left on the place. Then when I learned I was pregnant, I was so full of rage and hate."

"Hattie, you don't need to explain."

"They came back to our place once, did I tell you that," she added sitting up.

"No, I didn't know."

"I was ready with the rifle. I hit one of them; I figure it was Silas since he was walking with a limp at the store. Another I barked with splinters from the porch post. But I didn't hit Rafe. He's the one, the one I have to kill. He …." Her voice trailed away.

Each word was like a knife to him but he knew it was like any festering wound, she needed to talk to let all the poisonous hurt drain away. God grant him the strength to hear it all. "You can tell me," he whispered, his voice raw from swallowing back the rage and tears.

She shook her head, "I've wallowed in pity long enough Mr. Harper." She relaxed back into his arms.

A minute later she asked, "Why, why do you think they did this?"

He rubbed a hand lazily over her bare back, loving the soothing feel of her silky, damp skin. "I think someone sent them to do it. They did it because they wanted to punish us for the wedding."

"Wedding?" she laughed. "You mean the shotgun wedding where we both were threatened with being expelled from church, pulled before the preacher, and forced to marry."

Jackson shook his head, nuzzling her neck until she curved, spooning into his body. "Are you sorry to be Mrs. Harper?" he whispered, nibbling at her ear.

Hattie snuggled closer, trying to capture the hands that continued to skim over her skin, then boldly cupped her breasts and smoothed the softness of her stomach and lower.

She gasped as he entered her again. "No, Mr. Harper, I'm not sorry."

◇◇◇

Hattie knew she should still feel sad, but it was a beautiful day and with Rubye and James both to help, all the chores were finished by mid-morning. She sat with the cracked spice jars and the swept up pile of spices on a newspaper.

For the first time this morning, she felt the bitter frustration she had experienced yesterday. If there was one thing she didn't cotton to, it was being a victim. After the night she was attacked, she had vowed never to be one again. But if Jackson and all his men couldn't prevent raiders from doing this, then neither could she. Being angry about something that couldn't be changed was a waste of time. At least today she had her father's belt and gun around her waist and the rifle loaded above the fireplace. If they came today, she would be ready.

She listened to J.D. pounding on an empty pot with a wooden spoon in the space between the kitchen and dining table. These broken pieces had been precious to her mother, had come with her from the old world. Patiently Hattie fitted pieces together until she had two lids ready to glue and three bottles that had cracks or corners knocked off waiting for the porcelain sealer.

She smiled as Rubye told J.D. he was a great drummer, only to hear him pound even louder. Carefully, she applied the glue and set each piece aside to dry. If only she could repair her damaged life as easily.

The spices were a different problem. Sorting these out was like sorting out her emotions, an impossible task. After several minutes, she decided picking out dill or cinnamon might be doable, but it would definitely take more time than she had. She removed the three big nutmeg pieces and put them in their intact jar. There, simple. Like she had removed the fear of ever having any man touch her.

J.D. was already getting restless. He had managed to turn the pot over and she rose to hand him his wooden toys so he could drop them in the pot and then pull them out to drop again.

Quickly she moved to the kitchen where she found the tea sieve and then returned to sorting spices. She folded the corner of the paper, then poured them all through onto a new sheet of newspaper. With the ones remaining, Hattie shook the sieve for a few more minutes, then pulled the lighter dill from the top of the little basket. Her guilt over her father's sorrow. Maybe he hadn't been disappointed in her, but in his inability to protect her. She next put the bark fragments into the newly glued cinnamon jar with the bigger bark curls, and finished by returning the cloves to their own jar. Three down.

J.D. was complaining loudly and it was Rubye who moved, this time dumping the pot and turning it back over. The tall, gaunt woman stood bent over the boy, then handed him his wooden spoon.

When he did nothing, she gave it one good rap, then handed him the spoon again. Hattie smiled as he began to bang away.

This time Hattie went for the flour sifter, removed it from the flour bin in the pantry and carried it to the table. Again she shook the remaining spices together and poured them through the finer screen. Once again she shook the sifter, holding the newspaper underneath. This time she collected star anise in the top layer, black peppercorns in the next, and red pepper flakes in the third layer.

Unfortunately the pile remaining was all powder. She hated to waste anything, but even the best cookbook in the world would probably never have powdered cumin, mustard, turmeric, mace, and cayenne, all in one recipe. She took a break to change and feed the tired baby, asking Rubye if she had any ideas.

Rubye smiled as she removed the cornbread from the skillet. "Nope, I can't believe you were able to sort out so much with just two strainers."

J.D. leaned back and stared up at her. Hattie smiled. "Did you just think what I did?" He smiled before going back to nursing.

As soon as he was full, Hattie put J.D. back to work with his toys and the pot and carefully put up all the refilled jars and strainers. After wiping down and setting the table, she folded and tore six small squares of newspaper. Then she carefully folded a cone from the last newspaper sheet. Carefully she poured the spices in the cone. She pinched the tight end shut and slowly and carefully tapped on the side until she saw the top layer was uniform in color. Holding the cone over the first square, she released it until the color changed, pinched it, then moved to the next square. This time she couldn't get it to separate, the mingled colors and scents bled out over the edge of the square. She almost missed the moment when it actually changed. The last was all dark red. What was the last spice, cayenne? Was it hate? Could she separate it from her heart?

Men began to filter in and Rubye set food on the table, but Hattie continued until the last layer was emptied onto its square. Jackson had entered and stood behind her as she finished up.

"Well, I'll be," Jackson said as he held a kicking J.D.

Hattie smiled and relaxed. The inseparable spices were the mingled emotions in her heart. But the first was pure love, the last pure hate. These she could tell apart.

◇◇◇

"I think it's as good as I can get it. No one wants apple pie that tastes funny with mustard as part of its ginger, but we saved some of this expensive spice."

◇◇◇

Most of the men were finished by the time Hattie joined them to eat and took J.D. on her lap to feed mashed up beans and potatoes, as well as crumbled cornbread in milk. While he ate, he happily kicked his legs and bounced. Jackson reached out a hand to grab one small foot and kicking leg. "Whoa, fella, easy there."

J.D. looked up at him and grinned mischievously and kicked with the other foot. Jackson grabbed the other little foot and held it firmly.

"Slow down, bronco," he said more firmly and J.D. stopped and gave him a scowl. Jackson ignored the look and leaned down to whisper to the boy. "You need to be gentle with the ladies, partner."

As though he understood, J.D. stopped bouncing and Hattie finished feeding him and eating her own lunch.

"I think I can mend the sofa, then we'll only have the office to clean up."

Jackson nodded. "James is going to have to carve a new leg and rail, before I can finish the repair of the chair. The porch is done and the men have the coop back together. If it weren't for the damaged clothes, and the lost animals, we'd be back to normal."

Hattie nodded. The pause on the lost animals made her pause as well. She missed the big yellow dog, his grin of welcome and bounce of excitement when he would see her and the baby. There had been no reason to kill the sweet animal. But there had been no reason for them to shoot Shep, their old cow dog either. No reason for beating her father, robbing them, raping her. She shuddered, then straightened. "I think with Rubye's help, we can use some of the fabric to make a quilt, especially with the rag bag from James."

"Have you ever quilted before?"

She laughed and shook her head. "No, but I never repaired a sofa before or hemmed a dress until last week. With Rubye's help, I'll figure it out."

<><><>

Later, Hattie opened the door onto the office. The furniture was simple: a drop-leaf desk, a big desk chair, and a long book case. An empty, bare cot sat along one wall, the end legs knocked down. Only the desk had not been overturned. Unlike her bedroom, which had two, this room had no window.

Hattie left the door open for light. She pulled the mattress from the broken cot and set J.D. on it. She removed the gown with its spatters of beans and applesauce, his bare body reassuringly soft and pink as he rolled, waving his round legs in the air until he found a favorite toe to nibble. She loved the happy noises he made and she babbled along with him. "Let's set the furniture straight first."

She pushed the bookcase back upright and lifted the chair. She moved the leaf that formed the desk upright and was relieved that it wasn't broken and would still fasten. She lowered it again to reveal the clutter of papers and objects pulled from the tiny cubbyholes inside. She set the inkpot upright, relieved that it had stayed corked and she wouldn't have to try to remove spilled ink. Finally she carefully lifted and moved the frame for the cot and hollered to James. She left it outside in the sitting area near the chair so he could see if he could repair it too.

J. D. had abandoned his foot and watched her wrestle the awkward frame of the cot through the door before rolling over. He sat with his arms pushing down, his body raised, as though any minute he would push on up and help her. "Okay, son, what do you think, books next?"

At his complaint, she stepped through the door and returned minutes later with his pony, cowboy and rattle. He rolled back over and took the rattle. Eager to wave it and see if it would still make noise, he screeched loudly when it did. Hattie knelt for a second to kiss his bare belly and check that his diaper was still dry. "That's right, you little rattlesnake, shake that thing."

He did and she picked up a handful of books to set on the middle shelf. Tilting the cover to read them in the dim light, she arranged the books on ranching along the top shelf, sorting them by topic: animal husbandry, western cattle breeding, crop rotation, and the practical rancher's handbook. She wished she had been in this room before, to know what order Jackson had shelved them before they were dumped on the floor. But the mattress and laughing baby reminded her why she had not. Before two weeks ago, this had been Jackson's quarters and she would never have dared intrude.

On the second shelf, she arranged books that had clearly been Donna's. A cookbook, apparently unread, Dr. Padgett's Advice for Young Mothers, and several other textbooks from the Academy for Young Women in Dallas. Hattie stepped out to recover the book she had used last night. The encyclopedia of ladies needlework had dozens of pages that were dog-eared. The last section on embroidery had a scattering of patterns that had been traced from the pages, slipped back inside as markers. One was of a beautiful blue bird in flight.

Hattie tilted the page toward the lamp light, tracing the design with a finger as she recognized it from all the gowns and bonnets it had been embroidered on. The drawing in the book was labeled, "the blue bird of happiness." Beside her, Hattie heard J.D. baby-talking to his toys, shaking the little red rattle. Softly she whispered into the silent room, "It worked, Donna, listen to him. You gave him the elusive bluebird of happiness."

She closed the book lovingly and carefully placed it on Donna's shelf. By the time J.D. began to whine and complain, Hattie had organized and returned all the books, even stacked on the bottom shelf the copies of Godey's Lady Companion magazine and a stack of farm catalogs on Jackson's side. It was difficult, because she wanted to read it all.

She was surprised by the number and variety of novels. At home, they had only had a Bible, her mother's cookbook, and a volume on western ranch land that had been her father's favorite reading. Although she had told Rubye that her mother taught her everything, she realized she had gained a great deal of information from the old German cookbook. She had read and reread it, looking for traces of her mother in the pages. For a minute she debated carrying her two books to add to these, but decided she should ask Jackson for permission first.

Finally, Hattie began stacking the scattered papers onto the desk. She had managed to gather all from the floor when J.D.'s whine became full-out crying. She found him sprawled across the mattress, obviously too tired to sit or roll any longer. He was wet, as expected. She kissed his tears away, cleaning him and picking up the toys before settling down in Jackson's desk chair to nurse him.

In another hour, the men would be back for supper. Frustrated, she had wanted to finish straightening the study today. As the baby quieted, he became curious about his new surroundings. She watched him look around, before snagging a paper off the desk. Delighted with the noise, it took several minutes before she could wrestle it away and return it to the pile. Defeated, she cautiously closed the desk and carried the baby out to the dining table.

CHAPTER TWENTY-THREE

It was two days later before she returned to the study. By then, she and Rubye had made a pattern and cut most of the pieces for a quilt. They had argued heatedly for a while, between the patterns of Blue Bonnet or Lone-Star. James had declared the war had been settled quicker than they were ever going to agree on a pattern.

Rubye had argued that it was known by everyone that it was bad luck to sleep under a single star quilt. Hattie had argued that if they were going to do that much work, they ought to use the prettiest pattern they could find.

They had compromised. Their quilt would have a center, large sixteen-pointed star. They would make it with alternating triangles of the dark striped cotton from her dresses, and lighter, brighter scraps from the torn cowhand's shirts. Apparently, the prettier a man's shirt, the more likely it was to be ripped or tattered in a bar-room or bunkhouse brawl.

They would alternate smaller squares of six-pointed stars and plain squares of the dark fabric. The stars would be made from scraps of her shirts and a single color from each cowboy's pieced against the white from her ripped petticoats. The dark squares according to Rubye needed to be quilted in the blue bonnet flower design. Although a single blossom, it looked impossible to Hattie.

It seemed to Hattie that the million little pieces would never all be cut and organized, let alone sewn together again to make the quilt top. They were still arguing about whether to back it with a blanket and old sheet, Hattie's idea, or to use one of the new cotton batts and muslin.

◇◇◇

The baby grew heavier in her arms and she left the table, feeling outnumbered now that James and Rubye seemed to always be together in every argument. She again left the door to the office open and put the sleepy baby down on the mattress, making sure his arms were not caught underneath him. She kissed the warm soft cheek, satisfied that he would sleep for a while, then moved to the desk.

Everything was as she had left it. She opened the drawers on the bottom side of the desk, removing empty folders that had held the documents now piled high in the center of the desk. She set them in a row, open to the top and ready to receive papers.

One was labeled invoices farming, another invoices house, a third invoices stock. Another group was labeled land records, payroll records, etc. Satisfied that she was ready, she began with the first paper, the one that J.D. had wanted to keep and shred the last time she sat here.

Frustrated by the task, she lit the lamp and tried again. It was the invoice from Thompson's store. It had the clothes for her and food for the house – it took her back to that painful day that seemed years ago. The clothes were now tiny pieces of the soon to be quilt. Hattie put the slip into the folder marked invoices house and moved on.

She quickly decided to shift everything, putting all the folders away except the three labeled invoices. Next she moved papers that weren't invoices to the left side of the desk unread, those that were invoices she read and filed in the correct folder. One's that were like the first bill and had more than one category, she filed in the folder that had the largest amount of expenditure. When she ran out of invoices, she took each folder, sorted the papers inside by date, most recent on top

◇◇◇

In the distance, she heard James and Rubye laughing as they set the table and put food out for the men. She heard J.D. stir a little and hurried with her sorting. She found herself studying the plot map of the ranch, surprised to see how her ranch fit into the curve at the bottom corner of the ranch, nesting as she had against Jackson the other night. The memory brought color to her cheeks.

She was sitting there, when she looked up to see Jackson, standing and staring at her, a knowing grin on his face. J.D. raised his head and made swimming motions. Jackson lifted him up, accepting the hands grabbing his cheeks, reaching for his hat. He tilted his head back, making J.D. stretch to reach him. When he did, Jackson moved his head to kiss the soft exposed neck. The happy sound of the baby's laugh filled the room.

Hattie rose, pulled like a magnet to the tall man and laughing baby. She raised her head for a kiss and J.D. managed to snag the hat. He was quickly chewing on the dusty brim.

"No, yuck," she said, pulling the hat away and making a face at the baby.

He made the face back at her, but grunted and reached for the hat. Jackson swung it free and flung it back at the mattress.

"What's Momma been doing, Jackie?"

He walked over to the desk, stared at the plot map, looking over his shoulder at the shelved books, the drawer barely open, with papers filed, and the wild stack of papers still to file.

He smiled at Hattie and leaned forward to kiss her again. "Thank you. But what had that look on your face?" The gruff growl of his voice made her stomach tighten, her cheeks flush again.

She leaned and pointed to the map, tracing the curve of the border between the two ranches. Jackson's voice growled and she looked up to see his eyes dancing with devilment.

Rubye's voice called from the open door as she stepped in to take J.D. "Vittles are served, you folks better hurry if you're hungry."

"We're coming." Hattie started to scoot around him but he turned her so her hips were pressed against the bulge in his Levis. Jackson leaned in and breathed against her ear, "Later, pretty momma." He left first, winking at her as he picked up his hat.

◇◇◇

Hattie folded and filed the map in the folder marked land, then stared at the next document. Suddenly, all the joy fled as she read the deed that changed the title of the ranch from one Harriet Stoddard, daughter and heir of Tom Stoddard, to the name of Jackson Harper for an amount of money that made her gasp.

For a moment she thought it might be a mistake. Maybe it was recent, changed after they married. Texas was like every other state, a woman's property became her husband's upon marriage.

But when she checked the date she saw it was for six months earlier, the day she came to the ranch to be a wet nurse. All along, all this time, Jackson had already taken over her property. At that time he had not been contemplating marriage, he had just been grabbing her land.

Why, why had he called it the Stoddard ranch, let her send him there to check for her cattle, her pickling crocks, her missing furniture? Tears filled her eyes.

She sensed when he entered the doorway, waited while he closed the door and walked over to her.

"What'd you find now?" he asked, his voice still teasing.

But instead of going into his open arms, she shoved the deed at him and shot out of the seat.

"When were you going to tell me?"

"It's not what you think. It's still your land, our land. You remember, I promised you the taxes as salary, for taking care of J.D. But when I went to pay them, the amount was huge and overdue. Dawson was going to foreclose. So I bought the land for the back taxes, for you."

"With the deed in your name?"

"I planned to deed it back to you when J.D. was weaned."

She brushed past, swallowing the tears, hearing the words but not accepting their meaning. Feeling as empty and sad as she had her first day, she walked out.

She sat at the table to eat and take care of the baby. Her heart squeezed as the man she loved, the man she'd married, the man who had brought such joy to her even this morning, while that man walked out of the door without a look or word for her. Now that his secret was out, was he done with her?

Hattie swallowed, unsure of what she was eating. She knew from experience that to keep up with J.D. she needed food to make food. After all, that was her job, she was the milk cow.

◇◇◇

Hattie tried to carry her anger with her through the afternoon but there was the explanation that Jackson had given her and the feeling that she had been hasty and unfair. There was the rawness still of hurt as much from the look on his face as in her own heart. If you loved someone, didn't you have to trust and believe what they said?

She returned to the office, asked James to remove the repaired cot and mattress to the bunkhouse, folded the bedding and pillow and gave them to Rubye to store. After filing the last few pieces of paper, Hattie swept the floor, dusted the desk and chair and shelves. She checked the desk, sliding out the center drawer with its well-used pencils and shaved quill pens. She checked the sides, front and under the top for hidden panels like Jackson had shown her in the bedroom.

Those men had been looking for something. Hidden money, or something else of value. She checked the floor, satisfied that there was no secret floor board hiding hole. Jackson was a rancher. Somewhere there had to be a safe or hiding place for the money to keep the ranch running. He used the bank, she knew that he did. But where would he hide the daily money. More importantly, why had he looked so strange when he saw the empty space at the back of their bedroom closet? What was missing?

All afternoon, the thoughts churned as she stitched tiny scraps together to form another small star square. She tried to piece the facts into a truth, just like the fabric. Restlessly, she picked the garden, snapped late beans, put them on for supper. She fed the baby, folded clothes, settled down to piece a second square.

The house was quiet, Rubye had gone with James. They had promised her fish, something she had been longing for. Restlessly, she tended the baby, then made coleslaw while he played, made and baked cornbread, prepared pickled beets and eggs.

All the time she wondered how she could have behaved as she had. Then she wondered why she hadn't been angrier, yelled more. She felt sad, thinking of how wrong it was of her to not trust him if he were innocent. But what if he had been conniving, what if he were vile and evil like all men.

But she knew all men weren't evil. There was her father, and the men on this ranch, and Jackson. She would apologize, tell him she was sorry. After all, what did it matter? She was his and so was the land. But that made her even angrier. What was wrong with the world that a woman had such little value and why wasn't she entitled to property of her own?

Her head hurt. She made sure the lid was tilted on the beans, moved them to the back-eye. After straightening the bedding on the bed, she stretched out to give J.D. his late feeding. Finally, she put the sleeping baby in the crib and relaxed into sleep herself.

◇◇◇

In town, Jackson stopped at the teller's desk. "Smith, I need you to do me a favor."

He pulled out the deed, laid it on the teller's window. "I need to transfer this deed to my wife's name, and I need it witnessed and notarized."

"I'll need to check with Mr. Dawson."

"Why would that be? There's no money involved. I'm just changing the name on the deed and I need you to witness and notarize it."

"Well, Mr. Dawson is property assessor. All title transfers are done and recorded by him. I'll be happy to come and notarize your signature when he calls me back."

Irritated, Jackson turned to leave.

"I can let you wait in his room," Smith called after him.

"No thanks. I'll wait outside."

◇◇◇

Annoyed, Jackson crossed the street as soon as he saw Dawson coming back from lunch, walking from the big house at the edge of town. He tried to find a smile to match that of his father-in-law, but it was too difficult. Scowling, he followed him into the office, barely managing a nod for the curious clerk.

"What's troubling you son?" Charles asked.

"We were raided again Sunday. The house was broken into."

"Anyone hurt, anything stolen? Sunday, why have you waited so long?"

Jackson waited until they were both seated, facing each other across the desk. "Why did you send them, Charlie?"

His father-in-law stared at him. "What are you talking about?"

"They killed some animals, a mare and her foal, a dog. They wrecked the place but they only tore up Hattie's things, ripped her clothes to rags. They damaged things while they looked for something. What were they looking for Charlie?"

"This is crazy talk, Jackson. I don't know what you're talking about."

"I came to deed Hattie's place back to her."

"Don't be silly, Jackson. She's your damn wife. What's hers is yours anyway."

Jackson stared hard at him. "She found the deed, saw the title change, and was upset. I promised her I'd pay the taxes. Nothing was said about my taking the property. If legally it's all the same, then I just need the title to be in her name."

Dawson stared at him grimly. "You're a damn fool. The taxes will be at her rate, not yours. Why waste money?"

The thought of paying the outrageous taxes stopped Jackson. "Why would the tax rate be different?"

"It would be a small tract. Small ranches belong to squatters. The town council ordered that the rate for the small spreads would be ten times the going rate. You're a cattleman; you know that small outfits mean barbwire, closed ranges and hurt cattle. The town wants to keep them out; the taxes are a legal way to do it."

Jackson chewed on it for a minute, and then asked. "What about the Eastman place?"

"Fred Eastman lost that spread, the bank foreclosed, and I bought it. It's now part of Dawson range and has the lower rate. Whose side of this range war are you on?"

"I didn't know there was a range war."

"Damn, Jackson, it's being fought all over the west; Texas is just part of it. Now you've got a squatter for a wife, people are questioning your ability to think clearly. This nonsense of a title change will make them figure they're right."

"Is that why you sent them?"

The banker rose to his feet, his neck bulging, his face red in outrage. "That's twice you've accused me of this nonsense. Why would I be behind rustlers? If you want to report the raid, talk to the sheriff."

Jackson rose to his full height and glared down at him. "I saw them drinking with your man, the sheriff. Tony tells me they're all staying at the Eastman place, Hogue, one of the Sweats, and two strangers. You just told me you own the place, but you want me to believe you don't know about them? Come on Charlie."

"I'm telling you the truth, you're way off course on this."

"They opened the panel in the closet. Took Hattie's money and stole Donna's jewelry. Only you, Donna, and I knew about that secret hiding place in the closet. So why did you send them Charlie?"

"I swear on Donna's name, I know nothing about this."

"I saw where they stopped at your house. I followed their tracks there. You may be a big man in town and own the law, but I'll wire the Texas Rangers. If they come on my place, threaten my wife or child, I'll damn well kill them."

Dawson stood, florid with rage. "Get out, get out of here. You're crazy Jackson. If it weren't for Donna and J.D., I'd...," he stopped, the bluster swallowed at the intensity of Jackson's glare.

◇◇◇

On his way out of town, Jackson stopped and telegraphed the Rangers at Austin, then sat to wait for an answer.

He saw the fresh tracks as he rode toward home. Fear raised the hair at the back of his neck. He raised his gun and fired twice quickly, hoping his men would hear the signal and reach the ranch in time.

<>><><>

It was Red, the newest outlaw, who first noticed the kid watching the place. It took a day, but Able found out where he was staying in town, sleeping with a little Mexican named Maria. It was easy to waylay him on his way out to the ranch in the morning.

They argued about it, but finally left him beaten but tied up in the cabin. Red had plans to bring the little Mexican out for a visit. The plan pleased Rafe, but first he needed to take care of the Stoddard girl.

<>><><>

They outlaws smiled when they found the ranch empty. Then smiled even bigger when they saw the older couple walk up from the creek, giggling like kids and holding a string of fish. He sent Red and Pierce around to the front of the house, he and Able sprinted to the back corner of the building, pleased to see the curtains moving in the light breeze. Hogue peeked in to see the blue skirt on top of the bed. They waited until they heard the others enter the house. Signaling Sweat to be quiet, he eased the window up and climbed over the window sill.

Able followed him in. They stood listening to the breathing, then Able stepped over to the crib while Rafe stood staring down at Hattie.

<>><><>

Hattie woke, feeling like a snake was crawling over her, and screamed when she saw them. Able Sweat had his gun out and it was aimed at J.D. From the other side of the door she heard raised voices, James shouting, a crash, and then laughter.

Hattie sprang to her feet but Rafe held the gun up for her to see. "Not too fast, Mrs. Harper, you'll wake the baby."

Hattie shrank back against the dresser, her mouth dry with fear. "No, not again."

Able laughed, grabbing his crotch. "Oh yeah, again and again, ain't that right, Rafe."

Their laugher ran through her, leaving her knees weak. Hattie sagged against the bed, her eyes wide with horror.

"Take off your clothes," Rafe barked.

Hattie shook her head, "No, no I won't."

"Yeah, you will," Rafe snarled, "Pick up that baby, Able."

"No," Hattie screamed and J.D. woke crying, his little face a mask of fear.

Able laughed and holstered his gun. He grabbed J.D. and the baby screamed.

"Don't hurt him." She muttered, her teeth chattering. Woodenly, she closed her eyes and slowly began to unbutton her blouse, inching out of it even slower.

"Look at them titties, Rafe. She's got some titties on her now."

Hattie cringed, hating the see-through quality of Donna's fancy underwear. Even Jackson hadn't seen her in them. But stealing herself, she inched onto the bed, pretending to be struggling with the fastenings on her skirt. There was no rifle, behind her closed eyes she could visualize it in the rack above the fireplace. Why had she thought that meant it was ready to use as a weapon? But maybe the pistol was still there, still under the pillow. Was it, or was it in the gun belt hanging in the study?

When she had the skirt loose, Hattie rolled so the bed was between them, then she looked up, pretending to smile as she wiggled out of the blue garment.

"Who-wee, just like a pro," Rafe called. "Don't tell me you've grown to like it, cause I've been looking forward to having to fight you again, little hell-cat?"

Trembling Hattie draped the skirt onto the bedpost and sank down on the pillows. She could feel the hard edge of the pistol under her hips.

◇◇◇

Outside, Jackson waved Cliff to the front of the house, gun drawn and cocked as he inched closer to the window. He could hear and see everything inside.

Hattie stood again, almost blocking his view and he watched her remove and hang the skirt before sitting down. He didn't want to shoot her or J.D. by mistake. Then he watched her raise the petticoat and slowly begin to work a stocking off. For a moment, he was as mesmerized as the men inside.

"Damn," Able shouted and dropped J.D. into the crib. "Damn brat pee-ed on me."

Jackson heard the scream as the baby collided with the rails. God he was going to kill these animals.

But into the shocked atmosphere, there was the bark of gunfire from the living room and an answering echo from his bedroom.

◇◇◇

As soon as Able flung J.D. into the crib, Hattie aimed the pistol and fired, hitting him in the face, then she swiveled before Rafe could drop what he was holding to draw and fire his gun.

Jackson yelled from outside the window. "Grab, J.D."

Hattie rolled across the bed toward the crying baby and Jackson fired, shooting the gun from Rafe's hand, then shooting the horrible man through the chest and groin. Hattie lifted the baby from the crib, then aimed her gun at Able and echoed Jackson's shots, destroying the nightmares by shooting him in the groin and chest too.

Gingerly, Jackson came through the window, praying she wouldn't fire by reflex in his direction. She dropped her gun in the crib and sank back onto the bed to examine the bawling J.D.

From the other side of the door, Cliff called. Everything all right in there boss?"

"Yeah, we got these two, what about on your side?"

"Yeah, they're pretty well dead, almost as many holes as those ponies. Are the baby and your Missus okay?"

"Give me a minute to find out," Jackson called.

He turned to watch a half-dressed Hattie remove the last of J.D.'s clothes. Frantically she was checking the baby, gently feeling of his arms, legs, belly and back. Despite his crying, she carefully looked at every inch. Solemnly she looked over her shoulder at Jackson and nodded.

"They're both all right," he was gratified by the relieved sighs on the other side of the door.

He handed Hattie the discarded blouse, then helped her button it and handed her the skirt. He sank to lift the sobbing baby into his arms, cuddling him and kissing the red marks on his soft arm, the quickly forming bump on his forehead. Hattie fastened her skirt, pulled on her stocking, and then turned to take the baby.

Automatically she curved him against her body as Jackson lifted them both to sit in the open window. Hattie gave the baby her fuller breast while Jackson stood protectively over them.

"You were outside all along?"

"No, we just got here, but I heard most of it. I would never have let them put their hands on you. I just had to get a clear shot and know where you and the baby were."

"Although," he added, staring at her down turned face and the baby who suckled with one hand touching her face. "Looking at these bodies, it doesn't look like you needed a rescuer."

"I was terrified. I realized the rifle was over the fireplace. I remembered hanging the holster around your desk chair. I had to get on the bed to feel if the handgun was still there under the pillow."

"That was some performance. You were unbelievably brave. I don't think there's a braver or more daring woman in these 34 states."

"I didn't know if I could actually fire at them, but it was just like shooting the coyotes."

"I'm proud of you and your brave little momma, J.D." he leaned down to kiss the red spot on his forehead and arm again.

"I couldn't believe that monster had our baby." She curved down to kiss the bright red spot on his forehead too and J.D. released his nipple to reach up and stretch to a standing position. Jackson placed a steadying hand under the soft bare bottom as he wobbled between them. Finally, the baby managed to lean high enough to kiss her cheek with an open-mouthed sloppy kiss.

"You're right, he is giving a kiss." Jackson laughed. "Those little girl babies better watch out for our little Romeo. Right J.D?"

They heard a buggy roll into the yard. Jackson made sure Hattie was decent and opened the bedroom door, even as she managed to diaper the wiggling J.D. and get a short shirt on him.

"A couple of you men drag this crow bait out of here. We'll load them onto the buckboard and carry them into the sheriff."

Hank stepped closer to Jackson. "Boss, we've kind of got a situation out here. Reason those hombres were able to get into the house unnoticed."

Jackson looked over at James and Rubye. Both sat, red-faced, where the raiders had tied them into chairs. It was plain from their red faces and rumpled clothes that they had been busy at other things then watching out for outlaws.

"I see," he said. "Guess one of you men better ride for the preacher, soon as you let them loose and get this carrion hauled out of my house."

"Yeah, believe you're right, boss." Hank grinned as he stepped over to untie the mortified couple.

CHAPTER TWENTY-FOUR

Jackson walked out onto the porch, surprised to see Charlie Dawson climbing down from his buggy.

Charles hesitated below the porch, watching in horror as one after another, the desperadoes were hauled out.

Jackson stood there, studying his shocked reaction. "What brings you here, Charles, come to see who won?"

Dawson cleared his throat, looked up in relief as Hattie emerged from the house carrying a clinging J.D. "Thank, God, you and the baby are all right."

"No thanks to those hired thugs. You come to tell me what's really going on, Dad." Jackson said the last word with real anger.

Dawson seemed to shrink a little in his suit. "Yes, why don't you and Harriet walk a little with me? I need to tell you this in private."

Hattie looked confused, a little surprised at being included. "Give me a minute to get my shoes."

She handed J.D. to his father. The baby cried after her for a second, then curled up against his daddy. Dawson stared hungrily at the child, sighing when he noticed the red knot on his face, then the redness on his tiny arm. "They hurt the baby?" he whispered in horror.

"Used him to threaten Hattie, planned to rape her again, Charlie. But you already know that. Why don't you cut out the guff?

I know you were the one who sent them. You need to make a clean breast of it before you end up like the rest of these murderers."

"No, Jackson, you don't know, because I didn't. That's what we need to talk about."

Hattie came down the porch steps, carefully walking around the blood trail, and stopped to lean up and slip a soft lacy shawl over J.D. before taking him back from Jackson. The tall cowboy put a steadying arm around her and a protective hand on the baby's back.

As soon as they rounded the corner beside the garden with the scratching chickens and buzzing bees, Dawson began to talk.

"I've known for some time, Irene's not been right, not since after Donna had the baby. That business of being left alone with Donna and the baby, but of not really knowing what to do for them, it hurt her, she blamed herself. You have to understand, Irene has always been a sheltered, pampered woman. Such harsh reality, the death of our daughter, it caused a sort of break-down.

"Come on Charlie, you aren't going to blame all this on Irene."

"No, not all of it. There's blood on my hands too. When the other ranchers insisted we do something to get rid of squatters and the small ranchers, I approved and funded the first men. The plan wasn't to hurt anyone, I swear. I just wanted to frighten the squatter's into wanting to sell and move on. The sheriff recommended some men, men he rode with during the war."

"You hired the men who robbed us, who beat my father, who…"

He was protesting, but for several minutes she could hear nothing. She walked beside Jackson past the banker and away from the house.

Determinedly Dawson ran after them. "Harriett, I'm so sorry. I never meant for anyone to be hurt. When I learned what they did to you and Tom, I told Sheriff Tate they had to go."

She doesn't need to listen to anything you have to say. You're as guilty as that scum we just shot."

"No, I didn't plan for anyone to be hurt. I told the Sheriff to send them away, I wouldn't pay any of them anymore."

"But he didn't listen, right?" Jackson asked sarcastically.

"No, he told me I would keep my mouth shut or he'd tell everyone my part in it. I didn't have a choice."

"You had a choice; you just made the wrong one."

Suddenly Hattie turned back to face the red-faced banker.

"What about the money," Hattie interrupted. "Our money from the cattle we sold to pay the taxes."

"I have the money, well most of it. I used some of it to pay them."

"You used our money to pay them to savage and destroy us?" Hattie stared in horror at this man, who stood in his proper banker clothes and self-righteous pose. She clutched her stomach to keep from throwing up.

Jackson swore softly. "You made me pay for that land, when you'd already collected four times what they owed on the tax bill. Your problem Charles is you're a greedy bastard."

"Don't start about that ranch again. This morning you were insisting you wanted the title back in Hattie's name."

"Jackson," she grabbed at his arm.

He turned to stare down at her. "I never intended to take your ranch. I didn't think you'd ever believe me again unless I gave you the land back."

"But I did, after you left. I got to thinking about it; you've never lied to me, not once, about anything. I realized you were telling me the truth."

He stared down into her eyes, gave her a crooked smile. "You believed me."

"Of course. When I thought about everything, about everything I knew about you. Of course I trust you."

"Good, because I didn't get the title changed. Taxes will be sky high if it's in your name, just high if it's in mine. But it's your land girl, to do with as you want."

"Good, I've got plans for it."

"Are you going to tell me what they are?"

"Eventually," she grinned at him.

Jackson shook his head and grinned back. They were past the garden by the well. Hattie took the baby back as Jackson drew up a bucket and passed the gourd dipper of ice cold water around.

Jackson held the dipper, staring hard at Dawson. The man reached out to touch the handle but waited until it was surrendered. He swallowed, wiping his mouth and face with his handkerchief.

"Harriet, I will write a check for all of the money for the cattle sale before I leave today. I'm truly sorry, I wanted to return it as soon as Irene told me what they had done." Dawson said as he accepted more water.

"Go on about Irene," Jackson ordered.

"You said we three, Donna, you and me, were the only ones to know about the secret panel. But Irene knew too. She's the one who showed it to Donna, had her order it along with the rest of your bedroom furniture from that place in Boston. Cost a pretty penny, getting it made and shipped out here. But Irene could always spend money."

"Sounds like you're the perfect couple. Go on, tell it all."

"Jackson, when you had the shoot-out, Hogue came to the Sheriff with a bullet in the shoulder and Silas Sweat bleeding from a leg wound. Doc Jenkins fixed up Rafe and told them Silas was a gonner. He bled-out on the table like our Donna did. Sheriff Tate buried Silas's body that night and we sent Rafe and Able by stage the next day to Abilene."

"We asked around town, no one had seen them."

"Tate rode them out of town in his buckboard and they met the stage after it was at Red Rim. I thought it was the end of everything."

Jackson wondered how many men had been involved in the lie. None of the ones he'd asked had seen anything, especially the sheriff. The silence lasted until he asked. "Why did they come back?"

"It was Irene," Dawson paced back and forth, twisting his hands together. Jackson wondered if he was imagining Irene's slender neck between his hands.

With the pacing, they walked past the buckboard where the bodies had been loaded.

Hattie seemed to stumble and Jackson caught a glimpse of her chalk white face. He looped an arm behind her, lifted her against his shoulder. Frantically he ran, carrying her and the boy toward the house, shouting into the dark interior, "Rubye, come hold the baby."

Rubye did, but as she walked past the bloody floors, she didn't look any too steady either. The house smelled of powder and blood, and Jackson swore. Still cradling Hattie and the baby, he turned and walked back out onto the porch. "Get a blanket and some smelling salts," he yelled back into the house.

In minutes he had handed Rubye the baby and had Hattie wrapped in a blanket. He sat in the sun, cradling her in his arms as her teeth began to chatter. He pulled her closer, chafing her arms and pressing his face against hers. "It's all right, you're safe, it's all right darling."

When he looked at Rubye she was suddenly looking pale. "Dawson take the boy. James Boyd, get another blanket and come take care of your woman."

In minutes both women were stretched out, cradled in blankets.

◇◇◇

Dawson stepped onto the porch with the crying baby. Cuddling him close and talking to him softly, "What is it? What's wrong with them?"

"It's shock, damn females," Boyd muttered.

Jackson stared at the older man holding and rocking the staunch housekeeper who was as white as Hattie had been minutes ago. "Its shock all right, but you and I have seen it in men on the battlefield before. You can't expect anyone to go through what they've just done without any reaction."

"Hank, move that meat wagon into the barn and the shade. I wired the rangers, and I don't want to take these dead men into town until the afternoon stage arrives." Jackson called.

Hattie's color began to return and she turned toward the crying baby, taking him into the cocoon of her arms and the blanket. "I'm sorry, I just felt all wobbly for a minute.'

Jackson held her close and kissed her forehead as he motioned for Dawson to sit as well. "I believe we could all do with a shot of whiskey right now."

Charlie and James both pulled out bottles, the banker's flask was silver. Jackson held the flask to Hattie's lips, patting her back as her face flamed with color and she sputtered in reaction. Rubye managed a little better, grimacing fiercely, as she sipped James bottle.

Jackson drank from the banker's bottle, knowing the bonded Bourbon would be easier to swallow then Boyd's rock gut. Then he let James and the banker pass their bottles out to the men.

◇◇◇

"Might as well finish your story, Dawson, I'm not moving until I'm sure Hattie's okay."

"Of course, of course," he sputtered, "It can wait." But when the empty flask came back to him, he shook it, pocketed it, and resumed his tale, droning on in a monotone.

"Irene took Donna's loss real hard, really hard."

"You said that. Told us she knew about the secret panel. Tell us why Rafe and Able Sweat showed up."

"She sent a wire, asked them to come back."

"Why?"

"When Rubye White showed up at our place, all scandalized by the goings on out here, Irene decided to replace Hattie Stoddard for once and all. She kept going on about how unfit she was to be raising Donna's son. When that fool preacher stopped by and bragged about marrying you, I knew something bad was going to happen."

"That was the Sunday they came out and shot the animals?" Jackson asked.

"I think Irene sent the rustlers out with orders to bring back Donna's jewelry and anything else of value that they could find. She wanted them to scare Hattie into leaving. When Irene told me, I was furious. I told her you would never let Hattie go, but she wouldn't listen."

"Then when you showed up with her at church, Irene snapped. That's why when you told me about the jewelry being stolen, I knew it was Irene. That was one of the things she obsessed about, that horrible girl getting Donna's pretty things. It wasn't enough that she had Donna's son, now she had her husband, her house, everything. When Hattie showed up in Donna's clothes, Irene figured when she found the jewelry she'd wear it too. Some of the pieces were her families, Irene's mothers and grandmothers. She just couldn't bear to think of Harriet wearing any of them."

"Why didn't she just ask for them back?" Jackson asked.

"I don't know, she wasn't thinking rationally. As soon as I confronted her, she confessed it all. Showed me the money she'd made from the cattle they'd stolen. She told me we could use it to send J.D. to Harvard. 'It takes a lot of money to go to Harvard'," she said.

"I had Doc Jenkins come to stay with her, give her something for her nerves. He told me she would need to be sent off somewhere, to a special hospital, a sanitarium somewhere. I don't think she can stand it. I don't think she'll go. I don't know that I can stand it."

◇◇◇

Rubye started crying, "I'm sorry, that means all this was my fault."

Hattie sat up, handed Jackie to his dad, and then moved from Jackson's arms to hug the older woman. "No, no, don't blame yourself. You had no way to know how it would end."

"But I judged you, and you were innocent. The Bible says 'judge not that ye be not judged.' Then today, my lord, even Hank knew what we'd been doing. I never even saw you kissing. I just saw your eyes light up when you saw each other. The way you loved the baby and each other, I guess I was jealous."

James patted her, "It's not your fault old girl, its mine. Feeling like I do for you, never saying the truth to you. Just watching them fall in love made it that much worse. Knowing I didn't have any right to speak because I can't offer you a home, a decent life. I'm just an old cowhand, with nothing of my own."

Rubye laid a hand on his cheek and smiled at him. "I'm an old maid without anything of my own. All I need or want is you."

Hattie turned to smile at Jackson. "We would never have known what our feelings were if you hadn't forced us before the preacher."

"That's right. That's why we're doing the same for you two. Here he comes now," Jackson said.

"But," James started to protest, as Hattie rose with Jackson and the baby beside her. Charles Dawson stood as well. Impulsively Hattie put an arm around him. "It will work out, Mr. Dawson. No matter how terrible it might seem at the moment, it always works out."

He stared at her in shock, "That's what Donna always said when I would worry."

"She's always here, protecting J.D. Don't you feel her too?"

◇◇◇

Before he could answer, the preacher swung down from his buggy, already in mid sermon.

"I'm surprised to be back at this house so soon. I'm really shocked by what this young man had to tell us." He scowled at Rubye White and James Boyd, both of whom had the grace to blush and look at their feet.

The preacher winked at Jackson and continued in his sternest voice. "Shall we move inside to conduct the ceremony?"

"Not today Reverend. We thought a garden wedding might give us a little more room. But we have some things we need to take care of in Star. I'm sorry we ran you out for nothing, but if you can come back tomorrow around noon, with your missus, we'll have some neighbors in and a meal ready to celebrate."

The preacher stared, clearly surprised. "Will you promise James Boyd to do the right thing by Miss White tomorrow?"

The embarrassed cowboy looked up. "I want nothing more than to do the right thing and make her my wife."

Rubye stared at him and when he reached for her hand she squeezed his hand back. To everyone's surprise she blushed and her eyes filled with tears. James pulled her into his embrace, "You going to do right by me tomorrow, sweetheart?"

Rubye nodded, then leaned down a couple of inches and tucked her face into his shoulder, overwhelmed with embarrassment.

Jackson changed the mood. "All right men, let's mount up, remember to ride armed."

The preacher looked more confused. But in all the commotion, no one bothered to explain.

◇◇◇

The men had loaded the four dead bodies into the buckboard like so much cord wood. Jackson and Cliff tied their horses to the tail gate, then mounted up to drive, each checking and loading their guns. Jackson looked around, scowling. "Where's Tony? He should have been the first to ride in today. Hank ride ahead, see what you can find."

"I'll check Maria's house. Maybe he pulled a James today."

Jackson laughed, shook his head. "Did you see how red those two got?"

"Yeah, almost makes you feel guilty for teasing them. Almost." Cliff laughed.

"Oh, Hank, check the Eastman spread if you don't find him in town. He was supposed to be keeping watch there," Jackson hollered.

Hank waved as he put his horse to a gallop.

◇◇◇

Jackson looked back at the ranch, waving to the small crowd that remained. He knew the two young hands would stay close, rifles ready. James Boyd would not be distracted by Rubye again. He would be wary and guard them and J.D. Even as he watched, the irritated preacher turned around to head home. Behind the riders in his group, he saw Charlie Dawson in his red-wheeled buggy.

His father-in-law had been behind all this trouble, if not at the end, at least in the beginning. He had done it for profit. Probably the only thing that ever prodded Charles Dawson was his greed. For just a minute he was ready to shoot him.

With all Hattie had suffered, he couldn't believe she had stood to forgive the man, to offer him comfort. But that was Hattie. She didn't talk religion all day, but she sure lived it. Hadn't she shown the same grace to Rubye, forgiving her with love and a welcome home to the ranch. A welcome to a woman who had never offered Hattie one. No one else he had ever met had a bigger or more forgiving heart. More wonderful was the way she looked at him with love and trust. He couldn't believe she had already decided to forgive him about the ranch deed.

The deed brought him back to Dawson. Was the banker the real villain? Was he just putting the blame on his wife because she was temporarily loco.

No, Dawson hadn't come to the ranch because of greed. He had loved Donna, spoiled her rotten with his love, but had loved her. And, Jackson knew he loved the baby. Surprisingly, he seemed to be fond of Hattie. But why had he told them now? Did he expect Jackson to forgive him as easily as Hattie seemed to have? Despite all she had suffered, she always had the ability to look at other people with compassion. All the way into town, he pondered what could be in the man's mind and heart.

◇◇◇

Hattie used the strong lye soap solution to wash the walls and floor boards. She shuddered again about what might have been as she straightened the covers, remade the crib, and then went ahead and changed the sheets on both beds. Even though she was the only one on them, she shuddered at the sight of the bed and it was the only thing she could do to change the way it looked. Finally, she laid her father's rifle across the bed, left the pistol on the dresser as she worked.

She had insisted that Rubye rest and even though she wanted to refuse, James had made sure that she obeyed and layed down. James sat in the kitchen, drinking the hot, over-boiled coffee, his guns ready. The fish still soaked in a bowl of salted water, the uneaten meal still sat in pots on the cooled stove. Hattie didn't dare speculate on his state of mind. Finished in the bedroom, she picked up the pistol and moved it and the rifle to the dining room table.

She used the work, grateful to have it to keep her mind away from what was happening in town. J.D. was once again sleeping on the cot mattress in the living area. Hattie checked him, thrilled that he still slept. All the drama and his first experience with evil had exhausted him.

She fetched a new bucket of water, then stared at the dining room chairs where the older couple had been tied. For several minutes, she struggled with the knots on the leather thongs and finally freed the last one. She scrubbed the chairs too, horrified to realize it was blood on the top rung of the tall ladder back where James had been tied.

Nervously, she laid the rawhide strips on the table, pushing aside more plates and silverware. She set the bucket beside the damp chair seat and again attacked the floor, mopping and scrubbing the dark red stains away. She rinsed the floor in long sweeps out the door and across the porch. Satisfied that all the blood was up, she went back to carefully smooth the floor. Using a pail of clean water and a flat piece of sandstone she sanded where bullets had gouged the wood. She had to be careful that there would be no splinters for Jackie's' tender hands and knees as he moved from his swimming squirm to an actual crawl. Finished in the living room, she again moved the guns back to her bed and used the same method to smooth out and polish the bullet gouges in the bedroom floor.

Knees and back aching, hands red, Hattie was glad when J.D. began his waking fuss. She used the few minutes it would take him to become an angry complainer to clean up any water and grit and return broom, mop, sandstone and pail to the kitchen. She noticed James was sitting in front of the table playing with the rawhide strips, his hand over his face. Like her, he was reliving the raid. Unlike her, he wasn't worrying about the men entering Star, she knew if he were he would be busy, too.

It was Rubye who woke them both from their thoughts. "Isn't anyone going to take care of this little boy?" She held the baby, who had quit immediately when she bent to pick him up. Hattie hurried forward to take the wet boy to change and feed. As she left, she noticed Rubye wrapping an arm around James and bending to kiss his forehead. She was relieved to see him look up and smile before wrapping an arm around her.

◇◇◇

It was three o'clock when they arrived in the Mexican end of town. Jackson was relieved that both Hank and Tony were both waiting for them there. "Are you all right, Tony?"

He doffed his hat, and Jackson saw a white bandage. "Better, thanks to Hank showing up."

"You were right, he was tied up at the Eastman spread," Hank said.

"They said they were going to bring Maria back, and ..."

Jackson felt his own chest tighten as he relived the minutes before the gunfire at the ranch. He looked over his shoulder at the wagon, "You don't have to worry about that."

"That's what Hank said," he rode up and lifted the tarp anyway, then grinned.

◇◇◇

The street seemed deserted as they drew up at the jail, but soon curious onlookers began to gather, drawn by the wagon full of bodies.

The sheriff stepped out of the cool dark of the saloon and then ducked back in. From the corner of his eye, Jackson caught the motion. Stepping down, he motioned his men to join him inside the thick adobe walls of the jail, even as a gun fired from the window of the store across the street. Cliff returned fire and a dark half-breed fell from the window to the ground.

The sheriff shouted over at them even as onlookers scattered. "Throw down your guns, Jackson, and you and your men will be given a fair trial."

"Go to hell, Tate. Throw out your gun and badge, because we intend to see you hang. The rest of your "deputies" should do the same. Texas Rangers will be here on the next stage."

"Too bad you're not as clever as you think, Jackson. When Seth showed me the telegram, I sent an order to ignore it. That stage will be empty."

Jackson looked around the small room at the determined faces of the four men with him. Cliff reached over to the gun case and pulled out a shotgun and shells. "Guess, we'll have to wait and see who's right, unless you want to step out and surrender," he called.

It seemed to take forever for the hands to reach three-thirty and sweep past. When the stage pulled up, Jackson realized he was holding his breath. The driver stepped down, luggage was unloaded, horses changed. A couple stepped aboard, then the stage took off.

"Jackson, looks like you lose. I've got you surrounded. Come out," Tate racked his shotgun.

"Stay put, Jackson," a voice called from the saloon shadows, "Tate..." but before he could complete the order, the sheriff twirled and fired the shotgun at the shadows. The ranger rolled and fired and a second ranger sent bullets through the fat target.

A gun fired from the second story of the saloon brought answering fire from the rangers and the shooter pitched to the floor. Outside, fire was exchanged from Thompson's store and the stables with the cowboys inside the jail. When the smoke cleared, two wounded men were herded into the jail and Jackson met the rangers in the street.

"We got off at Red Rim, and rode in ahead of the stage. Knew when we got the second wire you needed our help." He nodded at Cliff, "Of course your man there had told us you were having trouble up this way. Told us he would wire us if anything else happened. Texas is so big, seems every town is having trouble between cattlemen and squatters these days. Sorry, we didn't come up sooner."

Jackson waited for him to pause. "Glad you arrived in time, it might have been another blood-bath here."

"Yeah, looks like you had one somewhere else, judging by that dead wood in your wagon."

"They showed up at my place after we left this morning. I wired you about all they did Sunday."

"One of the reasons we had to come. Men who shoot animals that way, tend to be the most dangerous."

"Today, they tied up our cook, yahooed our women, and held a gun on my infant son."

"Sounds like you were lucky to get back in time. This crew has made a bad name for themselves. Two of the three in the buggy are wanted for rape and murder from Kansas, Missouri, and now Texas."

"My wife had a gun under the pillow."

"Guess that explains the low aim on a couple of them."

"Yeah, I finished them by shooting them in the head. My men took care of the other two. If you want to charge us, we'll stand trial for it. But we didn't have a choice and I'd personally like to do it all again, maybe starting with those so-called deputies we have in jail," Jackson said.

The yells and protests inside the jail grew silent and the ranger grinned. "Reckon we'd better take this evidence and those birds back with us to Austin. We've got a judge there who will make quick work of them. What name do I have to wire any reward to?"

"Jackson Harper. I'll share it with my men if there is one."

"Yeah, as wide a swatch as these boys cut, it might amount to a pretty penny. We'll throw in Tate and the one in the saloon, since Rangers can't collect bounties."

Jackson nodded and started walking up the street toward the bank. "I'd like that, but while you're here, there's some shady dealings coming through from the city council and the tax assessor. I'd like you to check it out. I can't believe it's legal."

"Might be legal, just not be right." The Ranger told him in undertones as they walked toward the bank. "We might be able to convince them it's not legal, get it changed anyway. Just follow my lead. What's the assessor's name?"

"Charles Dawson, my first wife's father."

CHAPTER TWENTY-FIVE

In the small bedroom, Hattie helped Rubye into one of Donna's dresses, a simple one made up in ivory linen.

"It's not right, my wearing Mrs. Harper's dress."

Hattie laughed. "Thanks to you, I'm Mrs. Harper now. Admit it, I will be sewing until I die and I still won't get all Donna's clothes cut down to fit me. This dress fits you perfectly, it looks lovely, and even if I could get it altered, I would probably never wear it. You're the bride today, this is my and Donna's gift to you."

Rubye blushed, the high collared dress with its high puff sleeves flattered and softened her tall, angular build. She looked young, with her hair piled in a soft knot on top of her head, yellow rose buds tucked in amid the dark strands.

Hattie stood on tiptoe and kissed her soft cheek. "You're still young and beautiful. God willing this time next year we'll be watching our babies play together and J.D. will be the big boy, toddling around between them."

"I'm afraid I'm too old."

"How old?"

"Thirty-three. James is forty-two."

Hattie grinned at her. "God's blessings, let's hurry before you get one day older."

Finally Rubye laughed.

◇◇◇

In the garden, the cowhands were already gathered. James wore his dark church suit and a starched stiff white shirt that resembled Jackson's. His face glowed red. He was obviously fortified by spirits.

Hattie took the baby from his grandfather and quickly freshened him up as well. By the time she returned, the 'I do's' were being said. Smiling, she watched as Rubye and James exchanged smiles and then kissed to the delight of everyone. She and Jackson hugged the beaming newlyweds, then Hattie left the baby with Jackson. She brought out a perfectly glazed white cake, one she had baked in secret. Proudly she added it to the temporary table loaded with fried chicken, vegetables and more food the neighbors had brought.

◇◇◇

Later, over slices of cake, she and Jackson broached the arrangement that they had worked out that morning during their quiet pillow talk.

"We need your help, Mr. and Mrs. Boyd. I have eighty-seven head of cattle on my small ranch, you know, southeast of this ranch."

Jackson took over, "We need someone living there, taking care of the house and the animals. We would share the profit on all cattle sold, in times of drought, share the water. We still need help, at the house, during the day for the main meals. James you know I would still want to hire you for trail drives and rodeos to be camp cook. Of course if either of the gals were to have a baby, we would want you both to move back so we could help each other. Other than that, it's your place as long as you want it."

The new couple sat before them speechless. Before the tears forming in their eyes could spill, Hattie laughed. "You're good friends; we know you'll be good neighbors."

◇◇◇

Charles Dawson stared glumly at his son-in-law, his grandson, and Harriett, his daughter's replacement. Yesterday had been exhausting for him, the blow-up with Irene, the aftermath of the shoot-out at the ranch and in town, then the visit by the Ranger.

Jackson had seemed to gloat as he watched the ranger inspect the property appraisals. As he listened to the happy couples talk, Charlie wondered if Jackson already knew that the council was set to meet tonight. The agenda was the rewriting of the tax laws. Rates would go back to previous levels. The ranger had as much as threatened Charles if they didn't, hinting that the state planned to investigate further. He implied that Dawson was behind all the problems in the region since he had the most to gain. It had sent him scurrying to secure promises from the other council members before he drove out for the wedding.

The truth was, Charlie felt guilty for all that had happened. He had let greed and the prospect of gaining additional property lead him to fall for Tate's offer of help. All the violence, theft, and damaged lives were his fault. Despite all the celebration, he sat sad and apart from the others.

◇◇◇

In the series of hugs and kisses, J.D. leaned forward and shared wet kisses with Rubye, insisting she and James kiss his pony and little cowboy as well.

Suddenly Charles felt his fear and resentment slip away as he noticed the little cowboy doll. On the carefully pieced back of the cowboy's vest, appeared a vivid, embroidered bluebird. How many times had he heard Donna talk about this special pattern. He rose and walked over to shake hands with James and Rubye, leaning to kiss the blushing bride on the cheek.

"Jackson, you think you and Hattie could manage more acres while Irene and I are back east?"

"Charlie, maybe, if you want to give us the same option we just offered James and Rubye, fifty-fifty share in the profits. I'm sorry we can't manage the bank as well."

"Hopefully, it won't be for that long. Jim Smith will be in charge of the bank while I'm away. But I'll be back every three or four months to check on the ranch, the bank and visit my grandson.

Jackson walked his father-in-law to his buggy. "You were lucky Charlie. Tate's dying left no one to point the finger at you or Irene."

Charles scowled again then turned to stare up at the tall man. "I think so, although I'll always feel guilty for my part in things. My real luck was when Donna chose you at church that day. She told me you were all she'd ever need to be happy. I know you did that for her, made her happy."

Suddenly the tight suspicion that had tortured him about this man evaporated. When he stared at Charlie, all he saw was a tired old man facing months or the rest of his life watching over his insane wife and reliving his regrets. He held out a hand to help the man climb up into the buggy.

Suddenly he felt relief as he forgave the man.

"We'll all be glad to see you, especially J.D. Don't worry, I'll take care of things for you."

AFTERWORD

(One Year Later)

Hattie held onto Jackson's strong arm, Greta Jane a tiny bundle in her arm. J.D. trudged up the hill in his new boots, hanging onto his daddy's hand and talking all the way in his own language. Behind them, James Boyd walked with an arm around Ruybe, his son little James cradled in her arms and supported by his hand under the boy's back. Finally, they reached the crest of the little hill above the ranch, the one she had come to on that rainy evening so long ago.

Hank and Cliff waited at the top of the hill, each man held one of the beautiful carved crosses that James had made and brought out for the occasion. He had waited for the day that Hattie had a name for the smaller cross. It had taken awhile.

The preacher trailed up the hill behind them, the good book clasped in his hand. "I guess you know this is not the usual way things are done, but then I should know not to expect anything usual from the Harper's."

Jackson glared at the man, and he stopped his grumbling.

Hattie handed the baby girl, named for her and Jackson's mothers, into her daddy's arms. As usual, J.D. insisted that his Daddy kneel down so he could see his baby sister.

Hattie smiled at the older couple who meant so much to her, to all of them. She was so grateful that they had agreed to return to the ranch until both babies were born and she and Rubye could both be back on their feet. Hattie had been afraid it was her fault, that she couldn't give birth to a healthy child, and that she might lose this baby too. But her daughter was strong and healthy, just as Jackie had been.

She was surprised that Rubye was just as worried, fretting that she was too old. Both were grateful when she and James also had a strong, healthy boy. Two months and she knew they would soon leave, but she didn't know if she would be able to stand it.

She walked over to Hank and took the larger cross, the one with Thomas Matthew Stoddard, his years of birth and death chiseled below the beautifully carved name. James had painted both crosses white, and then painted black inside the chiseled letters and numbers. Proudly she positioned the cross at the head of her father's grave, but after pushing hard, she accepted Hank's help in getting it deep enough to stand straight. Then she took the smaller cross from Cliff and was able to get it deep enough on her own.

She let her fingers trail across the incised letters, Thomas James Stoddard, the single date, 1872. She had known he deserved to go into the next world with a name and the blessings of the lord, now at last he would. Gratefully she walked over and swept J.D. into her arms, leaned into the tall body of her husband as he rose and circled her back. Together they all listened to the words and prayers of benediction.

A sudden gust of wind blew, tugging at her bonnet and Hattie curved so that the new baby was sheltered in her embrace as well. For a brief moment she felt the brush of wings, smiled as she felt Donna's love surround them all. As she looked down, she saw Jackie's old bonnet framing Greta's face, its tiny bluebird vivid with the promise of happiness.

THE END

ABOUT THE AUTHOR

I'm a retired teacher who loves to write fiction. When I was little, my mother was always telling me to "come here and close that book right now." She wanted to convince me to stop wasting time reading and would add, "You know those books are all lies."

As a writer, I am always making up stories. I find the lies of fiction help me find structure and truth in all the confusion of real life.

DEAR READER

I hope you enjoy reading this book as much as I enjoyed writing it. If you like it and are so inclined, I would appreciate a kind review at https://www.amazon.com/dp/B00JC6DOLK

If you find errors or things that I should change, please send me suggestions at biery35@gmail.com.

MORE BY J.R. BIERY

From Darkness to Glory,
http://www.amazon.com/dp/B00LG1ZPMK
Potter's Field,
http://www.amazon.com/dp/B00KH7Q8C0
Killing the Darlings,
http://www.amazon.com/dp/B00IRRMO2A
Edge of Night
http://www.amazon.com/dp/B00J0LLQC6
Will Henry,
http://www.amazon.com/dp/B00K5POM0O
Happy Girl,
http://www.amazon.com/dp/B00MHHXMEA
Chimera Pass,
http://www.amazon.com/dp/B00KALJYRY
Ghost Warrior,
http://www.amazon.com/dp/B00M62NBEC
He's My Baby Now,
http://www.amazon.com/dp/B00N1X6ZFW

$9.99

LONGWOOD PUBLIC LIBRARY
800 Middle Country Road
Middle Island, NY 11953
(631) 924-6400
longwoodlibrary.org

LIBRARY HOURS

Monday-Friday	9:30 a.m. - 9:00 p.m.
Saturday	9:30 a.m. - 5:00 p.m.
Sunday (Sept-June)	1:00 p.m. - 5:00 p.m.

61143023R00158

Made in the USA
Lexington, KY
02 March 2017